W9-AVD-454

An autopistol appeared in Karkanian's hand like magic

"Whoa!" Butcher Boy protested, stepping out of the line of fire. "What's this for?"

"Have a look," Della said. "Show him, Spence."

A muscular blond man turned on the VCR. A CNN update of the San Diego attack popped onto the screen. The news anchor announced a breakthrough in the mysterious fire and reported gun battle in the canyon near downtown. The network had obtained exclusive rights to a videotape shot by a homeowner along the canyon rim.

At gunpoint, Mack Bolan watched the grainy tape, which showed a tall man running across a hillside, firing a machine pistol at a kneeling figure with a rifle.

Spence hit the freeze frame.

There was no doubt who they were all looking at.

DON PENDLETON's
MACK BOLAN®

ULTIMATE GAME

A GOLD EAGLE BOOK FROM
WORLDWIDE®

TORONTO • NEW YORK • LONDON
AMSTERDAM • PARIS • SYDNEY • HAMBURG
STOCKHOLM • ATHENS • TOKYO • MILAN
MADRID • WARSAW • BUDAPEST • AUCKLAND

First edition June 1998

ISBN 0-373-61460-8

ULTIMATE GAME

Printed in U.S.A.

My name is Legion: for we are many.
—The Gospel According to St. Mark, 5:9

I am nightmare's end, the tiger that eats tigers.
—From the Diary of Mack Bolan

CHAPTER ONE

Seattle, Washington,
Central District

Special Agent in Charge Lawrence Deeds crouched beside an overflowing garbage bin, straining to make out the voices in his headset through the buzz of static. The late-May afternoon was standard issue for the Pacific Northwest: forty-nine degrees with a gusty wind, and wet. The steady, misting rain had already saturated his FBI billcap and the shoulders of his nylon windbreaker; unfortunately it wasn't falling heavily enough to wash away the aroma of the trash heap.

He knew it would smell worse inside Aga Karkanian's lair.

A million times worse.

Though more than a year had passed since the Shreveport raid, the ghost of that particular stench still crept up on SAC Deeds as if it had been burned into the synapses of his brain, bringing with it a rush of slaughterhouse images and a wild beating of his heart. He shut his eyes. His heart was pounding now, high in his throat.

A burst of speech crackled in his ear, the words unintelligible over the power-line interference. He barely recognized the voice. "Bates, I didn't copy that," he growled into his headset's mike. "Are you in position?"

"Roger that, Number One," came the reply. "We have containment. Repeat, we have the lobby."

Deeds reached inside his jacket and pulled a matte black stainless-steel SIG-Sauer 229 from its paddle holster on his hip. With his index finger outside the pistol's trigger guard, he eased back the slide far enough to catch the silver glint of the first Black Talon round in the magazine's stack, the one already up the pipe. As he let the slide snap shut, more Shreveport memories came flooding back. Eighteen months earlier, fate had granted him the jackpot prize, a window of opportunity to avenge all the monster's victims, a chance to end the string of murders, singlehandedly and forever. He'd let it slip through his fingers.

Thanks to a tactical glitch, for a brief moment Deeds had found himself alone and face-to-face with the mass killer in the basement torture chamber on Benton Avenue. As Karkanian, half-smiling, put up his hands and dropped to his knees, over the sights of the SIG there was a split second of eye contact. The range from the muzzle of the .40-caliber pistol to the center of the murderer's high forehead had been less than six feet. Pumped by the heat of the chase, surrounded by the stink of death, by pools of fresh blood and a scatter of body parts, Deeds had held the wide combat trigger tightened right up to the break point. A quarter ounce more squeeze would have snapped the cap.

Karkanian had realized he was about to be executed.

The look of laughing contempt in his black eyes said, *See? See what you really are? When push comes to shove, Mr. Fed, you're no better than me.*

Deeds had paused on the brink of murder, but not because he gave a damn what Karkanian thought about him. He'd wanted the scumbag to stew in his own juice for a second or two, to feel what his victims had to have felt, before the frag round vaporized his head from the eyes up. The truth was, Lawrence Deeds had lost his professional detachment months earlier. When the job brought him into almost daily contact with brutally slain victims and their grieving families, how could it *not* become personal at some point? And in the end, it wasn't his years of training or the FBI's high standards of conduct that made him ease off on the trigger; it was the sudden, late arrival of his backup.

Even though his team had successfully captured Karkanian, even though he had gotten a commendation for his work on the case, the SAC still tortured himself with second guesses. He hadn't shared his pain with anyone, not even his wife of twenty-two years—to have done so would have meant exposing Cindy to the depth of this killer's evil, and that was something he couldn't bring himself to do. After the arrest, regrets and guilt hardened in Deeds's belly like knobs of limestone.

From the minute he was taken into custody, Aga Karkanian had played the justice system like a slide trombone. During court-ordered, pretrial psychiatric evaluations, he appeared confused and reluctant to discuss his hallucinations. A check of his background showed a history of bizarre behavior and lack of control over his frequent violent impulses. The panel of experts decided he was so lost in psychosis that he couldn't understand the charges filed against him. In the end, the court had had no choice but to judge Karkanian not guilty by reason of insanity and sentence him to a "high security" mental hospital. In that regard, he had succeeded where so many other mass murderers had failed. None of the evidence that Deeds and crew had gathered in their grueling, follow-the-trail-of-corpses investigation ever came before a jury, and the SAC was forced to watch the whole disgusting circus from the sidelines.

Deeds never had any doubt that his prime suspect was legally sane, a sociopath who knew right from wrong and didn't care. Karkanian had tested out as more intelligent than anyone ever arrested for serial murder. His crime spree had demonstrated that he was a meticulous tactician with a flair for the dramatic; equally important, he was a flawless actor, an ability that had helped him fool the court-appointed shrinks and briefly win the trust of his more than two dozen victims.

Though Deeds couldn't prove it, he believed that Karkanian had fabricated much of his own personal history, which was full of convenient blind alleys, deceased relatives, fires in county records and the like. Deeds also suspected that the killer had orchestrated the time and place of his capture, that he had, in fact, scripted his showdown with the law in Shreveport. Of course, there was no way to verify that, either.

Six weeks earlier, the mass murderer had furthered his grisly legend by escaping from the federal facility at Sparksburg, Nevada, with two male orderlies as hostages. Hospital authorities had discovered the corpse of Karkanian's staff psychiatrist in one of the interview rooms, strangled with his own necktie. The stolen hospital van was recovered a day later on a national-forest road near Reno, but the bodies of the orderlies were still missing. Karkanian had disappeared without a trace.

Deeds was sure he'd been helped by someone on the outside. Like other high-profile killers in captivity, he had attracted a small fan club of mostly young, sometimes pretty, but invariably vacant-eyed women. They had stood silent vigil in the hallways outside the sanity hearings. After his commitment to Sparksburg, they had sent him a steady stream of passionate, supportive letters. One of his more disturbed female admirers might have easily provided him with a getaway car, false ID and traveling money. If so, Deeds figured she was long dead, dismembered and dumped by now.

After the escape, things had remained quiet for more than a month, with no fresh body caches uncovered, but the ache in Deeds's gut told him that Karkanian was back at it. He was just being more careful about whom he killed and what he did with the remains. Then, out of the blue, as had happened in Shreveport, an anonymous phone tip had given the FBI the Seattle address. It could have come from a neighbor in the apartment building. It could have come from Karkanian himself.

Looming above Deeds, black with accumulated soot, was the rear wall of the six-story brick structure. On the alley side of the seventy-five-year-old Corinthian

Arms, there were a few small, narrow windows—bathroom windows propped open with blocks of wood or empty forty-ounce liquor bottles. Thick layers of white paint curled from the warped wooden frames. Water-stained rags of curtain hung limply inside, partially blocking the tenants' shower-stall views of the surrounding neighborhood: turn-of-the-century wooden houses, alternately abandoned and renovated, stairstepping up the hill; gang signs sprayed over the low concrete-block wall of the Korean church across the street; and beyond the Ethiopian takeout restaurant on the opposite corner, the tower blocks of Seattle's major hospitals that overlooked downtown and Elliott Bay.

Deeds switched the pistol to his weak hand so he could wipe his rain-slick right palm on the front of his body armor. As he did so, the back-and-forth chatter in his headset stopped. The eight-man unit awaited his go signal. They had the apartment building surrounded; all exits, including the fire escapes, were blocked. Karkanian could still jump off the roof, and that was okay with Deeds. There was nowhere for him to jump to, just ninety feet of free fall to the wet pavement.

Short of a successful suicide attempt, the SAC expected Karkanian to survive his recapture. He had given up without a fight in Shreveport and hadn't used firearms in any of his previous crimes. Karkanian relied on superior physical strength and edged weapons to subdue weaker or momentarily vulnerable targets. He was a predator, not a warrior. The Behavioral Sciences Unit's psychological profile had compared him to a spider, never moving far from the center of his web while on the hunt. From a home base in the Central District, he could prey on transients and runaways in Pioneer Square, on nurses and orderlies from the hospitals and on Rainier Valley prostitutes.

Though it would be small consolation to the families of his latest victims, Karkanian's insanity defense wouldn't work a second time. Ten years from now, after all his appeals were used up, the man would finally get what he deserved: he'd be strapped to a board and drip-lined barbiturates until his heart stopped beating.

Deeds drew in a slow breath between clenched teeth. It was time to see if Karkanian was home. "Let's do it," he barked into his headset mike. "Let's get this sucker."

He jumped out from behind the garbage bin and dashed across the muddy gravel of the parking lot. Two other agents angled in from their places of concealment, joining him at the dented sheet-metal door that was the apartment's back entrance. Deeds went through the door first, covered from the rear by his backups' stainless-steel 12-gauge Winchester riot pumpguns. The interior hallway of the Corinthian Arms was narrow, dark and dimly lit; decades of foot traffic had worn the midline of the black-and-white-diamond-pattern linoleum floor to a mottled gray. Waving for the others to follow, he headed down the hall on a dead run.

Deeds passed the building's elevator without slowing. Screened off with two-by-fours and chicken wire, it hadn't worked for years. There were only two possible escape routes open to the suspect: the front and back stairs leading to the subground floor, which was where the phone tip said Karkanian was living. The serial killer had shown a fondness for windowless basement apartments before. The things he enjoyed doing required privacy.

The flight of uncarpeted, wooden steps leading to the basement creaked underfoot, forcing the SAC to slow down and descend them cautiously. He stopped at the bottom of the stairwell and scanned another, similar hallway, this one harshly lit by a row of bare bulbs in the ceiling. Five doorways were spaced along each side of the gritty corridor. Deeds sniffed at the still air, identifying the smell of stale cigarette smoke, cooked cabbage and roach spray.

There was no telltale reek of carrion.

At least not yet.

On cue, at the opposite end of hall, two more bluejacketed men from Justice appeared. One of them, Agent Bates, carried a steel battering ram. At Deeds's hand signal, they all closed in on apartment B4.

Deeds put an ear to the outside of the thickly painted door and listened. Inside the apartment, an AM radio commercial blared. He could detect no odor of corpses, no overpowering smell of perfume or solvent meant to hide the scent of decay.

Maybe the tip was a hoax, he thought. Maybe the caller was trying to use the Bureau to get even with an annoying neighbor. It was also possible that Karkanian was living there, but had located his web and its ornaments elsewhere. In less than a minute, they would know.

Moving out of the line of fire through the door, Deeds put his back to the wall and reached around the jamb for the knob to apartment B4 with his left hand. When he twisted his wrist, to his surprise, the knob turned. He carefully pushed it inward, just far enough to slip the latch bolt.

At that instant, all the lights in the corridor went out.

From the pitch darkness to Deeds's right, Agent Bates said, "What the—?"

Bates never finished his sentence.

Strobe-flash bursts of yellow orange lit up the hall at both ends. The ambush of silenced autofire caught Deeds and company flat-footed and night-blind. A hail of bullets thwacked into walls, armored vests and flesh. As shards of Bates's disintegrating skull peppered the right side of Deeds's face and neck, slugs from the other direction stitched a ragged line across the SAC's chest. The impacts of half a dozen rounds spun him back hard against the wall and dropped him to a knee.

Under the body armor's steel trauma plate, Deeds's chest went numb, its nerves frozen by shock. He couldn't breathe. His brain screamed for his right hand to raise the pistol from his side, to answer fire.

It was a long-distance call.

Before he could aim his weapon, a flurry of bullets blasted his legs out from under him, and he toppled forward onto his face. Autofire continued to ripsaw the air above him, making it billow with plaster dust and flying splinters. Instinctively he covered the back of his head with his arms. After a moment, the muzzle-flashes stopped.

As Deeds lay gasping in the darkness, he heard heavy footsteps approaching. The bastards were coming to finish the job. He fumbled frantically over the floor for the autopistol that had dropped from his hand; it had bounced just out of his reach. When he tried to crawl through the slickness of his own puddled blood, pain from his shattered knee swallowed him whole and he blacked out.

Deeds came to, screaming, as he was dragged over the threshold of apartment B4 by his heels. His cries were buried under the roar of the radio. Someone hoisted him up by the armpits, and he was rushed through a low-ceilinged, brightly lit living room and dumped onto his back on a kitchen table. The jarring impact made his pain spike, and he lost consciousness again, but this time only for a few seconds. When he opened his eyes, he was surrounded by horned devils.

He forced his eyes to focus.

Not devils, backlit human figures with night-vision goggles pushed up on top of their heads, the twin barrels sticking up like antler stubs. One of them was a white female, with a stocky build and extremely short brown hair. Deeds didn't recognize any of their faces, which were distorted by the pressure of the goggle straps. The former-Soviet-issue optics were sub-state-of-the-art, the kind of surplus equipment found in survivalist mail-order catalogs. Their weapons were better quality—stubby 9 mm Heckler & Koch machine pistols.

His pulse racing, he told himself it had to be payback from some other case. Political terrorists. Or a hit squad hired by Colombian drug lords. Whoever they were, they'd used his pursuit of Aga Karkanian, which had been widely reported in the media, to lure him into a death trap.

When the gunmen looming over his head stepped aside, he felt the heat of intense light. Not just ordinary room lights, floodlights. The volume of the radio dropped, then something landed with a heavy thunk on the table beside his cheek. He turned his head and saw a tightly rolled, white bath towel. Powerful hands started to unroll the towel, but Deeds already knew what was inside.

The instruments lay in neat rows, bright and sharp.

The SAC tried to rear up, but two of the men pushed his shoulders back down on the table and held them there.

Another face leaned over him. It was so close it blocked out his view of everything else. Even upside down, with a newly grown, closely cropped black beard, there was no mistaking who it was.

"Goddammit, get a tourniquet on that leg!" Aga Karkanian said. "I don't want him bleeding out on me."

The woman jammed a wadded rag in Deeds's mouth and held it there while the others quickly cinched up his thigh with a twist of cord. The mass murderer waited until Deeds stopped screaming into the gag, then he waved for the woman to remove it.

"So, we meet again, Larry," Karkanian said, beaming down at him. "Not like the last time, huh? Not the way you expected, I'll bet. Right about now you're probably wondering who shot you and your men all to shit."

"What's to wonder?" Deeds snapped. "You hired some punks to do what you don't have the balls for."

That amused the Butcher of Benton Avenue. "No

money changed hands here," he said, gesturing at the shooters who ringed the kitchen table. "These are volunteers."

Volunteers? The idea made Deeds grimace. If it was true, it represented a sea change in modus operandi; like most serial killers, Karkanian had previously worked alone. The FBI man scanned the faces again. Who were they? Was this all of them, or were there more outside? It hit him then that the agents he had posted on the exits had to be dead, too, or they'd have surely closed in by now.

Deeds hadn't even considered the possibility of dying in the line of duty on this case. Now death—and a horrible one at that—seemed a certainty. He wasn't prepared for it. Neither was Cindy. He tried to swallow, but couldn't manage it. His mouth was too dry.

"Of course you don't believe me," Karkanian went on. "Like the rest of your breed, you subscribe to a static view of what you call my 'criminal type.' Having a set of carefully constructed pigeonholes—behavioral-science profiles—makes you feel better about your work, more in control of things, and it gives the tax-paying public the idea that the Department of Justice is doing a bang-up job, protecting them from the bogeyman with science. The trouble is, we both know your view of what I am and what I am capable of is based on endless reanalyses of the same few dozen, outdated cases. Do you know what a 'paradigm shift' is?"

When Deeds didn't respond at once, the killer answered his own question. "That's when the accumulation of contradictory evidence so weakens an existing scientific theory that it has to be replaced."

"The shrinks were right," Deeds snarled up at him. "You are fucking nuts."

Karkanian reached across the FBI man's chest and selected a small, wickedly curved scalpel from the unrolled towel. "Because of our long association, I've singled you out for a special honor. You're going to be the core of the new body of evidence that blows all the standard theories to hell. The guys in the lab coats down in Quantico are going to study what we're about to do to you for decades. Turn on the camera."

When the death squad stepped out of the way, Deeds saw the video unit set up on a tripod beyond the end of the table. One of the gunmen hit a button on the camera's side, and a little red light winked on as it began to roll tape.

"Better secure that gag in his mouth," the mass murderer said. "Things are going to get noisy in here."

The woman used her teeth to tear off a long strip from a roll of duct tape.

Though the serial killer's ravings made little sense to Deeds, he knew Karkanian was right about the video. If a record of his murder was sent to the Bureau, Behavioral Sciences would be looking at it for a long, long time. He knew that ultimately all that would be remembered about Special Agent in Charge Lawrence Deeds would be the minute details of his being flayed alive, his guts spread out like moist pink garlands, his pitiful mewlings for merciful death. Terror squeezed his heart, terror colder than any he had ever known. He beat it back savagely, with pure will.

Before they destroyed him, while he could still manage it, Deeds raised his head from the table. He looked straight into the rolling camera and spoke slowly, with exaggerated movements of his mouth, so anyone who saw the tape could lip-read the words without the sound. It was a final message to his wife.

"Cindy, I'm sorry," he said. "I love you. I'll always love you."

Port Flattery, Washington

BOBBIE MARIE POTTS rapped on the screen door of her Calhoun Street property with a single knuckle, careful to protect her new set of two-inch-long, flaming red fake nails. No one answered the knock. The front door was open, so she figured her new tenants had to be there.

"Anybody home?" she called through the mesh.

Beside the door frame, screwed onto the exterior wall, was a small wooden plaque, white with black letters. The sign read Byrum House, Built 1880. Every old house inside the city limits sported its own hand-painted nameplate, thanks to the Port Flattery Historical Society. During the tourist season, which didn't officially start for another month, out-of-towners wandered up and down the streets in droves, squinting at the little signs and trying to find the names of the houses on the free walking-tour map they got from Port Flattery's visitor-information trailer.

While she waited for someone to come to the door, Potts surveyed the Victorian house's wooden front porch. The bargain paint she'd paid to have put on last fall was already starting to chip and curl up in places.

It irked her that she couldn't afford to have the job done right.

After a long moment, a tall, tanned, blond woman in cutoff sweats stepped up on the other side of the screen.

"Afternoon, Della," Potts said. Like her nails, the warm, friendly smile was a fake. It was the same smile that in 1979 had helped earn her the title of "Miss Portage Bay." Even though Potts was dressed to kill in her red business suit and accessorized with heavy fake-gold jewelry hanging from wrists, neck and earlobes, when she looked at Della Gridley, who was without makeup and wearing fleece rags, it made her feel both dumpy and ancient. She didn't like that one bit.

"I don't want to bother you and Spence," Potts said, "but I thought I'd better check to make sure you two were settling in okay. I know the first week in a town this small can be a shock. We move at a snail's pace compared to what you're used to down in Hollywood...."

When the woman just stood there, silent, hand on hip, staring at her, Potts got nervous. She hurriedly added, "Oh, dear, I hope you don't think I'm being a nosy landlord."

Of course, she *was* being nosy, but she was also genuinely concerned about her tenants. It was in her self-interest to make sure the L.A. screenwriter and his wife were as happy as clams. Like every other "real-estate professional" in Port Flattery, Bobbie Marie Potts anxiously awaited an up-spiral in the depressed local market. Port Flattery was too far from Seattle—

three hours via two-lane highway—to ever become one of its bedroom communities. Realistically the next real-estate boom could only be fueled by an influx of rich people who didn't have to commute to the city five days a week.

Hollywood people, used to paying inflated Hollywood prices.

"We're doing fine," Gridley replied. Her blue eyes slightly slanted up at the corners, the angles matching the upturned corners of her wide mouth. The natural curve of her mouth made it look like she was smiling, but the expression in her eyes wasn't friendly.

Potts had a sudden, dismal thought. Maybe Mrs. Gridley had picked up on the touchy-feely game she'd been playing with Mr. Gridley. It was harmless stuff: she took every available opportunity to brush against him, pat his hand, stroke his arm. If Della resented the mild flirtation, Potts had made a terrible mistake. Having the woman against you was the kiss of death in real-estate sales. And real-estate sales was what this neighborly little visit was all about.

"I suppose you'd like to come in?" Della asked.

"Oh, I don't want to intrude," Potts said. "I know Spence is probably busy writing something exciting."

"Not at the moment," said a muscular blond man as he slipped his arm around Della's shoulders. He, too, was quite tall. Both of them looked like they worked out daily, and lived on fruits and vegetables. They had zero body fat and quick, corded muscles. They made a striking couple: tanned, graceful, reserved, intense. All alien qualities in this sleepy Pacific Northwest backwater. As Spence held open the screen for her, he said, "I'm still trying to get myself organized."

"I'll come in," Potts said, cranking up the wattage on her smile. "But I can only stay for a minute. I've got my meals-on-wheels deliveries to make."

The interior of Byrum House was typical of unrestored historic homes in Port Flattery, or "PF," as the locals called it for short. The two-story, farmhouse-style Victorian had ten-foot-high ceilings and fir-plank floors. A thick coat of high-gloss white paint covered the carved wooden bull's-eyes at the corners of the door lintels and the wainscoting that came halfway up the walls. Floral-print wallpaper added some faded color to the living room.

Through an open door, Potts could see into the downstairs bedroom where Spence had set up his office. He had a top-of-the-line computer system, which was turned on.

"Oh, I've never been inside a real screenwriter's office," she gushed. "Can I take a quick peek?"

"I'm afraid it's not very exciting," Spence said. "But sure, go ahead."

Behind her back, Potts felt fairly certain that Della was giving Spence an exasperated *Don't encourage her!* look. Potts didn't care. She wasn't faking her curiosity. The life-styles of the rich and famous fascinated her.

On the floor in the middle of the room stood a few open cardboard boxes marked Books. They hadn't been unpacked yet. She glanced at the titles of the ones on top. They were reference works, scholarly nonfiction books on crime-scene investigation. But for the computer, his desktop was clear. No papers of any kind. She noticed that there weren't any file cabinets in the office, either. He had to keep everything on computer, she thought. The monitor's screen-saver program was enabled—white cartoon ducks endlessly chasing each other across a cobalt blue sky—so she couldn't get a peek at what he was writing.

The office walls were blank, except for the big cork bulletin board Spence had hung up behind his desk. Thumbtacked to it in a double row were photos of young men and women that had been clipped out of magazines and newspapers. Some looked like high-school graduation pictures. Potts didn't count them, but there were more than thirty photos. She thought she recognized one of the men. He had wavy red hair and lots of freckles. She couldn't imagine where she had seen him before.

"Why do I know that face?" she asked, pointing at the picture.

"You probably saw it on the back of a milk carton," Della said from the doorway.

"A milk carton?"

"You know, the Have You Seen This Missing Child? campaign."

"She's exaggerating," Spence said. "He wasn't that young. He was nineteen when he disappeared from Tacoma a year ago. Paul Alan DeJong is his name. You probably remember his picture from the local TV news."

"Is he a relative of yours?"

Spence shook his head. "No, none of them are. They all disappeared without a trace, and under suspicious circumstances. It's part of the research for a made-for-cable movie script I'm writing on missing persons and their families.''

"Sounds like something everyone will want to watch," Potts replied.

"That's exactly what the producers are banking on."

Movies, producers, banks. Potts felt the urge to rush up and kiss him; if Della had been out of the room, she might even have done it.

"So, was there any particular reason you stopped by," Spence asked, "other than to see how we're doing?"

"Yes, of course there is. I wanted to tell that you're invited to a small, very casual party Saturday night over at Victorian View Estates, the new development on the north side of town. I don't know how many people you've managed to meet so far, but everybody who's anybody in PF will be there. It should be a nice mix of newcomers and old-timers."

The "party" was actually a high-pressure sales ambush in the project's model home. Though she had no direct financial interest in the development, Potts's commissions on sales of the yet-to-be-constructed, single-family, quasi-Victorian luxury houses were an integral part of her long-term economic plan. She needed capital to upgrade her handful of in-town properties so she could sell them for top dollar when the market finally turned around.

She had prepared herself for a polite but firm refusal from the Gridleys, so she was pleasantly surprised when, without hesitation, Spence said, "Thanks. We'd love to come."

"Super!" Potts pulled a slip of paper out of her pocket. "I jotted down the address and directions." As she passed the note to him, she managed to graze the back of his hand with her fingertips, a light, stroking pressure. The skin-on-skin contact was electric. She had no way of knowing if it was that good for him, too, but took the fact that his happy expression hadn't changed as a positive sign. "Oh, dear, I really do have to run now," she said, glancing at her watch.

THE FIRST THING Potts did after sliding behind the wheel of her cream-colored Mercedes was to check her makeup in the rearview mirror. Somehow her eyeliner had gotten smudged. She set about repairing the damage at once. Image was everything in real estate, which was the reason for the 300-class sedan.

She had Port Flattery's police chief to thank for the classy car. She'd picked up the late-model four-door for a tenth of its actual value at a federal-drug-seizure auction that Stan "Gummy" Nordland had put her onto, this shortly after they'd resumed dating. Gummy had been her high-school sweetheart, her first husband and was the father of her grown son. Before the Gridleys had moved in, he'd run a criminal-record computer check on them for her. They'd never even had so much as a traffic ticket in California.

As she started up the Mercedes and pulled away from the curb, Potts waved from the elbow, beauty-queen style, to the couple watching from the porch.

CHAPTER TWO

Airspace over the Shenandoah Valley, Virginia

Hal Brognola stared out the side window of the midnight black Sikorsky helicopter. One thousand feet below him, the shadow of the Justice Department chopper swept over a deep green sea of treetops, the densely forested flanks of Stony Man Mountain. With smooth air, like they had this morning, the trip between the Oval Office and the covert-operations center at Stony Man Farm never took more than an hour. This day it seemed endless. He popped the top of a plastic bottle and dumped its last three tablets into his mouth. He'd been eating antacids like candy mints since before daybreak.

On the empty seat beside him sat his locked briefcase, which held a pack of computer diskettes and a copy of a videocassette that had been anonymously sent to the FBI. Seventy-two hours had passed since the tape arrived at Quantico, addressed to current head of the Behavioral Sciences Unit. Because of the sensitive nature of its contents, the cassette had never made it into the Bureau's normal channels. That morning it had fallen to Brognola, White House liaison and head of Justice's ultrasecret Sensitive Operations Group, to brief the President on the unfolding situation and its wider implications.

After the big Fed had done that and played selected parts of the Karkanian tape, the President had asked him for his opinion on a course of action. Brognola had said he thought the Bureau should be left to handle the entire matter on its own, through its standard operating procedures, and that the SOG not be involved in any way. Otherwise, he'd reasoned, not only would Stony Man Farm be duplicating official efforts, but it also risked crossing paths with the Bureau's field investigation, which could compromise the secrecy of the fortified compound and its elite personnel.

Though Brognola had witnessed the temper explosions of his boss before, this day was the first time he'd ever been the primary target. This President didn't shout when he lost his cool. He was a leaner. He moved in real close and spoke in a normal voice, giving you the full force of his mouthwash. The natural response to such an invasion of personal space was a hasty retreat—of course, in this case, there was nowhere to go, unless you bolted from the room. Once he had you trapped, backed up against a wall or the front of a desk, he used both hands in your face to drive home his talking points.

"Screw the Bureau's standard operating procedure," the President had said. "What you've got down there is a freaking sieve, a goddamned rumor mill with a direct line to the networks whenever it suits somebody's private agenda. Can you imagine what those jackals in the media would do with something as sensational as this? For the sake of a few ratings points, they'd throw the whole country into a panic. A needless panic. People would be afraid to go to work or send their kids to school. I'll be damned if that kind of hysterical bushwah is going to go down on my watch.

"Spread the word to anyone who has seen that tape or has knowledge of it. This matter is under presidential seal. If you talk to your wife, or your barber, or your golf buddies about it, no matter who you are, no matter who you know, your career is history...and so is your pension."

"But, sir, that won't stop the ongoing murder investigations."

"The Department of Justice can investigate until the cows come home, as far as I'm concerned. In the meantime, I want you to turn your main man loose on it. And if he verifies this conspiracy theory, he is authorized to clean house, top to bottom. Every single one of these scum erased, understand? And, Hal, I don't want the bloody trail leading back to my door."

The President's parting shot had been a low blow.

Brognola didn't need to be reminded of the consequences of a screwup at his end, and they both knew it. In Stony Man Farm's many years of operation, not so much as a hint of backsplash had ever reached Pennsylvania Avenue. Though the remark had stung, Brognola hadn't gotten his back up. That would have been counterproductive.

The Sikorsky banked steeply right, snapping Brognola to the here and now. Beyond the concrete X of the landing strip, he saw the roofs of Stony Man Farm's cluster of buildings. The helicopter's sudden descent made his stomach lurch, which brought a fresh twinge of fire to the middle of his chest. In the hope of finding a lost antacid tablet, he rummaged through the bottoms of all his suit pockets. No such luck. He cleared his throat and swallowed hard, trying to force down the lava that was billowing up from his belly.

Even though the big Fed shared the President's frustration and anger at the situation, he had mixed feelings about the plan of action. The Chief Executive wanted the whole matter swept so far under the rug that no one would ever find it. Sure, the President was thinking about the safety of the general public, but he was also concerned with history and its view of his term of office. Criminal acts had destroyed presidencies before— who could forget Jimmy Carter and the hostages in Iran?

Because Brognola was a career man at Justice, not some political-hack appointee, it ticked him off that the ball had been taken away from the FBI. After all, his fellow agents had been murdered. Organization pride was at stake in the hunting down and capture of their killers. If the matter was resolved covertly, via executive action, the guilty parties would never be publicly identified. Closure would be impossible for the families and co-workers of the victims. Officially it would remain an unsolved case, forever.

Under the circumstances, a permanent stain on the department's record was the lesser of two evils.

From the evidence collected and analyzed to date, the United States faced a new type of international terrorist organization, one that gloried in murder not for political, social, economic or religious ends, but for its own sake. Given that threat assessment, the President had made the right decision. Brognola had to put aside department loyalty. The Bureau was too methodical, too conservative, too concerned with cases holding up in court to do what was required to nip the evil in the bud.

A job like that called for someone without a name, a face, or a government ID card, someone who could penetrate the conspiracy and at his own discretion, terminate those involved.

It was a job for the Executioner.

Stony Man Farm, Computer Lab

AFTER THE RECORDED portion of the cassette ended, blank tape continued to run, filling one of the lab's video monitors with black-and-white confetti.

No one moved to switch off the VCR.

No one said a word.

The only sound in the room was the steady hiss of the air-conditioning.

Though this was the fourth time Hal Brognola had sat through the whole tape, the spectacle of the federal agent's thirty-two-minute ordeal still numbed his soul. It had the same effect on Stony Man's cybersquad, men and women hardened to the aftermath of unspeakable violence—to death, the state of; not dying, the act of.

Because of what was done to the victim on camera, because he was alive and conscious right up to the finish, the video was a personal, intimate assault on anyone who witnessed it. As the ghastly last sequence began, Brognola had watched his colleagues turn away from the screen.

Only one person saw it through to the end.

The ice blue eyes of Mack Bolan stayed riveted on the man with the beard, the video's chief actor and director, the lone participant with a visible face. Post-recording computer editing had transformed the heads of Karkanian's accomplices into checkerboards of flesh-toned blurs. For all the emotion Bolan's face revealed, it might as well have been blurred out, too. Through even the worst of it, he sat perfectly still, his brow remained unfurrowed, his breathing slow and regular.

The Executioner's detachment sent a chill down Brognola's spine. Over the years, his old friend had done much killing, face-to-face, in the name of personal and public justice. Had the accumulated weight of all those taken lives finally made Bolan immune to human feeling, to human suffering? Brognola shook off the unwelcome thought. A highly skilled interrogator, he knew how to read body language. He knew that angry facial expressions and gestures almost always reflected deep-seated fear, indicating the wearer was much closer to flight than fight. By that yardstick, Mack Bolan's outward calm didn't mean he wasn't moved by the death agony of the man on the tape; he was simply—and completely—unafraid of it. To a trained observer such as Brognola, a placid expression during intense stress, such as interrogation or arrest, sent up a huge red flag. It revealed a focused mind working four or five steps ahead.

"God, I feel like I need a shower, inside and out,"

Aaron "the Bear" Kurtzman growled, breaking the heavy silence. He used the remote control in his lap to click off the VCR and monitor. Unlocking the brakes of his wheelchair, the computer-lab chief pivoted around to glare at Brognola. "I hope you had a damned good reason for making us sit through that."

"The video is connected to the ambush slayings of Justice personnel in Seattle last week," Brognola replied. "The man you just saw murdered was Special Agent in Charge Lawrence Deeds."

"The killing of federal agents by a gang of criminals sounds like something the Bureau should be able to handle without our help," said Barbara Price, Stony Man's mission controller. Her pretty, high-cheekboned face was starting to regain some of the color it had lost during the tape playback.

"If it was as simple as that, I wouldn't have asked you to watch the tape. The President believes, and I agree, that we have a much wider and more dangerous problem on our hands, something that requires the immediate involvement of this group."

Brognola turned to Carmen Delahunt, the compact redheaded woman sitting at a computer terminal beside him. He handed her the pack of diskettes from his briefcase and asked her to load them.

While the ex-FBI computer specialist was doing that, Brognola said to the others, "Are any of you familiar with the interactive computer game known as 'Legion'?"

"A computer game?" Kurtzman repeated. "Are we still on the same page here, Hal?"

"Stick with me, please. I'll explain the connection. Have any of you heard of Legion?"

"Sure, I know what it is," said Akira Tokaido, pushing back in his ergonomic chair. The youngest member of the Stony Man cybernetics team sported long hair sometimes worn in a samauri topknot, a stylishly holed, Nine Inch Nails concert T-shirt and prided himself on having the lab's most cluttered workstation. "It's got its own homepage on the Net. Legion's a role-playing fantasy game, like Dungeons & Dragons. Only it isn't about swords and sorcery. The players pretend they're serial killers on the hunt in a make-believe metropolitan city. The city is populated with a few thousand potential targets, men, women and children with names, faces, life histories, habit patterns. The object of the game is to acquire as many cyberkills as possible without getting caught and executed. The more kills a player gets, the higher he or she advances through the maze of levels."

"Now, there's a sick premise," Delahunt commented.

"If you're ready, call up the game disk," Brognola told her.

"Done," the redhead said, double-clicking her mouse.

A high-quality computer-animated cartoon popped onto one of the wall screens. It was drawn from the point of view of a pursuer, seen through his eyes as he chased a terrified female victim down a dimly lit downtown alley. The jerky, fast action was accompanied by the sounds of heavy breathing and footfalls. The pursuer quickly closed ground, crashing his prey into a row of trash cans. For an instant, the face of the cartoon victim filled the entire screen, then it was blocked off by a gleaming, raised knife blade, which reflected the face of the killer: black-hooded down to the nose with phosphor-green eyes behind narrow eyeslits.

A shrill scream erupted as the blade vanished downward. The knife came up, dripping red, then plunged down again. More red. More screams. The cries rapidly dwindled to nothing as the screen filled with spreading crimson; in its center appeared the Legion logo—a hooded face with glowing eyes.

"Whatever happened to Crusader Rabbit?" asked Dr. Huntington Wethers as the game's logo was replaced by a request for the player's name and/or identification number.

"Who?" Tokaido asked.

"My point exactly," the African American, former Berkeley professor said, slipping his unlit pipe back into the corner of his mouth.

Tokaido shrugged. "The way I understand it," he said, "the game was started as a gross-out prank a year ago by some grad students at UC San Diego. Since it went out on the Net, it's become much more complex, thanks to the input of various players from around the world."

"Have you ever tried it?" Brognola asked.

"I looked at it once. It didn't interest me."

"Well, it's interested the Bureau's Internet Crimes Investigation Division," Brognola said. "They've been monitoring Legion and its players for six months, hoping to track down real serials attracted to the game's concept. This thing started out as a gruesome twist on

D & D, but it's evolved into a subculture. There are chat rooms on the homepage connected with the game's various skill levels. ICID has been able to enter the rooms where beginners meet each other and discuss strategy, but the more advanced players exchange ideas in a restricted environment. Access to the upper-level rooms is by code, and inside the rooms all communication is in code.''

"Are these commercially manufactured encryption programs?" Wethers asked.

"Some of them are, and they're all top-of-the-line," the big Fed replied. "The problem our decoders face is that the active program changes every twelve hours. By the time we break the entry code, it's usually too late to use it. So far, we've only had a handful of peeks into the upper-level discussions."

Bolan shook his head. "To me Legion sounds like a complicated Justice Department scam," he said, "a way to sucker in and capture wanted killers. Real serials would be suspicious of it. Why would they take the risk?"

Brognola nodded. The Executioner could always find the knot in a problem, which was one of the reasons he'd been called in from the field for the planning of this mission.

"As I said," the big Fed continued, "we've managed to penetrate the highest-level chat rooms a few times and, days later unfortunately, cracked some of the coded discussions. From the content of these exchanges, and subsequent events, we believe that actual murders are being committed by the highest-level players."

"Body count," Bolan said grimly. "The ultimate security check for a mass killer."

"You got it. No way could the FBI stand by and allow innocent people to be murdered just to flesh out an entrapment setup."

"From what you've told us so far," Wethers said, "I take it that ICID hasn't been able to confirm any of this speculation by using the game to capture a real killer. Is there any direct evidence of a known serial's connection with Legion?"

"We know that Karkanian logged onto the Internet from a terminal at the Sparksburg facility just prior to his escape. ICID has also been monitoring the modem activity of a condemned California mass murderer, Bill Willie Pickett, and he is definitely into Legion."

"Prison authorities let *him* play the game?" Delahunt said. "God, I remember that TV-newsmagazine interview he did from death row a few years back. The bonehead interviewer was so cowed she let him cast himself as a philosopher. It made my hair stand on end."

"Pickett sued the state to get access to the Internet," Brognola told her, "supposedly in order to prepare his appeals. He linked up with Legion on the very first day. The ICID got wind of it and convinced the prison authorities to let him continue in the hope that they might get something of value."

"Has Pickett downloaded the daily codes so he can talk to the others?" Kurtzman said.

"Negative. He has never entered any of the chat rooms, and we haven't been able to prove that the e-mail he receives is encrypted. Much of it qualifies as fan mail. After all, he's a Legion celebrity player. He routinely gets sent detailed news reports of actual murders. He also has access to replays of selected cyber-kills.''

''A guy on death row doesn't worry me,'' Kurtzman said. ''He can't hurt anybody. But you think real murderers outside of prison are using the game as a contact point?''

''It's much worse than that,'' Hal said. ''It's gone way beyond the pen-pal stage. It looks like they've organized themselves into hunting packs. In the last seventy-two hours, we've logged five similar killings—two in Germany, one each in France, Britain and Canada. All were elaborately choreographed mutilations like the murder of SAC Larry Deeds. All the victims were ranking officers on standing serial-killer task forces.''

''So, the agenda here is revenge against international law enforcement?'' Price asked.

''We know only what they've done to date,'' Brognola said. ''We don't have enough information to make a guess at what they're really after, which is one of the reasons the President is so concerned. Our mission is first to define the nature and limits of the conspiracy. To do that, we have to infiltrate the upper levels of the game.''

''Which means we have to play it and win,'' Tokaido said.

''That's the only way to get Striker inside the organization,'' Brognola said. ''We've got to be careful at every step. We need a dossier for him that will stand up to intense scrutiny, and we can't make any mistakes after we get access to the chat rooms. These people are highly intelligent. They're certainly expecting penetration attempts by law enforcement. They might even welcome them. For all we know, they might let us into the loop just to get their hands on another law-enforcement victim. I don't think I need to remind any of you what that would mean.''

"What about the Bureau?" Bolan asked. "It's sure as hell not going to give ground on this one."

"We can monitor where the official investigation is going," Brognola replied. "Keep tabs on what it's uncovered. My job will be to keep us from butting heads down the road."

"Good enough," the Executioner said.

"Okay, people, let's get cracking on this," Kurtzman said as he wheeled up the ramp that led to his elevated computer station. "We've got a lot of information to digest, and everyone has to be up to speed before we go on-line."

CHAPTER THREE

Prison Library,
San Quentin, California

The smile on Bill Willie Pickett's face stretched practically from ear to ear as he rattled the keys of the library's computer. He used the system software to snip out a thirty-five-second piece of today's surprise from the information superhighway. One of his cyberpals had downloaded him a short segment of the Deeds video. As the gruesome loop cycled over and over, he swept a hand through his greasy, thinning, shoulder-length blond hair. It tickled him enormously that somewhere out in the real world, the federal agents monitoring his computer had to watch as he gloated over the murder of one of their own.

Life could be good, even on death row.

Though his scheduled date of execution was less than a week away, Pickett remained upbeat and confident. And why not? Everything was finally falling into place. As cyanide-time drew closer, the number of living witnesses from his first trial had shrunk considerably. That some should die over the space of a decade was to be expected; that so many would go in the past few months was a major break for Pickett's cause.

Luck had had nothing to do with it, of course. His fans from Legion had intervened on his behalf, permanently removing the most hardheaded of the prosecution's witnesses. The memories of the surviving do-gooders, fuzzy to begin with, would only get worse after his game buddies entered their homes by night and interpreted the rash of fatal "accidents" for them. Shortly Pickett's attorney would be filing a motion for a new trial, based on affidavits of recanted eyewitness testimony.

When he got out, Pickett intended to pay Shana Bledsoe of TV's *Deadline America* a visit. He wanted to thank her in person—and in his own special way—for his fifteen minutes of fame. Her exclusive, prime-time interview three years earlier had given him an international audience for his ideas. Seminal ideas, as it turned out.

Instead of following the standard *Dead Man Walking* script, telling the world he was sorry for all the killing he'd done and tearfully begging for mercy, or claiming he'd found Jesus and therefore had hope of a higher forgiveness, Pickett had taken the road as yet untraveled. He'd explained to the stunned newsmagazine reporter why the lives of his many victims didn't matter, why the suffering of the families of the victims mattered even less.

"They're nothing but bacteria," he'd told her. "Self-replicating eating machines. Double dittos, mindless copies of copies merrily gobbling up the world. You're one of them, Shana, you're a copy, too.

Think about it for a second. Think about your family photo album. Isn't it filled with ruddy-faced, ugly-git relatives? How is it different from your next-door neighbor's album? Or his accountant's? Or his accountant's car mechanic's? The ugly-git relatives are interchangeable, and each comes with interchangeable, heartfelt dreams. Adopted dreams.

"Whether you know it or not, Shana, every thought you've ever had, every desire you've ever felt, originated elsewhere. Originated outside your pretty head. All your programs were written by long-dead strangers and engineered with one end in mind—to increase your appetite for goods and services. The more sugar syrup your kind distills from the planet's juices, the more it has to have. You gorge yourselves into a stupor on the sticky stuff, on materialism and religion, because you know, deep down, there's no point to your being here—and that scares you shitless."

An outraged Shana Bledsoe had struck back. "You're no different. Murderers have been around since day one. There's nothing original about you, either."

"I never claimed that there was."

"I'm sure the audience is as curious as I am," she'd said. "What's the point in your being here?"

"Do you know that there hasn't been a meaningful dip in the human population curve since the Black Death of the Middle Ages? The sucker goes practically straight up, geometric growth right through the world wars, the modern famines and epidemics."

"That's thanks to science and medicine," she had countered defiantly. "It's called human progress."

"Whatever you choose to call it, one by one you've isolated and killed all the tigers, killed them so your kind can feed and breed in warmth and safety." A smile had twisted his lips. "Well, not quite *all* the tigers…"

When he'd suddenly reached across the table and stroked her hand, Shana Bledsoe had jerked back in her chair so hard that it had tipped over backward, sending her sprawling.

Nowhere in the brief interview did Bill Willie Pickett directly mention "his kind." But the implication was there, all the same. With a few well-chosen words, he had redefined the nature of the conflict, redrawn the scale of the battleground. Like a beacon, it shone for anyone who wanted to see it.

Other than being its inspiration, Pickett had had nothing directly to do with the creation of Legion. Two years after the *Deadline America* interview, the game network had come to him, fully formed, with an offer of celebrity-player status. His attorney had dutifully slipped him the message without realizing what it might mean. Pickett had seen the possibilities at once. He was a whole lot smarter than the California prison authorities gave him credit for—smart enough to take a dive on every jailhouse IQ test he had ever been given. Smart enough to make certain advance preparations before he showed his hand and tried to get access to the Internet.

After ten minutes of rerunning the Deeds loop, Pickett stopped the horror show, confident that the Feds would be hearing those shrill screams in their sleep. He screened back to the e-mail note attached to the video clip and reread it. "This is the pilot for an exciting new series," it said. "As you'll see, the guest star deserves an Emmy—he turned himself inside out for the part." It was signed "Herman Mudgett."

Using his mouse, Pickett dumped the entire transmission. He hated that he couldn't save any of the stuff Legion sent him, but that was the arrangement. It made it look like he thought he was being extracareful, like he thought he was putting something over on the Feds; as if he didn't know his every move was being monitored and recorded. His scrupulous housekeeping was a diversion, more play-dumb for the cops.

It took Pickett a little more than ten minutes to compose the six lines of his thank-you note to Herman Mudgett. When he was done, he e-mailed the message to him in care of the game network.

THE SERIAL MURDERER known as "Archangel" entered the darkness of the two-car garage through an unlocked side door. With a small, powerful flashlight, he examined the killing ground. The concrete floor gleamed like gray ice; the workbench was so clean he could have eaten off it. Except for a pair of forty-gallon plastic trash cans along the side wall, there was nothing to hide behind.

Archangel could see the trash cans were useless to him, no matter where he moved them. On the other hand, when his target parked in the garage and opened the driver's door, it and the rest of the vehicle would cover him from all floor-level angles of fire. The car's side windows and windshield weren't bulletproof, but the angle of the glass could deflect an otherwise well-aimed shot. A clean miss or a nonfatal hit would give the driver time to draw and fire his own gun. Archangel had no intention of letting that happen.

Looking up, he swept his light over the garage's open rafters. Stacked on them were a child's plastic swimming pool, assorted pieces of camping gear and some cardboard boxes. There were also a few pieces of lumber and lengths of PVC pipe, leftovers from a home-improvement project. With the flashlight between his teeth, the killer scaled the bare studs of the back wall and climbed up into the framework of rafters. Using the roof's cross braces for handholds, he moved to the center of the garage. Once there, he turned off the flashlight.

He didn't have to wait long on his dark perch.

A car pulled into the driveway almost immediately, its headlights edging the perimeter of the garage door in bright white light. A second later, a switch clicked below Archangel's feet. An electric motor whirred, the automatic door clanked as it started up and the garage's interior light came on.

Archangel stepped along the narrow board, positioning himself a little closer to the rising door. As the blue car nosed into the space below him, he drew a heavy-caliber autopistol from his belt holster, gave the sound suppressor a twist to double-check the seal and thumbed back the hammer.

The driver had no more than a quarter of a second to pick Archangel out from the stuff stored in the rafters—as long as it took him to pull ten feet into the garage. Past that point, the car's roof blocked his view of what was above him. If he'd been looking up at the time, he could have done it. But Homicide Captain Roberto Joven was concentrating on the trash cans, trying to not sideswipe them again this night. An ambush by the serial killer he hunted was the last thing on his mind. After all, he was home safe, and happy to have made it through another long and difficult day. That's what Archangel counted on—a momentarily lowered guard.

Before shutting off the engine, Joven honked his horn twice. In the distance, Archangel heard the back door of the house opening and closing, then high-pitched laughter. Joven's two kids were running out to greet him, part of the nightly ritual.

The garage door opener's electric switch clicked; the motor whirred again. As the door started down, a stocky man with close-cut brown hair got out of the car. Archangel let him straighten, then squeezed off a steeply angled, two-handed shot. The top of the homicide captain's head puffed crimson as the single bullet struck, bouncing him off the inside of the car door and hard onto his back on the floor.

Archangel hopped quickly from the rafters to the car roof to the concrete, careful to sidestep the spreading pool of red. He didn't pause to check his victim's vital signs. A glance at the exploded ruin of the man's lower face told him a second shot was unnecessary. He rolled under the closing door and came up running on the other side. As he dashed down the driveway, he pitched the gun into a bed of ivy.

By the time the screaming started at the Joven residence, he was around the corner, already jumping into his getaway car. When he twisted the ignition key, the engine didn't turn over. Instead, his black-gloved hand on the steering wheel, the warm glow of the dashboard lights, the suburban neighborhood he could see through the windshield—it all faded to black.

The words "Please stand by for your score" appeared on the computer screen.

Mack Bolan shoved the keyboard away. Though he'd aced the game's final test, there were no high fives from the Stony Man computer crew. After watching him hunt down and kill thirty-two virtual cops in the space of two days, his companions were in no mood to celebrate anything.

As advertised, the Internet game was as close to serial murder as you could get without committing a crime. Of course, *close* was a relative term. Better than anyone in the chilly lab, the Executioner understood the dividing line between make-believe and actual killing. A chasm a million miles wide separated the deaths of Roberto Joven, the computer construct, and the living man known as Lawrence Deeds.

Even so, the victory had left an evil taste in Bolan's mouth, too. It was a testament to the ingenuity of Legion's designers. He wouldn't have given a second thought to the amount of cyberblood on his hands or the fact that the "dead" were all law-enforcement good guys if it hadn't been for the game's carefully developed and highly realistic detail. Each of Bolan's victims had had a face and a personal history, a distinguished service record. Each left people behind who cared, people with faces, people who grieved. Fiction or not, the accumulated weight of all that loss, all that waste hung over the computer lab like a nauseating fog.

The idea to go after Legion City's police force had been Bolan's. Out of the game's thousands of potential victims, the cops were the biggest challenge. Always armed, they weren't shy about shooting back, or shooting first, for that matter. And when the Legion City PD opened up on a suspect, they let it all hang out. If a player was killed in an exchange of fire by police bullets, or captured by them and executed—official justice was swift and certain in virtual reality—he lost all the kills he had accumulated up to that point and dropped back to the game's beginner level. Because the police were so dangerous to confront and take down, Legion awarded double points for their murders.

According to the game's homepage archives, while many players had tried to specialize in killing cops before, no one had ever gone all the way to the top by that route. Since Bolan wanted to move up fast and stand out in the process, and since the only alternative—targeting unarmed civilians—was even more distasteful, there was really no other choice.

"Archangel" had kept an extremely low profile in the bottom-rung chat rooms. Through their game alter ego, Bolan and the Stony Man team had observed rather than participated in ongoing discussions of stalking, hunt strategy and killing techniques, and in endless Trivial Pursuit–type challenges about the careers of famous criminals. At the lower levels, there wasn't much to hold the interest of a real serial murderer. It was obvious from the superficial information being exchanged that the beginning players had never killed outside of cyberspace. Most of them came off as typical murder groupies, mildly disturbed individuals craving something powerful and dangerous in their lives, something that was also completely risk free.

The "Please stand by" message on Bolan's desk monitor and the lab's wall screen was replaced by a flashing six-digit number. After a few seconds, his point total vanished, and the screen filled with lines of type.

"Congratulations, Archangel!" the message read. "Your new total score means you've reached Legion's highest rank, level five. Entry is by access code only, and all communication in the chat room is encrypted. Your personal access code number is 8991. Memorize the number. Don't write it down. Respond to the level-five chat-room handshake with your access number, game alias and point total, and the current communication code will be automatically downloaded to your system. We're looking forward to hearing from you soon." The message was signed "Legion."

Kurtzman thumped his desk with a balled fist. "It's party-crashin' time!" he said. "Is everybody ready?"

Heads nodded around the lab.

Barbara Price turned to Akira Tokaido and said, "Disconnect and rescramble the phone link, then log us back on." As he did that, she cautioned everyone in the room. "Remember people, this isn't a one-way recon. These guys are going to be checking us out, too. Keep on your toes or we'll lose them."

At the handshake prompt, the Executioner entered the four-digit code and other information, and the Net site responded with a torrent of encryption program. When the data transfer to the Stony Man system stopped, the level-five chat-room page appeared on the desk and wall monitors.

"Wow, check the on-screen log!" Carmen Delahunt said. "There are sixty-eight players in the room with us. That's high. The Bureau estimates only about thirty serials are currently working in the U.S."

"Which means the Bureau's estimate is all wet," Tokaido stated.

"Don't forget that some of them could be from out-of-country," Kurtzman told him, "international killers linked up to the global network."

"It could also mean the players at level five aren't all mass murderers," Hunt Wethers added. "We might have to peel off another layer of this cybergarbage to get at our real targets."

Then a line of words began to unroll across the screens. Someone, somewhere along the information superhighway was typing in a message. "Archangel, this is Butcher Boy," it said. "I like your style of play. We all do. We think you have a special gift."

"Thanks," Bolan typed back.

"You might have heard the rumors that level five is a whole new ball game," Butcher Boy wrote. "Well, they're right. We do things differently up here. For starters, a few of us get together in person with each new level-five qualifier to explain how it all works."

"I like things just the way they are," Bolan told him. "Nice and anonymous."

"That's it," Price said. "Whatever they're offering, make them lay it all out."

"The face-to-face isn't optional, Archangel," Butcher Boy continued. "It's a requirement for you to be accepted into this level of play. If you refuse to meet us, your access code will be disabled, and you will drop back to level four forever.''

"How do I know you're not law enforcement?''

"Do you have something to hide?''

"Everybody has something to hide,'' Bolan replied.

"As far as we know,'' Butcher Boy typed, "you could be the cop. We've been watching how you insulate yourself from a call trace. Pretty neat. Maybe too neat.''

"All that proves is that I know a little something about telecommunications.''

"Then you know that sensitive matters are best discussed in person, in sanitized surroundings.''

"Why would I take that kind of risk?''

"Because you're that kind of guy,'' Butcher Boy responded. "You obviously get a kick out of putting it all on the line. You didn't climb the Legion ladder so quickly by playing it safe. Take that last kill, for example. For all you knew, that homicide cop could have been onto the fact you were stalking him. The garage could have been a trap. A setup. You took the chance because the prize was worth it.''

"It was a game. I wasn't risking anything.''

"That's the whole point. It doesn't have to just be a game. Legion doesn't have to exist only in cyberspace. When skilled players interact in real life, the rewards can be very special. That's part of what we want to talk to you about. We're offering you an entirely different kind of fellowship here. A unique opportunity. You could learn a lot from us. And vice versa, no doubt.''

"Sounds like we won't have to be turning over any more slippery rocks," Wethers commented.

Price agreed. "These are the bastards we're after. Go ahead, Striker. Close the deal."

"Where do you want to meet?" Bolan typed.

"What's the closest big city to your location?"

"Baltimore," the Executioner lied, knowing even as he input the answer that he wasn't fooling anyone. Given the care he'd taken to scramble his phone source, Legion wouldn't expect him to just meekly hand over his whereabouts.

After a brief pause, Butcher Boy gave him directions to a large shopping mall north of the city, off Interstate 695. "Be there tonight, at the south entrance, five minutes before the last movie lets out. Stand on the left side of the doorway as you face the building, next to the pay phones. Once you take up your position, don't move until we contact you."

Bolan broke the connection.

"The more I think about it," Kurtzman said as he rolled his wheelchair back down the ramp, "the more this meet thing gives me the creeps. We know what these bastards are capable of."

"The dossier on Michael Gene Butler is rock solid," Bolan said, referring to the new identity Brognola had provided him with. Hal had asked the Bureau's Violent Criminal Apprehension Program—VICAP—to create a serial-killer file under the Butler alias and send it out on the national law-enforcement computer network. "I know the bio by heart. I'm covered."

The cybernetics expert gave him a dubious look. "You're covered only if they bother to check your record. These guys aren't dumb. They might not even look at a computerized rap sheet because it's so easy to fake. Bottom line, we don't know what they want from you. They might put a scalpel in your hand and ask you to start slicing up somebody. Or they might just take you someplace quiet and dissect you for fun.''

"There's another problem here, too," Delahunt added. "Legion had no idea of our physical location. No advance warning at all. We gave them a city and bang, they came back with a meet site in under three minutes. That can't be a coincidence. What if we'd told them we were in Dallas? Or Boise? Could they have still gotten a team in position in a few hours? I think so. I think they have multiple, active cells across the country and the cells are supermobile.''

"What's your point?" Bolan asked.

"We know there are at least sixty-eight of them. We don't know how many enemy you're going to be facing.''

"Carmen, the opposition numbers don't matter," the Executioner told her. "This mission begins with a soft penetration. There's no way around that. And to pull it off, I have to go in with my hands up and my weapons holstered. If there's five of them or a hundred, I'm still at their mercy.''

"I don't like this," Kurtzman said. "Maybe we should contact Hal and run the new information past him before we proceed.''

"Hal's already given the okay," Price reminded him. "The new information is ninety-five percent supposition. It changes nothing. The mission is a go unless Striker says otherwise.''

All eyes turned toward the tall, dark-haired man.

It was a go.

"WHO IS HERMAN MUDGETT?" Hal Brognola asked, removing the unlit stub of his cigar from the corner of his mouth. In his other hand, he held a copy of Bill Willie Pickett's last e-mail exchange with Legion.

"Was," the agent from the Bureau's Internet Crimes Investigation Division corrected him. "The state of Pennsylvania executed Mudgett in May of 1896. Some of the Legion players take game handles from historical figures—their serial-killer heroes."

"Cute touch. What did this Mudgett guy do to get in the hall of fame?"

"He was a failed medical student. He killed women so he could take their life insurance, real estate and money. With the proceeds of his early crimes, he built an apartment building in Chicago, complete with secret passages and hidden torture rooms. After its basement graveyard was unearthed, it became known as the 'Murder Castle.' He lured young women with promises of stenographer jobs, seduced them, got them to sign over their possessions, then murdered them in various ways. He had two-hundred-plus kills by the time he was caught. One of his profitable little sidelines was selling the stripped human skeletons to medical schools."

Brognola chewed his cigar butt. The Quantico office smelled like stale coffee grounds, and it was so cramped you couldn't turn around without bumping into something or someone. Four other ICID agents were working elbow to elbow at computer terminals set up along one wall. Contributing in a big way to the space shortage, a third of the room was devoted solely to the study of Bill Willie Pickett. Bulletin boards on easels were decorated with blow-up photos of the interior of Pickett's San Quentin cell, showing every item he possessed. The ICID unit had collected identical books, magazines, calendars, toiletries, candy bars, cigarettes, towels, bedding and clothes, and spread everything out on long tables. Also on a table was a video recorder and monitor; both were running. The screen showed surveillance video of Pickett sleeping in his cell.

"That's a live picture?" Brognola asked.

"His afternoon nap," the agent replied. "Bill Willie likes his sleep. Hate to think what he must dream about."

The big Fed gestured at the Pickett shrine. "Where are you on all this?"

"We're sure he and Legion are communicating in code, but we haven't figured out how to break it, yet."

"You're watching him twenty-four hours a day and you don't know what he's doing?"

"We've been tracking his every move, cataloging everything he touches, in the order he touches it, and so far it's been no help. He'll pore over a particular book before writing an e-mail, but when we have the two compared and analyzed, there's no connection. As you can see, he's got a lot of stuff to work with. And he keeps adding to it every day. Books. Magazines."

"Doesn't that tell you something?" Brognola asked exasperatedly.

"Sir?"

"He's jerking your chain, for Christ's sake. You're not fooling him. He knows you're watching him."

ICID agents looked at Brognola like he'd just skidded a dune buggy across their front lawn. One of the privileges of rank, he was about to do a wheelie through their begonias.

"I want copies of everything you have," he said. "Electronic mail. Video. Dupes of all the publications and products he currently has access to. I want it all dated and assembled in order of acquisition. And I want a list of everything he's read in the past eighteen months.

"Sir, our surveillance doesn't go back that far."

"It does now, son. And one more thing. I want it all ready to ship before you leave the building."

CHAPTER FOUR

Victorian View Estates,
Port Flattery, Washington

Spence Gridley filled the viewfinder of his camcorder with the weather-seamed face of the Port Flattery police chief. From across the crowded living room of the model home, Gummy Nordland was giving him his Dirty Harry, hard-as-nails stare. The tough-cop look was supposed to intimidate him. It probably did scare the pants off preteenage shoplifters, but Gridley found it laughable.

He dropped the field of view to take in Nordland's big, soft stomach. No way could the man button the front of his sports jacket over that protruding gut. Gridley focused in on the ornately tooled leather belt that rode low on his hips, its buckle hidden somewhere under the overhang of his belly. Though Port Flattery's most serious crime problem was seasonal pilfering in the tourist stores, its police chief swaggered around at parties with his piece in full view—a blue steel Government Model .45 Colt with custom-made, contoured Brazilwood grips.

A soft, warm hand touched Gridley's forearm and lingered there.

"Oh, you're videotaping my Gummy!" Bobbie Marie Potts said. "Let me go get him. I know he wants to meet you."

Gridley lowered the camcorder. Her Gummy seemed much more interested in making time with a redhead in a short skirt.

Potts put an end to that in short order, actually stepping between the two of them to get her man's full attention. The police chief sipped from a plastic cup filled with bourbon and ice as his former wife and present girlfriend pointed over at the Gridleys. Nordland nodded without enthusiasm and followed Potts across the room.

"So, you gonna put me in a movie, or what?" Nordland asked, tapping the business end of the camcorder with his fingernail.

"No, honey," Potts replied, reaching up to cling to his wrist and in the process, firmly pulling his hand away from the video camera's lens. "Like I told you, Mr. Gridley writes movies. He's making a tape of the party to send to all his friends down in Hollywood. He's gonna show them how we live up here in God's country. Maybe some of them will even want to move to town. Isn't that nice?"

Nordland's dour expression brightened as he took in Della Gridley, spectacular in a fuzzy turtleneck sweater and tight jeans. "Pleased to meet you, ma'am," he said. When he turned back to her husband, the smile downshifted to a smirk. "Hollywood big shot like you," he said, "I'll bet you know all the stars. Heather Locklear? Nicolette Sheridan? Pamela Anderson Lee?"

Gridley paused a second before he answered. In the background, sixties soft rock competed with the laughter and loud talk of the party goers. "I've met them, sure," he said, "but I can't say I really know them. I hang out with producers and directors mostly. The people who control the purse strings. For a screenwriter, it's a survival thing down there."

"Kind of like a wood tick sucking on a dog's ass?"

"Gummy! You've had too much to drink. Say you're sorry! Say it right now."

The chief glowered down at Potts. He wasn't sorry, and he wasn't going to apologize. To drive home his point, he took a long swallow from his cup.

Della broke the impasse. "Phew!" she said, wrinkling her nose. "What's that awful smell? Is somebody cooking broccoli in the kitchen? If they are, they're burning it."

"Around here we call that 'the smell of money,'" Nordland said. "It's the smoke from the pulp mill down in Lower PF Bay."

"It hardly ever blows in this direction," Potts assured her, then changed the subject. "So, what do you two think of the house? Pretty classy, huh? We're all really proud of the way the design fits in with historic Port Flattery. Totally modern, affordable housing, yet with a Victorian flair."

"Yes, it's *very* nice," Della said.

Spence avoided making a direct comment by pretending to videotape the living room's decor. With its light wood-toned plastic veneers, beige carpet, white walls, simulated-brick fireplace and track lighting, it could have been any tract home, anywhere. Any cheaply built tract home. The exterior of the model house looked Victorian only if you squinted your eyes to slits and stared at it from a distance of seventy-five yards or more. Not only was it the only finished home in the development, but there weren't even any other graded lots. The rest of the hilltop acreage had been clear-cut for its timber; the 360-degree view was of half-burned slash piles, stumps and a few, sadly twisted, peckerwood madronas. It looked like Hiroshima the day after: landscaping by the *Enola Gay*.

"Oh, dear," Potts said as a tall, painfully thin, sixtyish woman in a purple silk kaftan, matching turban and layered gold necklaces approached them. "I'm afraid you're about to be accosted."

"You must be Spencer and Della Gridley," the woman said, extending her hand. "I'm Lyla Bamfield."

She spoke her name as if it should have rung bells. It didn't.

"Lyla used to be on TV," Potts stated. "Before she moved here a year ago, she was a character actress on that prime-time soap that got canceled. I can never remember the name of it."

"That's how I *finished* my career, dear," Bamfield said over her wineglass. She pointedly turned her back on the real-estate agent to better address Spence and Della. "As a young woman, I played leading roles, exclusively. I co-starred with Buddy Ebsen, Mike Connors, Robert Stack—all the greats. If you two are interested, I'd love to screen some of my early work for you. That was the golden age of television.''

"Lyla is in charge of the film society here in town," Potts said. Out of the scarecrow woman's line of sight, she rolled her eyes to add a sarcastic *Whoop-de-do*.

"Do you know when I first heard that you were coming to the party," Bamfield said to Spence, "I thought for sure I remembered your name. I thought we'd met once, years ago, over on the old Twentieth Century Fox lot, at a PR lunch for the *Barnaby Jones* show. But you don't look at all familiar to me."

Spence's smile didn't falter.

"The man I was thinking of was much older, even back then. I don't know who I'm confusing you with. The memory plays such tricks on us sometimes. It's so irritating. I know I've been seeing your credits for years and years. You must've started selling scripts in high school.''

"I'm not as young as I look," he said.

"I wish I could say that."

Spence glanced sidelong at Della. He knew they were both thinking the same thing. The first chance she got, Lyla Bamfield was going to call around down in Hollywood to check up on him.

"So you really played opposite Mike Connors?" Della said. "Was that in *The Fugitive?*"

"No, actually that show was called *Mannix*. I did do a walk-on on *The Fugitive*, though. David Jansen was such a professional. Such a complete gentleman."

As Della headed to the bar with Bamfield and Spence continued to videotape the room, Gummy Nordland hitched up his pants and slipped away in the direction of the redhead. Potts watched him go, staring daggers into his back, but didn't say a thing. Spence figured she didn't want to make a scene in front of Port Flattery's movers and shakers. Then she touched his arm again. "There's someone else I want you to meet. Come on."

The woman towed him through the middle of the party, past people he had already met. Spence nodded and smiled to Port Flattery's prosecuting attorney, the mayor, the developers of Victorian View Estates, the town's newspaper publisher-editor, several city-council members and the high-school principal. He hadn't bothered to commit faces, names and occupations to memory since he'd recorded it all on videotape.

Potts pulled him up to a stout little old lady sitting alone at one end of the couch. "Spencer Gridley, this is Mary Louise Gonerman," she said. "Miss Gonerman was my third-grade teacher. She's been like a second mom to me since I was a kid. I help her out now that she can't get around so well."

Miss Gonerman had hair like white cotton candy and eyeglasses with pink frames. She looked like a gaudy Christmas present in her satin-and-lace party dress. The firmness of her handshake took Spence by surprise.

The old lady tipped her head toward Nordland and the redhead who'd paired off again at the back of the kitchen. "Horndog's on the prowl again, I see. Haven't I always said there was something funny about that boy's wiring? Brains in the wrong place. I'm starting to think there's something wrong with you, too, for taking him back."

Potts pretended not to have heard a word she'd said.

"Can I bring you anything?" she asked the old lady. "More orange soda maybe?"

"No, thanks." The former grade-school teacher glared at Spence. "Bobbie Marie tells me you're part of that Hollywood crowd."

"What Hollywood crowd?" he asked.

"The one that's corrupting our youth with violence and filth."

Spence glanced at his landlord. "She told you that?" Potts looked horrified.

"No, of course not," Miss Gonerman said, "that's my own opinion. And I'm entitled to it. I'm eighty-four years old. Believe me, I've seen a thing or two in my time."

"I'll bet you have," Spence said.

"Are you patronizing me, young man?"

"No, ma'am. Just agreeing with you."

"We've got to circulate now, honey," Potts told her. "I'll swing back by to check on you in a few minutes."

"Your teacher doesn't think much of me," Spence said as they recrossed the living room.

"Oh, don't take that personally. She doesn't like anybody anymore. Except maybe me. And there she's got no choice. I'm the closest thing to family she's—"

Potts stiffened, and a flush crept over her cheeks. Spence looked over his shoulder to see what was wrong. In the kitchen, Nordland and the redhead were quietly slipping out the back door. Just about every head in the place turned to watch them go. The police chief had the flat of his big hand pressed against her lower back, just above the swell of the woman's round little behind. As the door closed after them, Potts's angry expression hardened and she got an unfocused, inward look in her eyes.

"Come on," she said, grabbing his hand, "you haven't seen the upstairs yet."

He let her lead him up the carpeted staircase to the second floor. The hallway was windowless, except for a skylight. While he pretended to video the master suite, she disappeared into one of the guest bedrooms.

"Spence, come over here," she called to him after a moment. "Look at this."

When he stuck his head in the doorway, she waved to him from inside the walk-in closet.

"Look what I found in here," she said, holding out her closed hand.

"What is it?" he asked as he stepped forward.

"A surprise." She dropped a small, wadded-up scrap of black nylon onto his palm.

Panties unfolded over his fingers, and they were warm.

It wasn't much of a surprise. What with all the casual body contact she'd been initiating, he'd expected her to come on to him at some point—it was a question of when, not if.

"This isn't smart," he told her. "There's way too many people around. Somebody could walk in on us."

"We can close the closet door," she replied, her face again flushed, this time with excitement. "There's plenty of room on the floor in here. It's all carpeted. It doesn't have to be a marathon, honey. A quickie will do."

When he made no move toward her, she said, "I thought you were a risk taker, Spence."

"It's a little obvious that you're using me to get even."

"So? We'd be using each other. What's wrong with that? Unless you don't want to make love to me..."

It was comical, really, Spence thought. Too bad he couldn't laugh out loud. Too bad he couldn't videotape the show for later viewing. Bobbie Marie Potts was a prime example of her species. Always confusing the urge to have sex with anger, hate, sadness, boredom, hunger, thirst—you name it, they confused it. Every sort of life experience put them in the mood. No wonder reproduction was the thing her kind did best.

Though she interested him sexually about as much as a chicken, or pond scum, he did want to do something to her, had planned on it in fact from the moment they'd met. But it wasn't the something she hoped. He was sorely tempted to pull the rabbit out of the hat right there, but he knew he had other, more-important things to do.

Lucky for her.

"Sorry," he said with a shrug. "Bad timing..."

As she snatched back her underwear, Bobbie Marie Potts had no idea how close she'd just come to being strangled with it.

CHAPTER FIVE

Eden Glen Mall,
Baltimore, Maryland

Mack Bolan stepped up onto the sidewalk and into the pool of bright light beside the mall entrance. Because of the glare of the widely spaced string of anticrime spotlights set high in the building's wall, he couldn't quite make out the edge of the rooftop. If there were shooters up there, they had him cold.

He leaned against the wall next to the hooded pay phone and scanned the fringes of the parking lot. Nothing moved, but there were plenty of dark spots on the far side of the street, less than 150 yards away, that would conceal a rifleman. Legion had chosen the meeting site well. With Eden Glen's cinder blocks as a backstop, they could turn the get-together into a firing squad at a moment's notice. Bolan knew they would only do that as a last resort. These guys preferred killing up close. Hands on.

To his left, on the other side of the pay phone, the rear exit of the mall's four-plex theater banged back against the wall. The last batch of moviegoers rushed out, trotted to their cars and drove away. After a minute or two, the theater's four employees, still in their red uniform vests, hurried out the mall's main entrance and headed home. Besides Bolan's white sedan, only a couple of other cars remained in the lot. None of the vehicles appeared to be occupied. The Executioner checked the time on his wristwatch. It was 12:14 a.m.

The entrance doors opened again, and a gray-capped security guard stuck his head out. "Is everything all right, mister?" he asked. The guard had his right hand close to the butt of his service revolver.

"Yeah, everything's fine, thanks."

"Well, the mall's closed until tomorrow. Better get on home now."

The pay phone on the wall rang.

"That's my call," Bolan told him, and turned for the phone.

When the Executioner picked up the receiver, a man's voice on other end said, "Archangel, get in your car and drive south on 695." Then whoever it was rang off. The guy spoke English with a foreign accent which could have been German or Dutch; the call was too brief to be sure.

As he'd expected, Bolan picked up a tail as soon as he left the parking lot, a dark van driving without lights. It followed him to the highway on-ramp, then with lights on, trailed him in the slow lane for a good five miles. The van kept well back. Legion was being extracareful, checking to make sure he was all by himself. The sparse, late-night traffic would have made it hard to hide a convoy of unmarked cop cars.

In the rearview mirror, he saw the van change lanes and accelerate. It pulled up alongside him in the fast lane. The woman in the passenger's seat had dark hair drawn back in a ponytail. She gestured with her thumb for him to follow. As the van drove ahead of him, he counted three other heads inside. Bolan got off at the next exit, behind the van. They traveled a short distance down an unlit road, then the van signaled and pulled onto the shoulder. The Executioner came to a stop a couple of car lengths back. The van's doors opened, and four people dressed in black jumped out. They all had autopistols, and as they ran toward his vehicle they aimed their guns at him through the windshield.

Bolan kept his hands in plain sight on top of the steering wheel.

"Turn off the engine, kill the lights and get out," said the crew-cut man who covered the driver's door. He was freight-train big, but doughy looking. "Hands first, then feet."

They made him spread-eagle against the side of the car. While the woman held a flashlight, Crew-cut frisked him. After the hand search, Crew-cut took out a metal detector and checked Bolan right down to the soles of his shoes.

"No weapons, no wire," he announced.

"Come on, Archangel," the woman said, grinding the muzzle of her Glock pistol between his shoulder blades, "somebody wants to meet you."

She herded him into the back of the van, then slipped in beside him on the bench seat. "Keep your hands on your knees," she ordered, digging the pistol into his side. "This baby's cocked and unlocked. You twitch, you die."

The driver hung a wheel-spinning U-turn and headed

back for the highway. Crew-cut, in the front passenger seat, adjusted the volume on a cop scanner. They were keeping tabs on police calls. That, by itself, didn't set off Bolan's internal alarm—after all, even if he wasn't wearing a bug, a Fed helicopter could still be tracking them with night-vision optics, drawing closed a wide net from high overhead. But add the scanner to the machine pistols and bulletproof vests he'd seen stacked by the van's back doors, and it looked like Legion had more than a quiet evening of conversation planned.

They traveled south on the highway for another ten miles before getting off at the edge of a residential neighborhood. The van slowed to twenty-five miles per hour as it rolled down tree-lined streets, past dark two-story brick-and-wood houses with well-kept lawns. The arsenal in the back of the van; the rows of middle-class homes; the smell of the woman's sweat, despite the cool night air, mixing with the perfume of her shampoo—it all gave the Executioner a familiar, tight feeling in his gut.

The numbers were falling on something ugly, and falling fast.

He wondered if he could move fast enough to twist the gun away from his ribs before the woman snapped the cap on him. If he could get control of the weapon, he could jam his thumb inside the trigger guard, force the woman's finger down, making her fire through the back of the front seat, killing the driver and passenger in short order. Since both his hands were free, he could easily bend her wrist back on itself, and in the same fashion shoot her point-blank in the chest. The high-powered slug would go through and through and hit the wiry, dark-haired guy on the other side. Of course, the van would crash without a driver, but they were going slow and he was in the back seat.

Another question nagged at him as he weighed the possibilities. Legion had been so careful about everything else so far, why would they give the lone woman in the squad the job of controlling him? Obviously they were pretty sure she could do it. She looked sure of it, too.

Under different circumstances, he would have put her to the test.

The driver turned into a dimly lit alley and parked behind a gray two-door sedan. He killed the headlights, but left the engine running.

Two guys got out of the car. Bolan saw them clearly as the van's front and side doors opened and the courtesy lights came on. One of them was tall, blond and Germanic looking. The other one had the same overgrown, wavy brown hair as the driver, the same wide nose and thin-lipped mouth. If they were brothers, the new guy looked a year or two older.

In the few seconds of available light, the Executioner took mental snapshots of his companions. They didn't match up to any of the varieties of stone killers he'd ever crossed paths with before. Take them out of their black outfits, he thought, put them in suits and ties and they'd pass for normal, law-abiding citizens.

Bolan knew at a glance that none of them had done hard time. Prison sucked something vital from a person's face—maybe the last spark of hope—and left in the eyes a flatness, a desperation. These guys hadn't ever looked into that particular pit. They weren't afraid of anything or anyone. They weren't high on speed or turned-on sexually. They weren't even angry. Instead of acting like the media stereotype—wild-eyed, random-slaughtering social misfits—these people were under control, and it was tight and total. This was a whole different ball game.

Then the doors shut and the courtesy light went out.

"I'm Butcher Boy," the German announced, half-turning to face him over the back of the front seat. "Glad you could make it, Archangel."

"If you're the guy in charge," Bolan said, "why don't you tell this woman to stow her piece? I've been patted down. I'm unarmed and I'm bug free. There are six of you and one of me. The way she keeps digging that Glock into my ribs is really starting to piss me off. Am I mistaken, or aren't we all supposed to be amigos here?"

"You're bug free or you'd be under two feet of loose dirt by now," Butcher Boy told him. "As for your being an amigo, we haven't established that yet."

"What about the way I played the game? Nobody's ever racked up scores like me. Didn't that show you something?"

"The game is nothing more than a carefully constructed screening device. A lot of very smart people spent a lot of time working it out so the poseurs and fantasy freaks could never make it to this level. We know you couldn't have moved up the way you did if you hadn't hunted live humans. But that doesn't change the fact that you've still got to prove you're one of us."

"Prove how? Do you expect me to give up my real name so you can pull my rap sheet?"

"We don't care who you say you are, or what some cop file says you've done. This is level five, Archangel. There's no role-playing here. No chat-room bullshitting. No virtual blood. We're not playing in cyberspace anymore, and there aren't any individual scorecards. In the real world, Legion operates in small groups, like this one. If we compete, we compete group against group. In the real world, players bond to the group through shared activities. What you do alongside the six of us tonight is the only way we have of verifying who and what you are."

"What sort of group bonding have you got in mind?"

"It's a problem we're taking care of for a shut-in pal. You ever hear of Bill Willie Pickett?"

"Are you kidding?" Bolan replied. "I think it's great that Legion put the text of that old TV interview of his on its homepage. Now, that is some powerful stuff. Bill Willie's a heavy-duty player, even from death row."

"Well, as a personal favor, kind of a group thank-you, we're removing an annoying obstacle for him," Butcher Boy said. "The house we're after is two blocks from here. A pair of armed sentries are sitting in a parked car out front. There are four more lawmen inside. Plus the obstacle, of course."

To Bolan, it sounded like a safehouse. The "obstacle" was under heavy-duty federal witness protection. He didn't ask for any more details because he knew that a bred-in-the-bone killer wouldn't have given a damn.

"What do you want me to do?" he asked.

"Ice the two guys in the car," Butcher Boy stated. "You like killing cops, so this should be right up your alley. Think of it as a final exam. If you flunk, I'll finish the job on the cops, then I'll finish you, too."

"I'll keep that in mind."

Butcher Boy waved the driver on. As the van pulled out, Bolan cleared his mind completely. There were times when thinking ahead didn't help, when all you could count on were your reactions and your instinct, and this looked like one of those times. He'd known from the get-go that the constraints of this particular mission might force him into any number of unpleasant tight spots. That included something that for him was unthinkable: having to take an innocent life in order to confirm his serial-killer credentials. That possibility now loomed large. The Executioner had supreme confidence in his ability to fight and maneuver when he was outnumbered and trapped in a narrow space, but before he actually did anything, before he committed himself to a course of action, he had to understand the boundaries of the box. In order to do that, he had to be patient.

The driver headed up the alley another block and a half, then stopped again, within sight of the cross street. Everyone bailed out of the van. The woman marched Bolan toward the back bumper, keeping the Glock aimed at the base of his spine. They watched as Crewcut opened the rear doors and ripped into the stack of assault gear. He started passing out ski masks, body armor, silenced 9 mm machine pistols and extra mags to the Legion players. He didn't offer one to Bolan.

"Don't I get a gun?" Bolan asked the German. "Or do you want me to bite their heads off?"

"Yeah, sure, you get a gun," Butcher Boy replied. Crew-cut passed the group leader a suppressor-equipped Beretta 92. Butcher Boy dropped the full magazine into his palm and quickly removed all but two bullets from the stack. Then he slapped the clip back into the pistol butt. "You get two tries," he said, jacking a round into the chamber. "Better make them count."

Bolan held out his hand for the silenced autopistol.

"Not yet, Archangel. Not just yet."

"What about a vest? Have you got an extra one for me?"

"Forget about it. If you screw the thing up, it'll make you harder to kill." Pulling the ski mask down over his face, Butcher Boy pointed the Beretta at Bolan's head and said, "Move. Follow the others."

Rattle-proofed, they hardly made a sound as they ran single file to the mouth of the alley. When they reached the street, Butcher Boy clapped a hand on Bolan's shoulder. The two of them crouched in the shadows until the others had crossed the street.

The Executioner watched them disappear down the alley entrance on the other side. The rest of the pack would be attacking the safehouse from the rear. There was nothing he could do about it, no way he could warn the Feds what was coming, not without blowing his cover and sinking the larger mission. The Executioner told himself that even without a tip-off from him, the Feds should be able to turn back the Legion attack. After all, they were well trained, and they had a secure defensive position, and if they were protecting a witness against Bill Willie Pickett, they had to be expecting trouble.

Butcher Boy poked him with the Beretta's suppressor. "We stay on this side of the street," he said. "Keep low and out of sight."

At gunpoint, Bolan moved from parked car to parked car, working his way to the middle of the block. Butcher Boy stopped him when they reached a silver minivan. Around the back bumper, the German pointed out a green four-door sedan with two men sitting in the front seat. The car was parked in front of a split-level home on the opposite side of the street. The house's porch and driveway lights were on, as were the lights downstairs.

A light went on inside the sentry car as the passenger's door opened. One of the Feds, a burly, bald-headed guy in a windbreaker, got out, ran up the driveway and knocked on the front door. When it swung inward, Bolan could see a guy in shirtsleeves and a shoulder holster standing inside. The holster was empty; the man's right fist held a chrome-plated, snub-nosed .357 wheelgun. The agent in the windbreaker said something as he entered, and the door slammed closed behind him.

"You lucked out, Archangel," Butcher Boy whispered. He shifted the Beretta into his left hand, and with his right he reached for the Heckler & Koch machine pistol slung on a nylon strap over his shoulder. With the H&K leveled at Bolan's chest, he thumbed the Beretta's safety on, then passed the handgun over, butt first. "Now you can do them one at a time."

The Executioner could feel the walls of the option box closing in around him, and the fit was coffin snug.

As he traded wolf grins with the Legion pack leader, Bolan weighed the pros and cons of taking the guy out. He considered doing it, even though the 9 mm hole in the end of the machine pistol's fat sound suppressor was pointed straight at his heart. The risk to himself didn't stop Bolan from giving the blond killer a pow-der-burn-rimmed, third eye socket; what stayed his hand was the risk to the mission.

There were more out there just like Butcher Boy and his team, playing the murder game for real, individual killers working with intense self-discipline, yet part of a unit, like a battle-seasoned rifle squad.

Like soldiers in a war.

The question was, a war for what?

Before he could begin the cleanup op, he had to have the answer.

"Don't follow me," Bolan warned Butcher Boy as he released the Beretta's safety. "I need room to work."

The Executioner darted back the way they'd come, then crossed the road in the shadow pools between streetlights, two driveways down from the parked car. Keeping to the gutter and staying in the driver's blind spot, he quickly moved up on the sentry car from the rear.

DELLA TURNED the Jeep Cherokee onto Port Flattery's waterfront main street, a short, narrow canyon of six-story, redbrick-and-gray-stone buildings bristling with Victorian turrets. "The old bat told me she lives up on the edge of the bluff," she said to Spence. "She's taking the scenic route."

Ahead of them, Lyla Bamfield's Miata veered on the wrong side of the center line, nearly sideswiping a parked car, then swung shakily back over the stripe. Despite the damp night air, the actress had the car's ragtop down: her height and headgear required it. The purple turban stuck up over the top of the windshield by a good six inches.

"She had a bottle and a half of merlot at the party," Della said. "I hope she doesn't get stopped by a cop."

"Slim chance of that," Spence said as they rolled past the Port Flattery police station. There were no lights on inside the two-room brick building. It was shut down for the night. The handful of city cops was all asleep, either off duty in their own beds, or curled up in the back seats of their cruisers, which they had parked at the end of some dark street.

Spence and Della drove behind the Miata, along the newer part of the waterfront, past the marina and around the lower curve of the bay where the road began to rise, climbing the white sandstone bluffs that bordered the southern end of the bay.

At the top of the hill, Lyla Bamfield signaled a left turn, then cut the wheels over way too slowly for her forward speed, missing the intersection and driving the Miata straight for a power pole on the shoulder. Slamming on the brakes, she fishtailed around it at the last instant.

"Damn!" Spence said as Della turned after the tiny sports car. "She almost solved our problem for us."

"As potted as she is," Della countered, "she could've walked away with nothing more than a few scratches. That's something we can't risk. We've got to make sure the culture queen of Port Flattery has seen her last rerun of *Hawaii Five-O*."

Spence grinned at her.

No way could they allow Ms. Bamfield to get up the next morning and call her former theatrical agent or a TV network cronie for the dirt on the Gridleys. Unlike a criminal-record check, which would show no entry under the Gridley name because it was clean, and unlike a credit-record check, which would merely give a recent rating unless further details were requested, if the retired actress bothered to look into the matter at all, the Hollywood grapevine would soon reveal that the real Spencer and Della Gridley still lived in a Los Angeles suburb, and that the couple had been happily married for almost sixty years.

The impostor Spencer and Della weren't married and had first met, face-to-face, just a month before. They knew each other only by those assumed names, by their Legion aliases, and by the pillow-talk confidences they had shared about their previous, solo-hunting exploits. The secrecy was designed for their own protection. If one of them was caught, he or she couldn't implicate the other. And neither of them could identify by real name anyone else in the level-five network.

Lyla Bamfield drove down the middle of the back road for three blocks, then turned into her driveway—a dark, tree-lined, gravel track wide enough for one car.

Della followed, hitting her high beams as she rolled onto the dirt-and-pine-needle parking apron in front of the two-story, cedar-shingle house-on-stilts. The ex-actress had already exited the Miata and was just closing the driver's door. Throwing up an arm to shield her eyes from the bright lights, Lyla staggered back against the side of her car. If the Miata hadn't been there, she would have fallen flat on her face.

"Hi, there," Della said as she and Spence jumped out of the Cherokee. "After you left the party, we were worried about your driving home. We wanted to make sure you got here all right."

"Sweet of you to be concerned," Bamfield said. "But I'm perfectly fine, as you can see."

She tried to open her purse and dropped it on the ground.

"Let me get that," Della said, scooping it up. "Come on, I'll give you a hand up the stairs."

"Wait a second," Spence said. "Don't either of you move." He ducked into the back seat of the Jeep to retrieve the video camera.

"Oh, God," Bamfield said as he attached a battery-powered floodlight to the camcorder. "Don't film me in this condition!"

"What condition is that?" Della said.

"I'm looped, darling."

"Well, you look great."

The actress carefully straightened her turban, which had slipped over to one side.

"Absolutely fabulous," Spence said. "Go on, help her up, Della."

"You two are so thoughtful," Bamfield said as the

young woman slipped a strong arm around her waist. "You really must come in for a minute. I'll give you a nightcap for all your trouble. And if it's not too late, maybe I could even screen you a little something."

Della supported her up the narrow flight of stairs. The back door and wide rear deck of the house were lit by a pair of spotlights. The painted planks of the deck glistened with beads of heavy dew. Stars twinkled down at them through the overhanging branches of tall evergreen trees. Off the bluff end of the deck, Port Flattery Bay gleamed like liquid silver, far below.

"You've got a wonderful view, don't you?" Della said. "Let's do have a look." She steered the actress across the slippery deck, over to the waist-high wooden railing.

Bamfield gripped the rail in both hands to steady herself.

"Why you can see the lights of town from here," Della stated.

"Lovely, isn't it?" the actress said.

Spence looked down over the rail. "Wow, that's a long drop to the water. Must be three or four hundred feet of straight fall." He stepped back from the edge, turned on his floodlight and started taping the two women again.

"Want to hit the beach?" Della asked the former actress.

"Oh, you can't get there from here," she replied. "You have to go all the way back down to the marina to pick up the trail."

"I know a quicker way," Della said. She scooped up the thin woman like a child, under backs of the knees and across the shoulders, and all in the same smooth motion, adroitly tossed her over the rail. Bamfield didn't put up a fight. By the time she realized what was happening, she was already in free fall. She was so terrified she couldn't even manage a scream until she was almost all the way down.

Spence tried to get tape of her drop to the beach, but the camera's floodlight wouldn't penetrate that far. With his naked eye, he could just barely make out her tiny, sprawled form at the waterline.

"I wish I'd caught the impact on video," he said. "I'll bet she bounced on the rocks like a bag of dry sticks."

Della reached down to pick up Lyla's purse and froze. "Shit," she said, "it looks like we've been playing touch football up here." Dirty footprints were smeared in the dew on the decking—different-sized footprints and fresh, right up to the fateful rail. "Anyone with half a brain is going to see that mess of tracks and figure out she wasn't alone when she went over the edge. Now it's too late to do anything about it. If we clean it up, we'll wipe away her footprints, too."

"So?"

"Unless the old bat could fly, Spence, how did she get to the railing without her feet touching the deck?" Della leaned out over top of the rail and tossed the woman's purse down after her.

"Now that you've actually met Police Chief Gummy Nordland," he said, "do you really think he's sharp enough to pick up on something like that? And miracle of miracles, even if he does, even if he suspects someone murdered her, he's got no motive and no suspects.

And most important of all, there's no time for him to do anything about it.''

Della threw her arms around his neck and planted a quick, moist kiss on his mouth. "You're right, of course," she said. "It was a clean kill. And fun, too. She was light as a feather."

"Can't you just see the obituary headline in the next issue of the *Bugle?*" Spence asked. "Ex-TV Star/PF Newcomer Falls To Death. Translation—drunken old biddy passes out and takes a header off her back deck."

"A tragic accident, but entirely predictable," Della added, "considering her well-known, habitual abuse of alcohol."

Spence located the outside water faucet, and together they hosed the footprints off the deck and steps.

TEN MINUTES LATER, with Spence behind the wheel of the Cherokee, they stopped on the main road on the outskirts of town. He pulled off the highway, right behind the city-limits sign. There were no cars coming in either direction. Port Flattery was the kind of place that rolled up the sidewalks at ten, even on weekends.

When she cranked down the window, Della let out a groan. The mill smoke had drifted up from the bay, over the road. It was so thick and so caustic it made her eyes and the inside of her nose burn. "That stink is unreal," she said. "It's probably poison to breathe it. Probably dissolves the brain stem. What the hell are we doing here?"

"I just need one more shot," Spence told her. "The capper. It'll only take a minute. In fact it'll take even less if you give me a hand."

"What do you want me to do?"

"Grab that packing blanket from off the floor behind you," he said as he got out of the Jeep. He picked up the video camera from the back seat. "Grab the blanket and bring it over here."

She followed him to the head-high, white-on-green-lettered road sign.

"Now what?" she asked.

Spence turned on his floodlight, then said, "Spread the blanket over the top half of the sign. I need you to cover up the town name. I can't have that showing in the frame."

She slipped the blanket over the sign and adjusted it, completely hiding the Port Flattery part.

"That's good," he said. "Now step around here behind me, out of the way."

He zoomed in on his subject and rolled fifteen seconds of tape, taking a picture of the bottom edge of the blanket and beneath it, the still visible words:

City Limits
Population: 1280

CHAPTER SIX

Baltimore, Maryland

From his position behind the back bumper of the sentry car, Mack Bolan took a moment to check the front of the house. Everything looked peaceful. The attack from the rear hadn't started yet, and the windbreaker guy was still inside. That's the way Bolan wanted to keep it until he'd dealt with the Fed in the driver's seat.

Bolan dropped to his stomach on the street and crawled alongside the car, below the range of the driver's-side mirror. At the edge of the driver's door, he drew himself up into a low crouch. From inside the car, a voice droned on and on. The Fed was listening to an audiotape. It could have been a bestselling book read by some actor or one of those self-improvement lectures; Bolan couldn't tell which. Maybe the Justice boys weren't as primed for the attack as he'd hoped.

Under the Executioner's personal rules of engagement, only one scenario would permit him to shoot at a law-enforcement officer: if the cop in question was corrupt, Mob owned, drug-lord bought and paid for, it was open season year-round. The current situation didn't fit the criteria. As far as he knew, the FBI sentries were squeaky-clean.

Uncoiling from his crouch, the Executioner straightened beside the open window. The Fed in the driver's seat jolted with unpleasant surprise as the tall, gun-wielding figure appeared so suddenly, a few inches away.

Bolan punched with the autopistol's steel butt. The powerful, short-arm right jab came from the soles of his feet and landed a head-snapping blow to the man's jaw. The Executioner hoped Justice had a good dental plan because he could feel teeth crack under the impact.

Better a few porcelain crowns than a gravestone.

The punch was a KO. Instant lights-out. As the agent slumped across the passenger seat on his side, Bolan reached an arm through the window and jerked him back into a sitting position. With his broad, muscular back partially blocking Butcher Boy's view of the action, he held the unconscious man pinned against the seat and pressed the muzzle of the Beretta against the headrest. Then he fired once, sending the bullet tracking a down angle through the seat and into the car's floorboards. The silenced pistol spit a single, bright casing, which ricocheted off the headliner and out of the car. It made a soft plink on the asphalt at his feet.

Bolan pulled out of the way far enough so Butcher Boy could see the slumping form in the driver's seat. From across the street, it looked like he'd whacked the Fed. He opened the driver's door and dragged the guy out, dumping him facedown in the street. Then he shoved the limp body into the shadows under the car's chassis, figuring if the man came to wedged in under there, he'd think twice about moving around and giving himself away.

As the Executioner got behind the wheel and quietly shut the car door, the house's front door opened and the agent in the windbreaker exited. He was carrying a couple of cans of soda and an open bag of cookies. Bolan watched him come down the driveway, confident that the darkness of the car's interior would hide his face.

The Fed approached the car without paying attention to who was or wasn't sitting inside. Reaching for the door handle, he said, "Hey, Woody, I got goodies." He didn't look in the window before he opened the passenger's door and backed onto the seat. With the door light on, he started to turn face front.

As he swung both his legs inside the car, Bolan hit him on the point of the chin with a stiff, bare-handed right. The man's head was moving toward the blow when it landed. Better for Bolan, worse for him. The impact bounced his temple off the inside of the door frame. His eyes rolled up in their sockets, then he sagged and started toppling off the seat, sideways out the open door. Bolan grabbed his wrist and hauled him back into the car, pulling him over the padded console between the front seats. Then he fired straight down into the lid of the console beside the man's head. The empty Beretta's slide locked back. He tossed it onto the back seat.

The second agent could be safely left in the car. The Executioner climbed over the unconscious body and out the passenger's side. As he tucked the guy's legs inside the car, he felt the lump of a holster. He tugged up the FBI man's pantcuff and found a blue-steel .380 automatic backup pistol in ankle leather. Out the driver's window, he could see Butcher Boy already moving across the street toward him. There was no time to grab and hide the weapon. He couldn't let the German get a close look at either "dead guy," since both were still breathing. He shut the passenger's door, and the interior light winked out.

Bolan was counting on the narrow time frame to keep Butcher Boy from checking the fallen Feds, and he counted right.

If, as Butcher Boy rounded the front of the car, he had any thoughts of taking pulses, they disappeared when the downstairs bay window of the safehouse blew out with a thunderous boom! The nearly simultaneous, double roar sent bits of glass and window frame bouncing across the well-manicured lawn.

Shotgun, the Executioner thought, and from the sound of it, a chopped-down, side-by-side 12-gauge shooting 3-inch Magnum rounds. Both barrels had gone off at once, and probably not by accident. A double blast of high brass buckshot could clear a room of bad guys, but quick. The Feds were fighting for their lives.

"Come on!" Butcher Boy said, darting past him up the driveway.

Before Bolan could take a step, a muffled clattering erupted from inside the house. It was punctuated by rapid-fire, unsilenced pistol shots. Shadows dashed across the bay window's torn, blood-sprayed curtains. As the Executioner closed on Butcher Boy's heels, he saw the house's front door open a crack. The inward swing stopped as a volley of slugs splintered through it. Madly tumbling bullets sparked off the front porch's concrete steps, spraying the yard with random, whistling death. The German dived to the lawn and rolled to the left, out of the line of the autofire. Bolan did the same.

As they moved to the cover of the house's wall, autopistols barked from the second story. High-powered rounds popped off in an unbroken string, the noise echoing through the quiet street.

In a second or two, Bolan thought, house lights would be coming on up and down the block. People in their pj's and nightgowns would be peeking out the corners of their front windows to see what the ruckus was all about. They weren't used to the sounds of pitched gun battles. It would take a minute for what was happening to register on them, another minute to get to the phone and alert 911. Police emergency-response time was probably between four and eight minutes. If the Feds could just hold out that long, the cavalry would arrive and save them.

The shooting stopped upstairs.

Butcher Boy signaled for Bolan to follow him, then charged the steps to the porch. When he reached the front door, he tried to boot it open. It swung back a foot, then stopped and bounced back. He booted it again, and again it stopped. Bolan put his shoulder to the door and pushed hard. It felt like the other side had been sandbagged. With both of them shoving, they managed to edge the door open wide enough to slip past and into the house.

The sandbags turned out to be a dead member of the witness-protection unit. Facedown on the foyer carpet, he'd almost made it out the door, would have if the Legion hunt pack hadn't nailed him to it with bullets in the center of his back. He still had his empty .357 pistol clutched in his hand.

Bolan stepped over the corpse. Ahead of him, Butcher Boy ran for the staircase. At the landing at the top of the steps, another dead Fed lay sprawled on his back. His torso and arms were a mass of heavily bleeding wounds; he had absorbed dozens of rounds at close range.

A burst of suppressed machine-pistol fire came from a open doorway down the hall. By the time Butcher Boy and Bolan reached it, the firing had stopped. The German entered the bedroom with his H&K leveled belt-high, but there were no more targets left.

"We got them," said the woman as she slapped a fresh mag in her machine pistol. "We got them all." She pointed at the wall on the far side of the queen-size bed, a wall pocked with bullet holes and splattered with gore.

Behind the bed, on the floor at the foot of the wall, two more FBI men were down for the count. Bolan could see that their semiautomatics were locked back, empty. They hadn't had time to reload before they were overrun and shot to pieces.

Then the wavy-haired brothers stepped out of the bathroom. Smoke still curled up from the barrels and actions of their subguns. "The annoying obstacle was having himself a bit of a soak," the younger one explained. "Still is, actually."

Butcher Boy and Bolan entered the bathroom. A hairy-chested man in his late forties lay in the bullet-hole-riddled fiberglass tub. The bloody soup he floated in was streaming out the perforated sides of the tub. Pink water spread across the white tile floor.

"Decorate the room with him," Butcher Boy told the brothers. "Do it quick."

The older brother pulled a sheath knife from his right boot. It was a Zipper model buck, rubber handled with a gut hook on the top side of the blade. While his brother held the shoulders of the dead guy pinned to the wall of the tub, he plunged the knife point in under the breastbone and, with a quick rip, slashed open the stomach cavity. Coils of gray intestine burst out of the wound, popping to the water's surface. The brothers dug in and yarded the dead man's guts out like so much slippery fire hose.

Whatever these people were, Bolan thought as he watched them drape intestines over the sink, the showerhead, the tub faucets, they weren't soldiers. To call them soldiers defamed all the brave and honorable men who had ever worn that title.

The Executioner hid his disgust behind an expressionless mask.

Whatever these people were, he told himself, they deserved no mercy. And they would get none when the time came.

A member of the Legion squad chose that moment to stick his head around the bathroom door. "We got a man hit downstairs," he said. "Better have a look quick. He's hurt real bad."

"That's enough," Butcher Boy said to the brothers. "We're done up here. Let's go."

The Legion pack abandoned the slaughterhouse they had made of the bedroom and double-timed down the stairs to the living room.

They found the crew-cut guy sitting on the floor in front of the bay window's tattered curtains. His back was propped up against the front of the couch.

One look at the murderer's legs and Bolan knew he wasn't going to kill anyone, ever again. He'd been hit high across both thighs with two rounds of double-aught. The sawed-off scattergun lay discarded on the rug near his feet. From the massive, powder-burn blackening of his flesh and the fabric of his pants, the range had to have been point-blank. Two dozen .31-caliber steel balls had hacked through both of his thigh bones like a chain saw. Though Crew-cut was in terrible pain, he remained fully conscious and alert.

In the distance, they heard the wail of sirens. It looked like the emergency response was going to be closer to four minutes than eight.

"Time to flee the scene," the older wavy-haired brother said.

They all looked at Crew-cut, who stared back at them with wide, fearful eyes.

"We can't take him with us," the woman said. "He'll slow us down too much."

"She's right," the younger wavy-haired brother said. "And the way he's bleeding, he'll be dead before we hit the alley, anyway."

The wounded man knew what was coming his way. With claw hands, he raked furrows in the bloody carpet. He moaned and averted his eyes as the German stepped closer to him.

"RIP, brother," Butcher Boy said. "We won't forget you." In a single smooth motion, he raised and fired the H&K, shooting Crew-cut once through the right eye. The guy's head snapped back, and a fan-shaped spray of gore splattered across the couch pillows behind him.

The deed done, Butcher Boy took the point and they exited through the sliding glass doors that led to the patio and backyard. Bolan ran in the middle of the file, out the rear gate and down the alley. With sirens closing in on them from two directions, the German called a halt in the shadows just inside the alley entrance. As they knelt along a cinder-block wall, a pair of cop cars screamed past the alley mouth, down the street toward the safehouse. Butcher Boy paused a second, then led them across the road and back to their parked vehicles.

Before they could get the doors open, bright lights from the other end of the alley swept over their position. For a second they were pinned in the high beams like so many jackrabbits. Siren shrieking, engine roaring, the third cop car raced straight for them.

"Get him!" Butcher Boy shouted, dropping to one knee and bracing his machine pistol against the van's front fender.

The four others followed suit, taking solid firing positions on either side of the alley. They opened up more or less all at once, emptying their weapons into the onrushing squad car. The front end of the cruiser absorbed more than a hundred hits in the space of ten seconds. Its headlights crashed out, the front tires blew, the windshield shattered and the hood popped up.

Unable to see where he was going, the cop locked his brakes, sending the car into a screeching, sideways slide down the middle of the alley. It just missed the Legion getaway vehicles as it skidded past them. The cruiser finally swerved to a stop across the alley mouth, completely blocking off access to it from the street.

Butcher Boy dug a hand into his side pocket and pulled something out of it. Bolan didn't see the bright green tennis ball or its two-inch-long fuse until the German lit it with a safety match. And by then it was too late.

"Fire in the hole!" Butcher Boy shouted to the others as he underhanded the homemade grenade through the car window and into the dazed cop's lap.

There was barely time for Bolan to duck for cover behind a telephone pole before it detonated.

A ball of orange flame rocked the cop car, blowing out all its windows and spraying the alley with glass shrapnel. Black smoke poured from inside the cruiser, rolling up over the roof, the plume rising into the night sky. The Legion team couldn't stick around to savor their victory, though. More sirens were coming.

"Archangel, you and me go in the sedan," Butcher Boy said as the others piled into the van. "You can drive."

There wasn't time or room to turn the car around. The driver of the van laid a long strip of rubber as he reversed his way out of the alley. Bolan did the same, hitting the brakes as he bounced the car out onto the cross street. He dropped the transmission into forward gear and tromped the gas, trying to keep the speeding van in sight.

"No, don't follow them," Butcher Boy said. "Go right, here! Go hard right!"

As the Executioner sliced the panic turn, two blocks over he saw another pair of squad cars zoom through the intersection, lights flashing. They were headed the opposite way, toward the safehouse.

The escape route back to the highway used narrow alleys and side streets. Bolan hit speeds of eighty miles per hour, running without lights, one foot on the gas, the other on the brake, while Butcher Boy gave him directions. Thanks to the convoluted route and his driving skill, they reached 695 with no cops on their rear bumper.

Once they were safely on the highway, Butcher Boy clapped him on the shoulder and said, "Good job, Archangel. You passed our little entrance exam with flying colors."

Bolan shot him a sidelong look. "Maybe so," he said, "but you haven't passed mine."

"How's that?"

"I don't mind doing Bill Willie Pickett a favor because he's been my hero for a long time," the Executioner told him. "But as for all this hunting-pack crap, I don't see what's in it for me. If I get the urge to kill a few cops, I can do it by myself. What do I need you for?"

"If all you want to do is off the odd beat cop every now and then, you're right, you don't need us. It's a different story if you want to make a real statement."

"A real statement? Go ahead, I'm listening."

"Take a look at the caliber of the targets we've selected and hit. We've staged successful strikes on high-level law enforcement in five countries. Legion is hunting down the very people who've been persecuting our kind for decades. That's something you could never hope to do on your own. We've managed to turn the tables on our enemies. We've issued them a warning written in their own blood."

"You mean the Jack the Ripper thing in the bathroom?"

Butcher Boy smiled. "You recognized the homage to him."

"Of course," Bolan said. "And so would anyone who had ever seen the Scotland Yard photos of his final crime scene."

"The dead hooker butchered in her bed," the German said. "Old Jack spread things around pretty good. A severed eyeball here, an eyeball there, kidneys stacked on the washstand, and her guts draped over the wall molding. It was his message to the future."

"Beware the two-legged tiger," Bolan said.

"Exactly. And that's the calling card we've left at every hit."

"Tipping off international law enforcement to your existence seems like a very dumb thing to do. It's like you're asking to get stomped on."

"The publicity is necessary."

"I don't see where all this is going."

"Then I'll spell it out for you," Butcher Boy said. "On your own, with a few dozen random kills, you could terrify a neighborhood, a city or maybe even part of a state. Because of its size and scope, Legion magnifies that impact hundreds of times. Our global network has the power to turn otherwise isolated acts of murder into something more meaningful, something more enduring. Think of it this way—alone, you cast a single, fleeting shadow over the lives of 'normal folks.' Working together, we become a tidal wave of darkness, we spread panic over the entire world. Bill Willie's bacteria people will soon discover that we can do whatever we want to them, whenever we want. We're going to burn the fear of us so deep into their ditto heads that they'll never feel safe again, no matter what they do.''

''What about comebacks from the Feds?''

''Looking forward to it, actually.''

Butcher Boy's cellular phone chirped. He turned away from Bolan to answer it The call was one-sided; he didn't talk, except for the occasional ''Uh-huh.'' After he hung up, he said, ''We've had a slight change in plans. Follow the signs to the airport.''

''You're going somewhere?''

''We're all going somewhere. That means you, too. We're short a man, after tonight. Do you have a problem with that?''

''No, no problem at all. What's the deal?''

''It turns out we've got another little hole to plug.''

''I take it we'll be traveling light.''

''Don't worry about that. Our Legion friends in San Diego will have everything we need waiting for us.''

Butcher Boy punched a number into the cellular phone.

A flicker of a smile passed over Bolan's face as the German set up an airport rendezvous with the other killers in the van. As planned, Legion was taking him into its fold, inside its guard. Very soon, the Executioner would be leaving his own gory "message to the future."

Beware the tiger that eats tigers.

CHAPTER SEVEN

San Diego, California

"You must've lit a fire under that pilot's butt, sir," the tall black man said as Hal Brognola stepped off the Bureau's Learjet and onto the gray tarmac of Lindbergh Field. "You made it here in record time." He extended a hand of greeting. "I'm Albert Wallace, the SAC."

Brognola shook it and said, "I don't have to stimulate you the same way, do I, Agent in Charge Wallace?"

"No, sir. You don't. This way, please."

They got in the back of the waiting Bureau car, and the driver headed for the landing-field exit at high speed.

"What has this Diaz guy given up so far?" Brognola asked as they turned onto Shelter Island Drive, following the curve of San Diego Bay toward the downtown skyline.

Wallace dug out his notebook. "I'll hit the points we've already verified," he said, flipping open the pad. "Ron Diaz was one of the six computer programmers who created the original Legion game. He says they lost control of the thing almost as soon as it hit the

Internet. They couldn't stop the new players from revising and expanding the basic program. They didn't think that Legion would attract real serial killers, or that the killers would have the computer skills to permanently alter the game.''

"What the hell *were* they thinking?"

"According to Diaz, it was just a hoot, a way to thumb their noses at the computer-game establishment. All these guys went to UCSD together. It was something they fooled around with in their spare time.''

"When did it stop being a hoot?"

"Three months ago, after the particularly nasty murder of the sixth designer, a guy named David Gale, in Pacific Beach. Diaz and the other four got scared and decided to become invisible. They scattered to hiding places up and down the state. According to Diaz, the other four were all hunted down and murdered. He's the only survivor. The poor bastard thought he was being followed yesterday afternoon and freaked. He called up the office here and demanded to be taken in. He offered to give us everything he had. How much he can help us, we don't know yet.''

The driver crossed the intersection with Pacific Coast Highway and started up the hill. When he reached India Street, he turned left, away from the city center. The area they were in was multiple-zoned commercial. The commercial part was primarily light manufacturing and auto repair, with some apartment buildings and a few restaurants sprinkled in.

"We're not going downtown?" Brognola said.

"No, we've got our informant stashed in a small office block just up the street. It's a much more defensible location, and less dangerous for the general public if we have to return fire. We moved Diaz after ICID filled us in on Bill Willie Pickett and the hit last night.''

''We lost one witness and four federal marshals,'' Brognola stated. ''The two men who lived through it couldn't ID anybody. I hope to hell you're not underestimating these bastards, Wallace. They're smart and they enjoy what they're doing.''

''Wait until you see our setup, sir. If they mean to hit the informant, they've got their work cut out for them.''

The driver turned left, then left again onto Kettner Boulevard. He went south half a block before he pulled into the driveway of a four-story, dark gray concrete building with black-tinted glass windows. The ground floor was a parking area; access to it was cut off by a heavy, barred security gate. As the gate rolled out of the way, three agents in armored vests, headsets and carrying CAR-15s waved them inside.

''See what I mean?'' Wallace said, holding the car door for his superior. ''This place is airtight. No way they're getting in here.''

The armed agents escorted them to the elevator. Brognola and Wallace rode the car up to the third floor. As they exited, the big Fed saw the row of baffles on skids lined up in front of the floor-to-ceiling windows. Half-inch steel plate protected the interior from gunfire through the tinted glass. Wallace led him to a small office on the windowless side of the building.

Sitting slumped in a corner of the couch was Ronald Diaz. Gaunt faced, with thinning black hair, he looked much older than his twenty-five years. On the coffee table in front of him were jumbo soft-drink cups and a pile of other takeout refuse.

After Wallace had introduced them, Brognola took the chair across from the informant. "SAC Wallace has filled me in on part of your story," he said, "but I have a few more questions, if you don't mind."

"Sure, whatever," Diaz replied. His hands shifted nervously in his lap, fingers lacing, unlacing.

"Why did you and your friends decide to create a game like Legion in the first place?" Brognola asked.

"Believe it or not, when we started out, we were trying to do something constructive," Diaz said. "We were all disgusted by the blood-and-guts trend in computer games. Our brilliant idea was to write the ultimate, excessively violent computer game, something so gross and amoral in concept, so outrageous that everyone would be offended. We believed that public outcry against Legion's superviolence would force the game industry to reevaluate and clean up its own nasty act."

"Things didn't work out the way you'd hoped."

"We weren't marketing experts or psychologists. We were just a bunch of grad students playing around with the tools of our trade, trying to make a point in a way we thought was obvious. We were sure everyone would view Legion the same way we did and be totally repulsed by it. Of course, as it turned out, we had our heads up our respective butts. People wanted to play the damned game *because* it was so sick, *because* it cranked the violence so far past all the previous limits. Christ, what a total screwup! The last thing we ever wanted to do was to whet somebody's appetite for killing. If we'd stuck to writing accounting programs for banks and savings-and-loans companies, the others would all still be alive. I wouldn't be the only one left.''

''We know about one of your friends, a guy named David Gale. He was found murdered in his condo in Pacific Beach.''

''Not just murdered,'' Diaz said. ''They didn't just murder him. They pulled his insides out. If you ever locate the bodies of the others, trust me, you'll find the same thing happened to them.''

''Why do you think that?''

''If you'd ever played the Net version of the game, you wouldn't ask me the question.''

''I've seen it played,'' Brognola said.

''You know about L-5?''

''If you mean level five, yes.''

''Then you know why they messed Dave up like that, why they had to have messed up the others. Because it was fun for them. These people aren't like you and me, Mr. Brognola. They aren't like anybody we've ever seen, not in our worst nightmares. These are serious, highly intelligent people who love to kill other people—I ought to know, me and my dead friends helped get them organized.''

''What's this L-5?'' Wallace asked.

Brognola silenced him with a wave of his hand. ''I need to know why they came after you.''

''Because we hacked into their private garden.''

''The secure chat room?''

Diaz nodded. ''Level five wasn't part of our program,'' he said. ''It didn't exist when Legion first went out on the Net. It appeared a few months later, fully developed, with its own lock and key. We were already getting spooked by the kind of players Legion was attracting—Christ, they brought that murdering maniac Pickett in as an on-line celebrity—and by the unauthorized changes being made in the lower levels of play. I'm not talking about someone tinkering with the eye-hand-speed parameters. The really critical changes involved hunt strategy and killing techniques. At L-4, the revised Legion program puts players into situations where book research can't help them. To win and advance, they have to have had hands-on experience.''

"Why did you try to break into level five?"

"Because that security system really pissed us off. It was the ultimate insult. I mean, this was our concept, we invented it, developed it, and there we were, locked out of the highest level. We poked around until we found a way past the gate that was undetectable. The conversations we monitored inside the chat room confirmed our worst fears. They convinced us that the L-5 players were taking the game outside of cyberspace, killing people in the real world, for sport.''

"The chat room transmissions weren't encoded?"

"No. They trusted their access block. Back then, they must've thought it would do the trick. That was before they caught us inside the chat room, snooping on them. I'm still not sure how they got wind of us, but we screwed up royally. That's what started them hunting us down and what started us running.''

"You think they picked up your trail again?"

"No, I'm sure of it. I barely got out of my apartment in time. I've been ducking these people for three months. I watched them get my friends, one by one. I know how they operate. They work in cells, five or six to a cell. And the cell that's assigned to kill you doesn't do the reconnaissance. The first time you ever see those people is when they come to make the hit.''

"If you and your friends had turned yourselves in," Brognola told him, "you would've saved yourselves a lot of grief."

"Hey, we all panicked after Dave got killed. Not just because we were scared of what Legion might do to us. We were afraid that we'd be held responsible in some way for what was going on. After all, it was our idea.''

Brognola read the programmer's face. He didn't need a lie detector to tell Diaz was giving him the truth, whole and unvarnished. "The question is," the big Fed said, "what are you willing to do now to help us catch these guys, in return for full federal protection?"

"What do you want?"

"Can you still get in the chat room?"

"Unless they found our back way and sealed it, I can. Look, Mr. Brognola, I'm afraid to go to sleep. Afraid to go out. Afraid to contact my family or friends. I don't have a life anymore. Just get me the hell away from these people, and I'll do anything you ask."

"Okay, okay, calm down. You're safe now. I need to debrief you a little more, then we'll jump on a plane."

THE FBI SNIPER GUARDING the roof of the Kettner building slow-cooked in his black SWAT uniform. The afternoon sun was hot. So was the reflection off the roof. From his position at the north end of the building, he watched the traffic flow toward him down the one-way street. It amazed him how fast people were going between the stoplights, which were spaced every four, short blocks. They'd put pedals to the metal as soon as they got the green, then be forced to tromp on the brakes to keep from running the next red. Acceleration was futile, unless you were driving a fuel dragster. The lights were timed that way. You had to be going two hundred miles per hour to make them all.

Three blocks away, a twenty-foot-long yellow rental truck signaled and changed lanes, moving into the right one, the lane closest to the FBI outpost. The sentry noticed it even at that distance because it was the same kind of truck, from the same rental company, that had been used in the Oklahoma City bombing. As the truck approached the driveway in front of the building, it slowed. The sniper moved closer to the edge of the roof, raised his binoculars and scanned the cab. There was one guy inside. He had on a dark blue baseball cap and sunglasses.

The sniper watched as the driver stopped the truck in front of the building's driveway and killed the engine. The sniper hit the transmit button on his belt pack and spoke into his headset mike, never taking his eyes off the truck cab. "We have a possible—" he began.

The driver bailed out of the passenger's door and ran across the street.

"Damn!" the sniper said, dropping the binoculars and reaching for the sling of his Remington Police Special rifle. Before he could get the Leupold ten-power scope to his eye, the driver had ducked between two buildings and vanished.

"Get on that truck!" he shouted into his mike. "Goddammit, hurry!"

The security gate rolled back far enough for two of the parking-area guards to slip past. They ran over to the truck. One of them checked the cab while the other examined the rear sliding door. The guy at the rear didn't try the door; instead he took a giant step backward.

"Oh, fuck," the man said into his headset. "We've got big problems down here. This baby stinks like cow shit and fuel oil. No timing device is visible. Notify the SAC. Notify the SDPD bomb squad. We'd better evacuate the area, and fast."

BROGNOLA KNEW the news was bad when he saw the SAC's face.

"Somebody might have just parked a truck bomb in front of our driveway," Wallace said. "We're going to have to leave the building at once."

"It's them, isn't it?" Diaz stated. "Good God, it's them!"

"Get him a vest," Brognola said. "This could be a ruse to smoke him out."

Diaz pulled on the body armor as they headed for the fire stairs. Brognola had his stainless-steel .357 Smith & Wesson in his hand. Counting Wallace and himself, there were a dozen agents in the building, a dozen standing between the witness and Legion.

Under any other circumstances, it would probably have been enough.

Brognola hit the fire door right behind Diaz and started down the concrete stairs. The problem was, all twelve of them couldn't stick with the programmer. Because of the destructive threat to the surrounding area, most of the agents would have to go door to door, getting civilians out.

When they reached the ground level, the rest of the agents were waiting for them. Wallace assigned four to evacuate Diaz and Brognola. "Take the Suburban parked in the restaurant lot around the corner," he said to a guy in a shirt and tie and armored vest. "Get them to the airport ASAP." The SAC wasn't going anywhere. He would stay with the bomb until the situation was resolved.

When the security gate opened, Brognola and Diaz ran out with the agents. Brognola could smell the fertilizer. They turned around the corner of the building, darted down a narrow breezeway and hopped a low cinder-block wall into the parking lot. As promised, the Suburban was right there, dark green, with black-tinted windows.

"Everything's going to be fine," the shirt-and-tie agent said as he opened the driver's door.

Brognola heard the rifle crack a fraction of a second after the man's head exploded.

CHAPTER EIGHT

Port Flattery, Washington

Gummy Nordland squatted over the crumpled body on the beach. Dead about ten hours, Lyla Bamfield was cold and stiff. She'd landed on her head, then flopped over on her back. The impact had crushed the top of her skull and turned her shoulder-length brown hair into a clotted mass of blackening blood and spilled brains. The horribly bruised remnants of a shattered neck joined the ruined head to the torso. Lyla's arms and legs had bends where there shouldn't have been bends.

Despite the fact that the four-hundred-foot fall had broken just about every bone in her body, she still held the purple turban clutched in the fingers of her right hand. She had to have been trying to keep it on her head as she fell, he thought.

Reflex was a strange thing, sometimes.

Nordland craned his head back to look up the side of the sheer white bluff. He could see the underside of her rear deck. Nothing stood between it and him but tangy sea air.

The ex-actress had gone skydiving without a parachute.

"So, do you think it was suicide?" asked the man who stood on the bluff side of the body. The editor-publisher of the Port Flattery *Bugle* had an open notepad, and his pen was poised to record Nordland's answer. He wore shin-high gum boots, suspenders on his blue jeans and a red-and-black-plaid flannel shirt with the cuffs rolled back over spindly, hairless forearms. Though Fred Ferguson wasn't a "born-here," he tried hard to pass for one. He'd only been in PF since his junior year of high school, twenty-five years ago, a second-class citizen, and a fourth-class newspaperman.

Nordland grunted in a way that could have been taken for a yes or a no. He knew better than to commit himself. The *Bugle* almost never got anything right, hardly ever printed a correction, and when it did, the corrections were usually wrong, too. Even so, every year Ferguson published a full-page article-promo about all the awards the rag had won in national competition. Which didn't say much for the other small-town papers in the running. Or maybe it was one of those deals where everyone who paid the entry fee got a prize. Like the rest of the town's residents, Nordland had never cared enough to find out.

The dead woman's purse lay on the water side of the body, about forty feet down the rocky beach toward the marina. That, he didn't understand. And what he didn't understand, he didn't like. The pair of kayakers who discovered the corpse around nine said they hadn't touched anything, and Nordland believed them. They were locals.

As purses went, Lyla Bamfield's was about the size of a cigar box. It weighed practically nothing and was too light to have bounced that far from the body on impact. The shoulder strap was intact; if it had been over her arm when she hit, it would either have broken or it would have kept the purse next to her. So, he figured the strap was hanging loose.

If she'd had the purse with her when she went over, she was holding the thing in her hand. Then why wouldn't she have death-gripped it like the turban? he wondered. Why would she toss it away from her on the way down? Of course, if she had killed herself, she could've thrown the purse down first, then jumped after it—although he couldn't imagine why in the world she would do a thing like that. The only thing Nordland was sure of was that the body and the purse had hit the beach separately.

Using his handkerchief, he opened the purse without moving it on the rocks and removed her house keys. Then he addressed the uniformed deputy standing behind him. "Teddy, get me some Polaroid pictures of the positions of the body and the purse. When you're done, cover her up with a tarp and tape off the beach. I'm going on up the hill."

Nordland started to trudge toward the marina. He wasn't alone.

"What do you think?" Ferguson asked. "Was there foul play?"

"When I know something, I'll fill you in, Fred."

"But you've got your suspicions, right?"

The police chief kept on walking. Even if he had suspicions, which he didn't at that point, they were the last thing he'd share with Fred Ferguson. He'd been stung by that bee one too many times.

He and the *Bugle* editor-publisher parted company briefly at the marina. The chief got in his squad car and the newspaperman got in his. Then Ferguson trailed him up to Lyla Bamfield's house.

Two other cars were parked below the deck when the chief arrived—another police cruiser and the prosecuting attorney's silver Lexus. As Nordland shut off the engine, a uniformed deputy and a round, balding guy in a three-piece navy blue suit walked to the edge of the rear deck and looked over. Behind them, the house's deck lights glowed yellow.

When the chief got out of his car, Ferguson got out of his. "Stay where you are," he warned the journalist. "This is a potential crime scene."

"You think it was murder, then?"

"Don't come any closer."

Nordland didn't notice the surface of the parking area until he saw the mess of pine needles and gray dirt the deputy and prosecutor had tracked up the wet steps leading to the deck. He checked the soles of his own shoes and saw they were covered with the same kind of debris. Some of the stairs had standing water on them. The chief knew it hadn't rained the previous night, so where had all the water come from?

"Doors are all locked, Chief," the sandy-haired deputy said as he reached the top of the steps. "I didn't try to break in."

"I got her keys from her purse," Nordland said. Then he turned and looked at the deck, which had some standing puddles on it, too. It was clean except for the muddle of tracks where the two men had stepped to the rail to look down at the beach.

"Were there any footprints on the deck when you got here, Brian?" he asked.

"Sir?" the officer replied.

The chief moved closer to both men and kept his voice down so Ferguson couldn't overhear. "Before you two boneheads thoroughly screwed up the crime scene, did either of you happen to notice a woman's footprints heading for the rail?"

"Gee, Gummy, I didn't think."

"That goes without saying." The chief looked at the prosecutor. "What about you?"

Hughie Pearson shrugged. "Not that I recall. I wasn't paying much attention, either. Sorry about that."

Nordland kicked off his boots. "Nobody goes on that deck with shoes on from now on," he told the deputy.

The chief padded around the edge of the deck in his stocking feet, giving the tracks the two men had made a wide berth. When he reached the back rail, he hunkered down. He was lucky he'd gotten there before the other two men smeared the grime on their shoes all over the rest of the deck, destroying whatever evidence remained. Though Nordland looked hard, he couldn't see any women's prints near the rail, only the marks made by Brian O'Hara's huge brogues and the prosecutor's size-seven, kiltie tassle loafers.

The deck definitely looked like it had been recently washed off. Because of the deep shade of the surrounding trees, the scattering of puddles hadn't evaporated yet.

"Brian," he said as he followed the rail to the house's back door, "go down to the beach and relieve Teddy. If he's done taking the pictures I asked for, tell him to bring his camera up here. And tell him I want him to bring both of the woman's shoes in an evidence bag."

When Nordland glanced down the steps, he saw Ferguson sitting on the front fender of his squad car, scribbling like mad in a notepad.

"Fred!" he shouted. "Get the fuck off my car!"

"Sorry, chief."

"Dumb son of a bitch," Nordland muttered as he turned the key in the door's lock.

"Can I come in, too?" the prosecutor asked.

"Kick off your shoes first," the chief ordered, stepping into the kitchen. "And don't touch anything." He knew Pearson would obey. He'd rather break his own neck than upset somebody "important." Pearson was a renowned local suck-up. In any other profession, in any other place, the man's shameless brownnosing might have cut short his climb to power; but being both a lawyer and a born-here, the sky was the limit.

The ex-actress had been an extremely neat housekeeper. The only things out of place in the kitchen were the rinsed glass in the sink and the half-full liquor bottle she'd left on the counter. Lyla Bamfield had drunk a very large, fortifying Scotch whiskey before she'd left for the party.

There were a few lights on inside the house, just enough to keep her from stumbling over something on her return. Hung on the walls were framed glossy photos that looked like stills from old TV dramas—Lyla Bamfield at various ages was in all of the pictures. Her videotape library and a supersized TV took up half the living room. Though he searched every likely spot, Nordland could find no goodbye-cruel-world note.

"She didn't strike me as the suicidal type," Pearson said, careful to keep his hands at his sides. "That woman had an ego the size of Mount Rainier."

"She liked PF because here she was a big fish in a little pond," the chief agreed.

"She sure didn't look depressed at the party," Pearson added. "She had those newcomers cornered, talking a mile a minute about Hollywood and the good old days—all her usual stories. Better them than me, I thought."

"We're going to have to pony up some money to the state M.E.," Nordland said.

"Pay for an autopsy? We already know she was drunk."

"An autopsy can tell us if she was alive when she hit the ground. Or whether she got conked on the head up here before she went over the rail. She might have scratches or bruises from a struggle."

"It's way more likely that she passed out from all the booze, or had a heart attack or a stroke and fell off the deck."

"Maybe. There's only one way to tell."

"Jesus Christ, Gummy," the prosecutor groaned. "Is it really worth the trouble?"

Trouble had nothing to do with it. It was all about money. Hughie Pearson was a regular mother hen when it came to his office budget. He was convinced that staying in the black every year made him look better to his superiors in city government. Because Port Flattery was too small to afford a full-time coroner, it relied on the state to conduct the forensic part of murder investigations. The money to pay for outside analysis came directly out of the prosecutor's funding.

"Look at it this way," the chief said. "If she wasn't a suicide, and we find and convict her killer, you can ride the case all the way to that judgeship in superior court."

Pearson thought about it for maybe a tenth of a second. "If it's okay with you," he said, "I'll make the call from here."

Gummy Nordland knew how to hit the sweet spot.

FIFTEEN MINUTES LATER, with state crime-lab techs en route, Chief Nordland got in his patrol car and headed for Bobbie Marie Pott's rental house. As far as he knew, the Californians were the last people to talk to the deceased, so they were first on his interview list.

He had Lyla Bamfield's shoes in an evidence bag locked up in the trunk of the car. A closer search of the parking area turned up fresh impressions that matched the shoes. The footprints led right up to the steps, then stopped. The former actress had certainly walked that far the previous night. But had she washed the prints off the steps herself, then cleaned her shoes when she was three sheets to the wind? And only afterward, when everything was spotless, did she finally get around to chucking herself off the deck?

As neat as Bamfield was, it seemed highly unlikely.

Nordland drove past the town's elementary school.

Kindergarten kids were climbing on the yellow bus that would take them home. When he honked and flashed his roof lights, they waved at him from the bus windows.

As he turned down the street to Bobbie Marie's Victorian, he thought about how dumb he'd been to ditch the Victorian View Estates party. Not that the evening hadn't turned out as he'd hoped. He and the redheaded former wife of the mill manager had ended up at her beachfront bungalow. But there was a price to pay. Always. Nordland told himself he was going to have to go see Bobbie Marie after he was done with the Gridleys and face the consequences.

Getting together with her again had been a big mistake. When it came to women, he never seemed to make little ones. All his adult life, it had been the same thing—a case of greener pastures, the rolling stone who couldn't leave it alone.

Which tended to severely complicate life in a place as small as PF. There were those even in the born-here community who didn't think a womanizer like Nordland should be the town's representative of law and order. No matter what anybody said, he'd never let his hobby interfere with his work; unlike the previous chief, who had been a Bud man. And even though at any one time there were always a few people pissed off at him—a former lover or her husband or her mother, father, siblings—they seemed to get over it pretty quick. After a few weeks, he'd honk and wave, and they'd honk and wave back, all forgiven.

It was a gift he had.

People just liked him.

Nordland also had a talent for the job of small-town police chief; the scale of it fit him to a tee. He didn't mind trading punches with local-boy drunks to keep the bars safe for tourists. Most of the work like that he did by himself. He didn't need to recruit top-notch deputies because nothing ever happened in Port Flattery. The last homicide, which had occurred on his predecessor's watch, had been the result of a domestic dispute that got out of hand. That was four years earlier.

Whenever Nordland heard about brewing trouble like that, he always paid the folks a visit. He took the man out behind the barn or the toolshed and made it clear to him that the legal system was the least of his worries. The chief wasn't shy about pulling his .45 automatic when it was just one person's word against his. He'd never had to cock the pistol to make his point.

The crime in town amounted to a few break-ins of vacation homes by teenagers looking for liquor, lots of drunk-driving arrests and, of course, shoplifting. Guys like Brian and Teddy who couldn't make the grade as cops in Seattle or Portland usually worked out just fine in PF.

When he pulled up to Byrum House, the garage door was open and Della Gridley was inside. Dressed in shorts and a sleeveless T-shirt, she bent over some long wooden crates. Nordland sat there for a moment, admiring the view through the windshield. The blonde had a behind that wouldn't quit, all muscle and tight, cheeks like meshed gears. God, you could crack walnuts in there, he thought.

When she glanced over her shoulder and saw him,

she smiled and straightened from her work. The chief pulled on his game face as he got out of the car.

Della Gridley didn't look the least bit worried as he walked up the driveway. When he broke the news about Lyla Bamfield, she said, "Oh, no! Oh, that's just terrible! We only met her last night."

"That's why I wanted to have a word with you. Did she seem out of sorts at all? Depressed? Sometimes alcohol has that effect on people."

"No, if anything, she was bubbling over. I think she was excited because there was someone else from Hollywood in town."

"How much did she have to drink?"

"A lot. I couldn't keep up with her. What happened? Did she crash her car?"

"No, it looks like she fell off her deck."

"An accident?"

"Most likely. I have to investigate, though. It's my job. Did she leave the party alone?"

"Yes. At about midnight, I think."

"You didn't know her down in Hollywood?"

"No, like I said, we never met before last night."

"And your husband? Maybe he ran into her because of his work. He writes for TV, as I remember."

"No, he didn't know her, either."

"Is he around?"

"Yes, he's in the house, writing."

"Well, he should be out here helping you lug those heavy crates around. What in the world have you got in there?"

Della smiled. She looked really good when she did

that. "Actually it's heirloom china. I didn't trust the movers. These were the strongest boxes I could find."

"Maybe I'll just look in on your husband, if that's okay. He might have seen something that you missed."

She took him into the house by the back door. He hadn't been inside the old place for a long time. He and Bobbie Marie had used it for sex whenever her auntie June was away. That had been their junior year of high school. They'd done it right there on the kitchen floor. Watching Della Gridley walk in front of him, he couldn't help but wonder how hard it would be to talk her into something like that.

She called out to her husband from the kitchen doorway, "Spence, we've got company. Police Chief Nordland's here. There's been an awful accident."

To Nordland, it almost sounded like a warning.

"Come on back," Spence called.

Spencer Gridley greeted them at his office door with a concerned expression on his face. While Della explained the reason for the visit, the chief surveyed the office. The screenwriter's computer system was up and running. There was a still color photo from the party on the monitor, a picture of Mary Louise Gonerman and Bobbie Marie. Spence had transferred the videotape image to computer. For what reason, Nordland couldn't guess.

Spence expressed shock and regret at the news, but claimed he could add nothing to what his wife had already said.

"I wish there was something more I could say," the writer told him.

The chief thanked them both for their help.

Back in the squad car, he rubbed his face. He didn't like outsiders much. He liked Californians least of all. In this case, his natural suspicion seemed to go nowhere. And his previous check on the Gridleys had turned up no rap sheets. He could get more information on them, but there didn't seem too much point yet.

The problem was, to kill somebody you had to have both opportunity and motive. He asked himself who had gained anything from the actress's death. She hadn't been robbed. Or, God help us, sexually attacked. Even without sex, the "gain" could have been from the act of murder itself, a thrill killing—although that, too, seemed improbable. If Lyla Bamfield had made any enemies in PF, they were the jealous, nasty-rumor-spreading type, not the throw-you-off-the-cliff type.

Murder didn't make sense.

But the scene shouted murder at him.

Nordland started the patrol car and pulled away down the street. He needed to let things simmer for a while, to focus his mind on something else. Though he'd intended to catch Bobbie Marie at the realty office and straighten things out, he found himself heading in the other direction, toward the beachfront bungalow where the redhead was staying.

CHAPTER NINE

San Diego, California

Mack Bolan stood under the red-and-white-striped awning of the deli-restaurant. Beyond the mostly empty restaurant parking lot, backlit by the afternoon sun, he could see the windowless backside of the FBI building. Like a medieval castle, it was designed to repel attack from without. Like a castle, its defensive positions were layered—after the outer wall was breached, its fighters could retreat to the next layer and fight on. Taking the building in a direct assault wasn't impossible, but it meant sweeping the place, confronting its heavily armed and well-trained personnel floor to floor and room to room, which would be a time-consuming and dangerous procedure. And the longer it took, the better chance the Bureau had of calling in reinforcements, cutting off the attackers' retreat and killing or capturing them all.

Legion's battle plan was devilishly simple. Forget about the building. Make the rabbit run. Create so much panic and confusion in a quarter-mile radius that local law enforcement wouldn't be able to help the Feds protect their informant.

The Executioner had nothing to do with the prep on the rental truck. That had been completed before Butcher Boy's pack arrived in San Diego. The Legion hunt team already in place had taken care of everything, including supplying the new guys with weapons and a change of clothes. Its leader, the short, compact, heavy-boned woman who stood next to him at the deli-restaurant's entrance, was in charge of the two-pack operation.

Under the hood of her gray sweatshirt, her brown hair was cut mannishly short: bare skin, white walls, showed over the ears. She had the hood pulled up, despite the sun's heat, to hide her headset microphone. Her age was difficult to judge—somewhere between thirty and forty, he guessed. Her face showed weather damage, windseaming at the corners of the eyes. She had martial-artist's knuckles: callused and calcified, oversize for her blunt fingers. Her game name was Lizzie—after the ax murderer, Lizzie Borden—and the phony truck bomb had been her idea. She'd even used the same rental-truck company as in Oklahoma City in order to play on established fears.

On the plane on the way in, Butcher Boy had made a joke about her nom de guerre and how it didn't reflect her personal taste in murder. "She should call herself the Knacker Man," he'd said. "Because what she knackers is men. She's got a collection of trophy neck-laces hidden away to prove it. Keep your legs crossed when you're around her, Archangel, or she'll add your boys to the string."

Lizzie Knacker Man definitely had the look, Bolan decided.

The Legion look.

It was there in her narrowed brown eyes and the set of her mouth. Arrogant. Uncompromising. Fully focused and in the moment. Ready to snuff out lives by the dozen. Unlike her long-dead namesake, this Lizzie wasn't insane, and she wasn't tiptoeing daintily along the edge of Hell—this Lizzie was clogging the brink, her face thrust into the sulfurous wind.

The Executioner picked up the paper shopping bag at his feet. In it was a silenced, German-made machine pistol and 30-round stick mags of 9 mm parabellum bullets taped back-to-back. Butcher Boy and the others trusted him enough to let him carry a fully loaded weapon. Lizzie held a bag just like it cradled to her chest.

He looked over at the building. He had little hard information on the identity of Legion's intended target. From scattered bits of conversation on the plane, he gathered that the troublemaker was a man, and that he'd had something to do with the development of the game software, not with the alliance of serial killers or with Bill Willie Pickett. Bolan figured the guy was a major threat to the conspiracy or it wouldn't have been willing to risk a dozen of its people in a daylight gun battle with the Bureau just take to him out.

If this computer programmer was that important to Legion dead, then he was that important for Bolan to keep alive. The problem was, he could only be in one place at a time, and the potential field of fire was huge. There were eleven other level-five players with guns and eight vehicles scattered around the area, each positioned to cut off a possible avenue of escape.

There was another problem, too. Any rescue attempt he mounted would require his killing all or some of the players in the San Diego op. If he killed them all, he'd lose his hard-earned connection to Legion and with it, any chance to clean sweep the conspiracy would be gone. If he killed some of the players, he risked being seen by those who survived, which could not only cost him his Legion membership card, but could prove fatal, as well.

The Executioner was just starting to get a feel for the way the organization operated, at least at the pack level. As individuals, Legion's shock troops were used to hunting and killing on their own. In pack mode, they didn't blindly follow the commands of a charismatic psychopath, like the Manson family. Off the field of battle, where a strict command structure was unnecessary, a pack leader like Butcher Boy or Lizzie became more of an arbitrater than a supreme dictator. Members had their own opinions and expressed them freely. But in the end, they put aside their egos in order to make the thing work as smoothly as possible.

That was the most disturbing part.

These lone predators believed in their cause enough to submit to military, if not majority rule.

A man's voice hissed in his earpiece. It was the driver of the rental truck. "Lizzie," he said, "I've just passed the last stoplight. I'm two blocks away, changing lanes now. The driveway is clear."

The stocky woman moved toward Bolan, past the open entrance door to the deli, bringing with her a pungent whiff of salt cod and garlic. She spoke softly into her hidden mike. "Stay on your toes, everybody," she said. "Get ready to close in."

Lizzie stuck her right hand inside the paper bag, taking hold of the pistol grip of the H&K.

After the driver left the truck in the driveway, it seemed to take forever for anything to break. Bolan knew there was a standard procedure and chain of command that the Bureau followed. First the guys on the street had to identify the nature of the presumed threat. Second they had to pass the on-scene evaluation up the line. Third they would evacuate the premises as quickly as possible. In the meantime, the numbers fell in slow motion.

Bolan and Lizzie couldn't see what was happening on Kettner, but the players stationed on the other side of the FBI building could.

"They're bailing out!" an excited voice said in his ear. "The Feds and Diaz. They're coming your way, Lizzie, toward the parking lot."

Bolan caught a brief glimpse of six dark figures as they scrambled over the low wall at the back of the lot across the street. They moved quickly to cover behind an off-road-equipped Chevy Suburban, too quickly for Lizzie to open fire with her SMG. Someone else had a clear shot, though. A high-powered rifle cracked once, and one of the Feds spun out from cover, bouncing off the Suburban's hood before he disappeared behind the fender. A flurry of rifle shots followed as the remaining FBI men and their informant piled into the four-wheel-drive vehicle. Its engine kicked over, and it started to move even before the driver got his door closed.

Down the street to Bolan's left, a blue Legion van

pulled away from a parking meter and sped toward them.

"Cut them off, Butcher Boy!" Lizzie said into her mike as the Suburban roared for the lot's driveway and India Street. Its massive tubular steel front bumper was aimed straight at them.

The plan was for the blue van to cut off the parking-lot exit, but it was traveling too slowly to get the job done. The Suburban bounded out of the driveway before the van arrived and turned left on the one-way street, opening its entire side, from bumper to bumper, to Lizzie's and Bolan's autofire.

"Shoot!" Lizzie said, raising her concealed SMG. The end of the paper bag shredded and burst into flames as she raked the side windows of the four-wheel drive with slugs. The black windows pocked but didn't break. Tires smoking, the Suburban headed north on India Street.

The blue van braked hard, screeching past them and coming to a rolling stop forty feet up the street.

Lizzie pulled the burning bag from her weapon and tossed it aside. "Why didn't you fire?" she demanded of Bolan as they ran toward the Legion van.

"A waste of good ammo," he told her. The van's side and front passenger's doors were already swinging open for them. "It had armored glass and body panels."

That shut her up.

Lizzie got in the back with Butcher Boy. Bolan climbed in beside the driver, who was the older of the two wavy-haired brothers from the Baltimore hit.

Sudden acceleration pushed the Executioner deep

into his bucket seat. Through the windshield, a block and a half ahead, he saw the Suburban racing away from them in the middle lane. Half a block farther on, two Legion cars abruptly pulled out from opposite curbs of the one-way street. Angling toward each other, into the center lane, they tried to cut off the Chevy's retreat. The heavy vehicle plowed between the converging bumpers, parting them with a crash of shattering glass and groan of twisting metal.

Out of control, the car on the left did a complete 360-degree turn; when it hit the curb it went airborne, nosediving through the plate-glass facade of a wholesale plumbing-supply house. The second sedan slammed into a parked car, crashing out both its passenger's side windows as it came to a sudden, unplanned stop. At least the Legion car was still pointed in the right direction. The driver recovered from the impact almost instantly. He stomped the gas so hard he fishtailed out of control, scraping the paint and side mirrors from a line of parked cars. He was back in high-speed pursuit before the blue van reached him.

"My brother's okay," Wavy Hair announced with relief. "Man, oh, man, would you look at him go."

"Get closer!" Butcher Boy shouted from the back seat. "We've got them penned in now!"

As the Suburban approached the next intersection, its brake lights flashed on. Two more Legion vans had pulled out from the cross street, jumping the stoplight to intercept it. They were willing to take a broadside in order to end the chase right there.

The nose of the Suburban dipped and veered right as it went into a four-wheel slide.

FOR AN AWFUL SECOND, Hal Brognola froze there in the parking lot. The sight of the dead FBI man slumping to the asphalt, his brains and blood splattering across the Suburban's hood and windshield, paralyzed him. He'd thought he was ready for an attack; the reality of it proved him wrong.

Before he could move, another heavy-caliber rifle slug whistled past his head. It skimmed off the vehicle's roof, slashing a ragged rent in the sheet steel a foot and a half long.

He grabbed Ron Diaz by the back of the neck and shoved him headfirst through the Suburban's open driver's door. More bullets slammed into the outside of the door as Brognola used both hands to push the programmer over the console and into the passenger's seat. Then he reached around the door and jerked the car keys out of the door lock.

There was no time for everybody to change places so one of the experienced local agents could do the driving. Not if they wanted to live. While the big Fed was getting behind the wheel, the other three agents piled into the back seat.

Brognola found the ignition and started the engine. He gunned the big diesel once and blasted out of the parking space with spinning rear wheels. He could hardly see out of the windshield for all the blood, but he couldn't miss the street exit, which was dead ahead. He was almost there when he saw the blue van coming up India Street to his right, trying to block the driveway.

"Hang on!" he roared, cutting the wheel hard over. The heavy vehicle responded with a gut-wrenching lurch and screaming tires. As the Suburban swung left, Brognola glimpsed a pair of figures stepping out from under the awning across the street. Instinct told him they weren't innocent bystanders. "Incoming!" he said.

Bullets rattled the length of the vehicle, chipping the dark windows, penetrating the side panels of the doors and ricocheting off the hidden steel-plate armor.

Brognola jammed the gas pedal flat against the fire wall. Tires smoking, the Suburban peeled away from the ambush, accelerating up the street. The speedometer's red needle climbed from sixty to seventy, then hung, quivering at eighty miles per hour. He was still flying blind, though, and quickly found the the washer-wiper switch. A jet of cleaning fluid and a couple of swishes of the blades cut a double arc through the gore on the outside of the windshield.

"Look out!" one of the agents cried over the seat back.

Brognola had already seen the problem.

Ahead of them, two cars were converging from the outside lanes, trying to form a roadblock. They misjudged his speed. Keeping the gas pedal mashed, Brognola slammed between them. The Suburban's cow-catcher of a bumper wedged the sedans violently apart.

The armored vehicle weighed close to seven thousand pounds, and it was going twice as fast as the lighter cars. Like a three-and-a-half-ton cue ball, it didn't veer off course upon impact. The sedans spun away from it in opposite directions. Brognola was past them in an instant. He glanced in his side mirror in time to see the car on the left hop the curb and fly into the storefront. One gone, he thought. He was less pleased when he checked his rearview and saw the other sedan recover from its spinout and resume the chase. Right behind the sedan, the blue van was coming, too.

"Maybe you'd all better put on your seat belts," he suggested. "This isn't over yet. Not by a long shot."

The traffic light in front of them was green. One hundred feet from the cross street, two panel vans on the left side of the intersection jumped the red, one moving slightly ahead of the other, blocking off the road from crosswalk to crosswalk.

Brognola squashed the brakes, locking up the wheels, and steered into the sickening skid to the right. Just missing the rear of a parked car, he jumped the curb and ran the Suburban up on the sidewalk. Between the back of a bus bench and a line of storefronts, the clearance was virtually zero. Sideways momentum slammed the right side of the vehicle into the building, bounced it back against the bench, then they were through the gap. He clipped the street sign with the left corner of his bumper, bending it horizontal, as they bounded off the sidewalk, past the first of the two road-blocking vans, and onto the cross street. Pouncing on the gas again, he powered out of the left-hand slide and shot away from the vans.

"Is everybody okay?" he asked, glancing at Ron Diaz, who didn't answer. The programmer was hunkered down in his seat, and he had the soles of his feet braced against the dash, prepared for head-on impact. His eyes were shut tight, his lips pale.

"Hey!" one of the FBI men in the back exclaimed.

"We're going the wrong way, we're headed away from the airport."

Brognola didn't need to be reminded of that. The road ahead climbed away from the bay and Lindberg Field, up toward the foot of a broad, canyon-riddled mesa. The top of the mesa was a heavily populated part of San Diego, a place they didn't want to go. The more people and cars on the streets, the more likely it was that they'd crack up, maybe even kill somebody innocent on the way to being killed themselves.

"We're all going to die," Diaz said.

"Shut up," Brognola growled, even though he was thinking the same thing.

He looked in his rearview again. Now three vans and a car were chasing them uphill at high speed. "Get on the horn," he told the agents. "Get us some help."

The Fed in the middle of the back seat unbuckled his safety belt and reached over the console to grab the vehicle's radio mike from under the dash. When the agent tried to get through to SDPD, he couldn't. The dispatch system was jammed with traffic related to the truck bomb on Kettner, but not just police. They were calling in fire and emergency units from all over the city.

It was a triage situation.

The bomb had priority.

Which meant they were on their own.

As BOLAN'S VAN CLOSED IN on the traffic light, things got crowded in a hurry. Wavy Hair the Elder had to brake to keep from hitting the rear of the car driven by Wavy Hair the Younger, who in turn was braking to keep from clipping the two vans that were racing out of the intersection.

"Dammit, move your butt, Dennis!" Wavy Hair the Elder snarled as he cranked a squealing right turn inches behind his brother, maintaining a dead-last position in the Legion file.

"Cain, this is Lizzie," the pack leader barked into her headset. "We're heading up Taylor, in hot pursuit of a dark green Suburban. Intercept it at Bogner. Ram them. Don't let them get past you."

The Executioner caught a hint of delight in her voice. There was no doubt about it; Lizzie was having a blast. For her, this was the best of all games. Move and countermove.

But with real blood spilled.

Real lives taken.

Because they were speeding uphill and there were vehicles ahead of them, Bolan didn't actually see the collision. He heard it, though, a brief, piercing squeal of brakes, then a grinding, metallic crash. A horn sounded and kept on blowing.

In the blink of an eye, they were on top of the intersection with Bogner. The sedan, black smoke billowing from under its crumpled hood, was still rolling backward from the impact with the Suburban, away from the glittering scatter of broken glass. Entangled in his deployed air bag, the Legion driver waved a bloody arm at them. If he wanted help, he got none.

Wavy Hair the Elder screeched a hard left, following the rest of the pack.

"If he doesn't turn left in the next two blocks," Lizzie said, "we've got him."

Bolan could see what she meant. The street they were on ran along the base of the mesa. It gradually curved right, turning into the hillside. Ahead, a huge canyon arm cut across their path. The road curved some more, and the canyon mouth loomed before them. Expensive homes perched high on its rim; below their fire-retardant greenbelts, the undeveloped slopes were covered with scrub trees and tall, dried grass.

A yellow Dead End signpost whipped past them on the right.

"'Dead Meat' is closer to it," Butcher Boy said, laughing as they headed up the desert canyon, past a landscape of boulder fields, arroyo and stunted, gray-green brush.

The two-lane street narrowed, its painted dividing line vanished and it started to wind. Wavy Hair feathered his brakes. In front of them a cloud of pale brown dust appeared, obscuring the lead vehicles. Then the smooth, paved street suddenly turned to rutted dirt under them.

A fire road, Bolan thought when he saw the steel access gate emerge out of the dust cloud. It had been padlocked shut; now it gaped open, smashed apart by the speeding Suburban.

As the canyon sides closed in tightly on them, the dirt road deteriorated even more. It became a two-rut track cut by erosion gullies, dotted with exposed, stream-smoothed boulders. On the right the ground dropped off into a rocky, dry creek bed. The track climbed as they raced deeper into the canyon, increasing the sheer fall to the creek.

Wavy Hair locked up his brakes as the daisy chain

of vehicles came to a screeching halt. The Executioner jumped out with the others to see what was wrong. The lead van had hit a ditch wrong and skidded sideways off the track. Its front wheels hung over the edge of the drop-off, nose pointing down into the creek.

Up the canyon ahead of them, the Suburban was still roaring.

"It doesn't matter," Lizzie said as the driver and two passengers exited the decommissioned van via the side door. "The Feds are going to have to ditch their wheels, too. The car track ends just ahead. It narrows to a footpath that goes all the way to the top."

"Then they could get out that way," Butcher Boy said. "Out into the neighborhood."

"Not if you take the van and beat them to the head of the canyon," Lizzie told him. "We'll push them toward you. Go on, move it!"

Bolan watched Butcher Boy and Wavy Hair run back to the van and pile in. Wavy Hair stuck his head out the driver's window as he reversed his way down the narrow track. The van disappeared in a swirling cloud of dust.

The tension that had built up in the Executioner's neck and shoulders melted away. He had been waiting for just such an opportunity, and now it had finally arrived. The moment the pack leader split up her force to trap the Feds, those that remained in the canyon became viable targets for him. With Butcher Boy and Wavy Hair safely away from the combat zone, and the battlefield largely out of their view, Bolan didn't need to keep any of the others alive. He could maintain contact with level five through the German and his driver.

Lizzie shouted for the rest of them to advance, on the double, up the weedy canyon path. The Executioner fell into an easy, loping stride behind her, the machine pistol in his right fist. They trotted in a ragged line through chest-high, golden grass, past dead eucalyptus trees and live stands of prickly pear cactus.

A warm breeze touched Bolan's face; as the wind moved down and across the canyon, it carried with it the sweet, spicy smell of sun-dried grass and wild fennel. Uphill, the howl of the Suburban's diesel stopped. Sirens wailed from the freeway behind them. Police and fire units were converging from all directions on the Kettner Boulevard building.

In the space of twenty-five yards, the two-rut car track became a one-rut footpath. Where the track narrowed, fresh tire marks veered right, gouging furrows in the earth in the direction of the creek. Bolan and Lizzie followed the tire marks to the edge and looked over.

Crushed by the weight and four grinding tires of the Suburban, the first ten feet of the dirt bank had collapsed into the creek. The Fed had driven off the path and down into the streambed. The vehicle's tracks were clearly visible in the loose gravel. It was still headed up the canyon.

Bolan half slid, half stepped down the broken bank into the dry creek. Then he stood to one side and let the two players carrying bolt-action sniper rifles go ahead of him before he continued on. One of the snipers was from his pack, the ponytailed girl from Baltimore. She nodded to him as she walked by, all business.

The going wasn't easy up the creek. The grade was steep, and the streambed was clogged at every bend with viny, misshapen trees. While thin, their ground-dragging branches were so densely packed that the Suburban hadn't even tried to plow through them. From the tracks, the driver had run one set of wheels up the side of the bank to get past.

As he followed the deep ruts around a clump of stunted trees, the Executioner saw the abandoned Suburban, not thirty feet away. It had finally found an obstacle that it couldn't overcome: the width of the creek bed in front of it was blocked by an enormous, fallen eucalyptus. The Feds had left, and the front and side doors of the vehicle were standing open. The rear ones, too. Bolan looked inside the back of the vehicle as he passed by. The floor mat was pulled up, exposing the spare-tire compartment.

Uphill from him, out of sight, silenced machine pistols started clattering. The answering fire when it came barked loud and full-auto.

And close.

Somewhere in the dense brush ahead, Legion had found its quarry.

"SHIT!" Brognola shouted as the Dead End sign popped up one hundred feet away on the right. He started to hit his brakes, but realized at once that he had already blown it. He was going too fast to take the last possible turnoff without rolling the Suburban and turning its occupants into hamburger. The side of the canyon loomed in front of them.

They were boxed in.

"It might be a little late to ask this," he said over his shoulder, "but is there any way out of here?"

"There's a fire-road entrance up ahead," one of the FBI men said. "If we can get past the gate, the road might go to the top of the canyon."

The fire-road barrier was no match for 3.5 tons of on-rushing Suburban. The gate parted from its latch post with a resounding clank. Past it, Brognola shifted into four-wheel drive on the fly. Because of the swirling dust in their wake, he could no longer see the pursuit in his rearview mirror. He didn't kid himself that the prospect of a little off-road travel would scare Legion off the chase. They were still back there, and they still wanted Diaz dead.

The unmaintained fire road quickly became a challenge, even for the heavy four-by-four. The Suburban bounded over ruts and exposed boulders, its power train screaming. Ahead, the space between the hillside slope on Brognola's left and the flood plain of the creek on his right narrowed to nothing.

"Maybe we'd do better if we got out and ran?" one of the FBI men in the back suggested.

"Not yet," Brognola said. Downshifting, he turned toward the creek and the drop-off.

"Hey, wait a minute!" one of the Feds shouted.

Gunning the engine, the Justice man drove right up to the edge. The cliff gave way beneath them, and the Suburban slid down an avalanche of its own making, yawing madly from side to side before its front wheels clawed hold of the streambed.

Brognola rampaged up the creek, swerving around the brush and Volkswagen-size boulders, using every inch of passable space. Another two hundred feet up the canyon, he hit the brakes. The smooth trunk of the downed eucalyptus tree was headlight high, and something he couldn't go over or around.

"That's it, we've had it," he said. "Everybody out."

Brognola took a moment to look around him. The vegetation in the canyon bottom and up the hillsides was tinder dry, the wind blowing gently down the creek, toward the canyon mouth. The idea that popped into his head was drastic, a last resort.

"Where's the car's emergency kit?" he asked one of the FBI agents. "I need to see it quick."

The big Fed ignored the spare tire, the jack, the tire iron, the first-aid kit and snatched up a pair of road flares from the bottom of the compartment. Then he grabbed Diaz by the front of his belt and towed the man behind him as he broke trail through a maze of ground-scraping branches.

They had no choice but to keep following the creek. The footpath was twenty feet above them now, and unreachable because of the undercut dirt bank. On the other side of the streambed, the canyon slope was accessible, but the slope itself was supersteep, close to seventy-five degrees. And it had no usable cover. Its eucalyptus trees were widely spaced, as were the stands of tightly packed scrub bushes. Trying to cross the open ground of the grassy hillside would draw a sniper's bullet.

Brognola paused another second to listen. He no longer heard vehicles roaring up the canyon path; instead, he heard the sounds of boot soles scraping on loose rock in the creek bed below them. They had to get moving.

Farther uphill, Brognola pushed out from under the branches of a stunted peppertree, dragging Diaz behind him. To his left, a four-foot-wide, corrugated-steel culvert angled down from the path and into the creek bed. Set in concrete on the hill above them, it fed runoff from a side canyon into the main stream channel protecting the footpath from erosion. A slope of basketball-size riprap supported the exposed length of pipe.

He and the others scrambled behind the cover it provided.

"If two of us stay here," one of the Feds said, "we can hold them off for a while. That'll give you a chance to reach the top."

A flurry of slugs whined overhead, clipping through tree branches, skipping off stream boulders, sparking off the top of the steel culvet pipe.

They had cover, but they weren't hidden.

Two of the agents poked their CAR-15s over the pipe and sprayed the creek with a few short bursts of unaimed autofire.

Whatever they did, the odds were against them. If they all stayed there, they'd all probably die. If they all made a break for the path, they'd all probably die. Even if just three of them made a break, they'd still all probably die. But Brognola wasn't about to leave anybody behind to hold the fort, not after seeing the Karkanian tape.

"Three of us will try to get to the path," he said as the agents pulled their weapons back. "It looks like it takes a sharp bend up there. When we reach the bend, we'll give you covering fire and you can follow us. Watch the hillsides, though. Whatever you do, don't let them flank you." Brognola pointed at the third agent and said, "Let's hit it. You take the point."

They crawled up the riprap slope behind the culvert to the edge of the path. Then, on the count of three, they scrambled onto the trail. They got about ten feet down the track when a single rifle shot from above and behind sent the agent in the lead sprawling. It hit him low in the right buttock, below the protection of his body armor. With more single shots kicking up the dirt around him, Brognola grabbed the wounded man by the ankle and pulled him off the path, behind the protection of the culvert.

As he rolled the agent over onto his back on the rocks, Brognola's heart sank. Bright blood pulsed from a ragged exit wound at the join of thigh and hip. The man's femoral artery had been severed, and every second counted. The big Fed used both hands, trying to get pressure on the wound, but it was too massive. Maybe, if they'd been in an emergency room, instead of a creek bed, he could have been saved.

Maybe.

As it was, in the space of a minute, the man bled out into the riprap and died.

Brognola cursed as he pushed Diaz back down the pile of rock. The computer programmer was muttering to himself. He slumped in a heap beside the culvert, his face ashen, staring slack-mouthed at the blood smeared all over Brognola's suit jacket. He jerked like a puppet every time a bullet clanged off the pipe. They would have to practically carry the guy out; it was either that or leave him for the butchers. The pair of snipers on the opposite hillsides already controlled access to the footpath. Now they would work their way up the canyon until they could get behind their targets, then they'd pick them off, one by one.

"We can't stay here any longer," Brognola said. "We've got make a break for it. If we can get around the bend in the path, we've got a chance."

"They'll shoot us dead!" Diaz whimpered. "Like they shot him!"

"We're going," Brognola said evenly, "and you're going with us. What we need is some cover, and I'm going to get it for us. But to do that I've got to climb up there." He pointed at the opposite hillside, above the creek. "The sniper I'm worried about is on the path side. He's the one who'll have the clearest shot at me, assuming I make it across the creek. Keep him and the others busy for a few minutes and I'll be back."

Making sure the pair of flares was safely tucked in his waistband, Brognola drew his .357 pistol and made a mad dash for the far side of the creek.

CHAPTER TEN

A spray of 5.56 mm tumblers erupted from behind the culvert, sending Bolan to his belly on the rocks. As he rolled to his left, Lizzie and the rest of the pack moved the other way, ducking for cover behind a pile of big boulders. Two heads popped up over the top of the drainpipe—heads and CAR-15s. The assault rifles flashed and barked, chipping at the edges of Lizzie's position with a barrage of full-metal-jacketed rounds. It was covering fire.

One of the Feds broke away from the culvert, running full tilt.

The Executioner recognized his old friend, and in the same instant knew there was nothing he could do to help him. Before he could raise his weapon, it was going to be over, one way or another. Hal Brognola sprinted under the sights of a half-dozen enemy guns. Silenced 9 mm rounds pelted the rocks behind the man from Justice, but they couldn't catch up with those sturdy, pumping legs. With a final lunge, Brognola reached cover behind the trunk of a tree that had tipped over into the creek. Staying behind it, he continued to move up the hillside.

It pleased Bolan to see Brognola could still run like

that. Of course, it wasn't just quickness that had saved his life. The big Fed was going in an unexpected direction, away from the path, not toward it. His dash had surprised the Legion players so much that they'd frozen for a fateful second.

With a resounding boom and a solid thwack, a heavy-caliber rifle slug blasted a chunk out of the top of the tree trunk where Brognola's head had just been. The shot had come from the hillside on Bolan's left, and it was answered by a double burst of aimed autofire from behind the culvert. Out of Bolan's sight, Brognola would be running again, hell-for-leather.

The Executioner guessed that the head Fed had come to San Diego to collect the informant and take him somewhere safe for debriefing. What he was doing now, risking a sniper's bullet in the back to scurry up the slope, was more puzzling. Bolan caught sight of Brognola again halfway to the top of the hill, a dark form against the gold of the dried grass. Then the man crawled under a broad patch of bushes and vanished. A volley of Legion bullets shook the mass of branches, raising a cloud of dust that the wind lifted and spread downslope.

The Executioner smiled. Rolling to his feet, he turned away from the culvert. As he ran down the creek, Lizzie shouted at his back, but he didn't stop. Bolan knew what was going to happen, and he knew how it was going to happen. He knew it before the flare glowed bright red on the parched hillside. He had already decided which targets he'd take first. If he wanted to bag them all, with no survivors, they had to go in order.

A rifle shot echoed through the canyon as he raced past the abandoned Suburban, then another. Both snipers were working now, crisscrossing fire from opposite sides of the canyon, trying to knock Brognola out of the box, Brognola who stood silhouetted on the grassy slope like a paper target at a shooting range.

Putting his arm through the H&K's shoulder sling, the Executioner used exposed tree roots to climb up the undercut bank to the path. He didn't follow the track, but ran straight up the hill. The slope was so steep he had to take it on all fours, with the SMG slapping against his side. Halfway up, he stopped. He could see the sniper down on one knee in the tall grass on the ridge of a branch canyon that overlooked the culvert. Paralleling the hillside, Bolan closed the gap on a dead run. Even as he approached, the sniper fired again. The scoped rifle bucked hard, driving the ponytailed woman's shoulder back. As she recovered from the recoil wave, she turned her head and saw the big guy coming for her.

Something registered when their eyes met.

Predator recognizing predator.

Whatever it was, she *knew*.

The ponytailed woman worked the bolt of her gun, chambering a live round as she whipped the muzzle around.

The Executioner fired his SMG on the run, stitching a line of bullets across the woman's upper chest. Slugs hit her shoulder, collarbone, windpipe, collarbone and shoulder. Her mouth gushing blood, the sniper clutched at her throat and collapsed on her face, dead, in the flattened grass.

Reslinging the Heckler & Koch, the Executioner picked up the rifle the woman had dropped. Built around a Remington Model 700 bolt action, the M-24 System was the U.S. Army's sniper weapon of choice. Bolan knew it well. Shouldering the rifle, he peered through the Leupold M-3's eyepiece. Above the crosshairs of the Duplex reticle, he could see Brognola scrambling down the steep slope, the lit flare in his hand. Behind him, a line of flame sprang up in the tall grass. Whipped by the wind, the fire leaped higher and higher as it spread. It angled out from its starting point, sweeping along the flanks and down the sides of the canyon. Burning grass, underbrush and oily eucalyptus leaves sent up clouds of cottony white smoke, which the wind blew ahead of the flames.

Brognola had risked his life to start the blaze at exactly the right place: well above the position of the other sniper on his side of the canyon. Fire now beat down on that rifleman, forcing him to retreat and expose himself.

Bolan acquired the moving target in the scope's viewfield. He swung the telescopic sight past the running man, holding the crosshairs low to compensate for the down angle of the shot. He tightened the trigger's slack; it broke crisply, and the heavy rifle boomed and bucked.

The Executioner rode the recoil wave, working the bolt to put a second round under the firing pin. When he reacquired his target, the man was flat on his belly, sliding at high speed down the grassy slope. As the sniper slid, his arms and legs flopped around like they were made of rubber. Bolan held his fire, watching the sniper slam headfirst into a gully and bounce out onto his back. After that the guy didn't move.

Bolan swept the Leupold scope over the creek bed. Everything in the fire's path was burning. Not just grass and weeds, but the trees, as well. Thick smoke boiled along the canyon bottom. Through the scope, he could see panicked figures dashing down the creek bed to keep from being roasted alive.

The Executioner discarded the sniper rifle. Even with a good gun, it was too easy to miss targets that were running and ducking in and out of tendrils of smoke. Besides, he knew where they were going.

There was only one way out.

He raced along the side of the slope, back the way he'd come before descending to the path and cutting off Legion's escape.

Bolan was waiting when they struggled up, one by one, from the creek bed. There were six of them, coughing, their eyes streaming with tears.

Dennis, Wavy Hair the Younger, squinted at him through the pall of smoke and said, "How'd you get here so fast?"

Lizzie didn't let him answer for himself. "Didn't you see?" she croaked. "He ran. The cowardly bastard turned tail and ran."

"Is that right?" Wavy Hair said.

The Executioner stood with the muzzle and sound suppressor of his SMG cradled in the crook of his arm, his hand wrapped around the pistol grip, index finger inside the trigger guard. "Depends on how you look at it," he replied.

"How so?"

"If we take in the big picture, from start to finish, you could say I was just acting as pointman for the pack's hasty retreat. Hasty and inevitable. Lizzie there gets all the credit for the strategic withdrawal.'' Bolan grinned at the stocky woman. "Those Feds outfoxed you but good."

Lizzie thumbed down the safety on her shoulder-slung H&K and started swinging it up in a tight arc. "Congratulations, Archangel,'' she snarled, "you just earned yourself a free ride to hell.''

"Ladies first,'' Bolan said, firing through the crook of his arm as he pivoted his torso.

Lizzie's head jolted back as three tightly spaced parabellum rounds caught her under the nose. A slurry of brains and blood exited a yawning wound at the back of her head, splattering across Wavy Hair's cheek and shoulder. The shock of instant death was galvanic. Every muscle in her body contracted. The dead woman's hand squeezed the SMG's grip as her knees gave way, and it spit a furious line of slugs through the space where Bolan had just been.

Like a wisp of smoke, the big guy slipped away, intangible man, inflicting tangible pain. With the machine pistol's trigger pinned, its breech spewing an unbroken stream of spent brass, the Executioner circled the bunched targets. Dennis took half a dozen slugs through the side of the neck. Like Lizzie, he dropped before he could even cry out.

There were faces behind his, slack-jawed faces with eyes wide, nostrils flared. Bodies shifted in slow motion, leaden hands trying to lift weapons that suddenly weighed tons.

Bolan stepped forward and emptied the 30-round mag into them.

Killing at point-blank range wasn't neat, but it was quick, so quick that none of the players managed to shoot back. The Executioner left them there, dead in the dirt, and disappeared into the swirling smoke.

"IF YOU GO OUT THERE with that dinky little gun of yours, Tom Carvey, you're an even bigger fool than I ever imagined."

The sonic boom of another high-powered rifle shot rattled the living room's bell-shaped picture window.

Carvey inched back the slide on his Colt automatic pistol to make sure he had a live .32ACP round chambered and ready to shoot. "I know what I'm doing, Martha."

"That's what I'll have them put on your tombstone," snorted his wife of forty-four years.

Carvey engaged the safety and slipped the compact handgun into the side pocket of his red jogging suit. The weight of it made his waistband sag over one scrawny hip. He hitched his pants back up, retied the drawcord more snugly and headed for the door.

"Tom, wait for the police, please. Let them handle it."

"The cops aren't coming, Martha. You tried and you can't even get through to the cops."

"It could be dangerous out there."

"I'm just going for a little look-see, that's all. I'm not going to plug anybody, unless they ask for it."

He threw in the last part just to rile the old bird. He

liked to poke a stick in her cage every now and then, to try and even up the score, as hopeless as that was.

"Tom!"

"Yeah, yeah, Martha," he said, waving her off as he stepped out the front door onto the porch of their Spanish-style home. Another pair of rifle shots echoed up from the canyon across the street, followed by a cluster of reports that sounded like firecrackers.

They weren't firecrackers, though. Carvey had seen action in the South Pacific, and he knew what kind of noise a machine gun made. Some crazy bastard was popping off a fully automatic weapon down there. That didn't surprise him much, not with the way everything nowadays was going to hell in a handbasket. The cops were so overworked they couldn't even protect a nice neighborhood like this one anymore. There was gang graffiti on the stop signs and the perimeter walls of expensive homes. Low-rider cars cruised past at all hours, driven by Hispanic males in do-rags and sunglasses, blasting that idiot rap music through giant speakers, scaring God-fearing folks out of their sleep. The fear of being killed in your bed was a prescription for instant insomnia.

Carvey straightened his thick eyeglasses and, with a quick hand, smoothed his slicked-back fringe of gunmetal gray hair. He had convinced himself that all the trouble in the neighborhood, not to mention the city and the state, had come up from the south with the influx of illegal Mexican immigrants. It didn't take a genius to figure out that the aliens had brought the crime and drugs with them, like rats carrying the plague. On the local news every night, there were stories that supported his theory. Martha couldn't see it, of course, no matter how clearly he laid it all out for her, but she never agreed with him on anything, anyway.

Before he set foot off his porch, Carvey paused to take stock of the situation. Parked across the street in the turnout next to the canyon rim was a dusty blue van. Because of the van, he couldn't see the steel gate that blocked four-wheel-vehicle access to the canyon footpath. The city had put up a sign beside the gate telling the dirt bikers to keep out, too. Of course they ignored the sign and drove around the end of the gate. Dirt bikers made a hell of a racket and tore up the canyon, but they didn't shoot off guns down there and they didn't spray-paint garbage over the trunks of the eucalyptus trees. All the off-road motorcyclists Carvey had seen were white Americans, something that, he felt, went a long way to explaining the difference in behavior. The blue van might be connected to the shooting; it could also be just hauling dirt bikes. There was no way to tell without having a closer look.

As he crossed the street, Carvey saw some of his less-brave neighbors peeking out their front doors or standing on their porches with hands on hips. He waved for them to come on over with him and check it out, knowing they wouldn't.

"WHAT THE HELL IS THAT?" Wavy Hair said, shielding his eyes from the glare of the setting sun as he peered down into the canyon. "Is that smoke?"

Butcher Boy looked where his Legion pal was pointing. It was smoke, all right. A pillar of gray spiraled up from the hillside far below, and at the base of the plume, orange lights danced.

A last rifle shot rang out, then it was quiet.

"Was that it, do you think?" Wavy Hair said. "Did they get them all?"

"I can't see anybody moving," Butcher Boy told him. "Our guys or theirs."

"Jesus, our guys better get moving," Wavy Hair said. "With the way the wind's blowing, the whole fucking place is going to be burning in a minute. I hate to say it, but my brother probably started it. He's a goddamed firebug."

"I don't think it was him," Butcher Boy said. "I don't think it was any of our people, at least not on purpose."

"An accident, then? From a sustained burst of autofire, the heat of a muzzle-blast?"

"Or maybe the Feds, using the smoke to make their getaway."

"What's going on, gentlemen?" a brittle voice said behind them.

As Butcher Boy turned, a dried-up little old man in a red jogging suit was walking toward them, along the side of the van. He had his right hand in his pants pocket. His hand wasn't alone in there, by any means. Butcher Boy looked at Wavy Hair, who saw the gun, too. Their own weapons were momentarily out of reach, on the floor in the front of the van.

"You tell us," Wavy Hair said. "We stopped by the side of the road when we heard all the noise."

"Probably goddamed teenage gangsters," the old guy said, "killing each other over drugs. They cross the border, do their crimes, then sneak back.'' He sized up the two strangers, decided they looked like honest white Americans, and took his hand out of his pocket. More than half the bulge in his pants remained; the pistol slapped his skinny thigh as he stepped past them and walked around the fire-road gate.

Butcher Boy ducked inside the van's open passenger's door as the old man turned to look over the edge.

"Dear sweet Lord!" the old guy shouted. He gestured helplessly at the raging wildfire. "The whole canyon's going to burn. I'd better get Martha to call the fire department.''

When Butcher Boy turned from the van, he had the silenced machine pistol in his hand. "Hold on to that thought,'' he said, then he shot the old guy once through the back of the head. For a second, the man remained standing, as if he didn't know he was dead. A puff of exit-wound blood mist glittered in the sunlight. Then his legs gave way and he dropped to his knees, tumbling forward, headfirst into the canyon.

Wavy Hair leaned over the edge and watched him cartwheel seventy-five feet before slamming into a clump of manzanita bushes in a gulley below. The impact of 130 pounds of deadweight raised a cloud of brown dust. Other than that, the old guy simply disappeared, red jogging suit and all, swallowed up by the foliage.

Coyote food.

"Get your gun and some extra mags,'' Butcher Boy told Wavy Hair. "We'd better take a hike down the trail and see what's happening.''

As Wavy Hair pulled his subgun out from under the

driver's seat, the German said, "Stay alert. If the Feds set the fire to screen their escape, they may be running right at us."

THE SHOCK WAVE of a high-powered bullet fanned Brognola's hair. It plowed into the hillside above his head with a solid whack that he could feel through the soles of his shoes. A little farther, Brognola told himself as he scrambled higher. He felt like a bug under a microscope, about to be impaled on a pin. There was no cover, nowhere to run. He zigzagged as best he could, trying to put the snipers off their aim. When he reached the midway point of the canyon's side, he ripped the fuse of the first flare. With a flash, it ignited. As he turned, a bullet screamed past his shoulder. He could see the dark form of the sniper on his side of the canyon.

"This is for you, pal," he said, touching the blazing tip of the flare to the grass. With an air-sucking whoosh, the vegetation burst into flame. Brognola had to jump away or be caught up in the fireball. He hadn't anticipated how quickly everything would burn or how much heat it would generate.

Dragging the flare through the grass behind him, he ran down the slope. A wall of fire bloomed behind him, roaring, crackling. He raced ahead of the boiling smoke.

A rifle barked on the other side of the canyon, but the bullet didn't come close to him this time. The slap of impact was down the canyon.

If he'd hoped for a little smoke to conceal them, Brognola got much more than he bargained for. White and thick, it looked like CS gas rolling before the leaping flames. It burned his eyes, nose and mouth like tear gas, but it was hot enough to melt skin. He lit the undergrowth right up to the edge of the creek, then moved upwind, giving the blaze a minute or two to get going good. Smoke poured down the creek bed, completely obscuring it. Over the sounds of the fire, he could hear cursing, coughing and the skitter of boots running on stream gravel.

The Legion players were in full retreat.

He hoped Diaz and the two agents had had the sense to stay put. Because of the way he'd set the fire, they were in no real danger, except for breathing the odd bit of smoke.

When he guessed the fire was far enough along, he shouted out, "Don't shoot. It's me." Then he recrossed the creek to the culvert, which was dimly visible in the haze, and found the three men huddled there behind it.

"Is everybody okay?" he asked. The agents nodded; Diaz just sat there, glassy-eyed. "The opposition took off to keep from getting fried. Let's get out of here while we can."

Pushing the programmer in front of him, Brognola climbed the riprap pile to the trail. He crouched there and looked for signs of Legion. Drifting smoke made it hard to see more than ten yards in any direction.

When the agents joined him at the edge of the trail, one of them said, "Which way should we go? Down or up?"

"We'll keep going up," Brognola said, towing Diaz onto the trail. "If we go out the top, we should be okay."

"Wrong, Hal," said a deep, familiar voice from behind them.

The Feds spun, hip-aiming their assault rifles as a tall, dark-haired man stepped out of the pall of smoke.

CHAPTER ELEVEN

"Don't shoot!" Brognola commanded, clapping his hands on the agents' shoulders. "He's on our side. He's working undercover."

The agents lowered their weapons and relaxed.

"There's a couple more level-five players up at the trailhead," Mack Bolan said as he stepped closer. "They're supposed to ambush if you make it that far."

"We can take them no problem if there's only two of them," the taller of the agents said.

"No," the Executioner replied. "I need them alive. Otherwise, I'm cut out of the loop."

"What about the rest?" Brognola asked.

"Taken care of, permanently."

"This guy killed them all?" the tall Fed said in disbelief. "Is that what he's saying?"

Brognola shot the agent a button-your-lip look, then said, "Why don't you and your partner take Mr. Diaz up the trail a little ways and wait for me there. I'll be right along."

"Yes, sir."

Brognola made sure they were well out of earshot before he turned to Bolan and said, "What have you got?"

"Not much, considering I've sat in on two of their operations now."

"You were part of the Baltimore hit?

Bolan nodded.

"I thought it was strange that two agents came through the attack with nothing worse than sore jaws."

"I couldn't do anything for the others. I'm working at a big disadvantage here."

"We all are," Brognola replied. "At least it looks like Legion trusts you now, or they wouldn't have let you carry a gun. Have you got any idea where this thing is going?"

"Yeah. Someplace bad. These people are well funded, well armed and well organized. And they've got a grudge to settle."

"Against law enforcement."

"That's just part of it. I think they want to get back at everybody who isn't like them. Everybody normal. They see themselves as oppressed by a society of inferior beings. Law enforcement is the instrument of social control, so it's an obvious target for a lot of reasons, symbolic and practical."

"They want some sort of payback for this supposed oppression their kind has suffered. But how?"

The Executioner shook his head. "Your guess is as good as mine. Whatever they're up to, you can bet it's going to be a first, something that will go down in history. That's the kind of people these are. They have huge egos. They think large."

"At our end," Brognola said, "we haven't had much luck, either. The level-five chat room has been a tough nut to crack. We haven't dented their codes so far. I'm hoping that the programmer, Diaz, will help us there. He knows the Legion program inside out. If we can get a line on where this is all headed, we can arrange to get you some backup before the shit hits the fan.''

Bolan knew Brognola wasn't talking about official backup: FBI, state police or National Guard. To use any of those organizations would blow the secrecy of the mission all to hell. If the idea was to eliminate Legion without stirring a ripple, reinforcements would have to come from Stony Man's covert-op tactical units—either Able Team or Phoenix Force, or both.

"I don't have a problem going solo on this," Bolan told him. "I'm going to operate as usual, as if no backup is coming."

"If you find out what the plan is…''

"Don't count on me relaying the information, Hal. There may not be time to make a call. You turned me loose on this. It's my play to make.''

Brognola started to protest, then thought better of it. He didn't have to point out the obvious, that as expert as he was, his old friend hadn't been able to completely control the situation by himself. Better than anyone, Bolan knew lives had been lost, and he knew many more were at stake. In the past, when called, the Executioner had always risen to the occasion. Brognola expected no less from him now.

"I've got to regroup with the players at the top of the path," Bolan told him. "Stick around down here for another five minutes before you start up. We'll be long gone by then."

"Understood."

"There's one more thing, Hal. You need to make all the bodies in the creek disappear. If Legion finds out that they're full of bullet holes, my cover is blown."

"I'll arrange to have them picked up as soon as it cools off down there."

"And keep the media away."

"Striker..." Brognola said as the tall man stepped past him.

"Yeah?"

"Watch your back, pal."

BOLAN HEARD THE CRUNCH of Butcher Boy's and Wavy Hair's footsteps on the trail long before he saw them cautiously rounding the turn ahead. He stopped in the middle of the path and let them come to him.

"What happened? Where is everybody else?" Butcher Boy demanded as he and Wavy Hair ran up.

"I don't know for sure," Bolan said with a shrug. "I got split up from the others in all the smoke. I came this way, they went the other, back to the cars, I think."

"Did you see my brother?" Wavy Hair said anxiously. "Did he make it out okay?"

"I couldn't see anybody very clearly. Too much smoke. It was like a barbecue down there."

"What about Diaz and the Feds?" Butcher Boy asked. "What happened to them?"

"All dead," Bolan said. "We shot them to hell."

"And the fire?"

"One of the Feds started it before he got nailed."

"Then the job's completed," the German stated. "Let's get out of here, quick."

As they started back up the path, Wavy Hair said,

"Are we going down to the mouth of the canyon, to make sure everybody got out?"

"No, we're headed for the airport," Butcher Boy said. "If the others are okay, they'll meet us there. That was the plan if we got separated."

AN HOUR LATER, the troops still hadn't shown up at the Lindbergh Field terminal. While Bolan and Butcher Boy sat and watched, Wavy Hair paced back and forth in front of the terminal's television monitor. Every few minutes, there was a breaking news flash about the forced evacuation of one-half square mile of San Diego. The truck-bomb story preempted any mention of the fire in the nearby canyon. Wavy Hair was upset.

Butcher Boy got up and brought him back to the first row of chairs in the passenger boarding area.

"My brother's dead," Wavy Hair said. "I know he is. I should've been there with him. If I'd been there, this would never have happened."

"Calm down," Butcher Boy told him. "You couldn't have stopped the fire. And you don't know anything for sure yet. They might have had an engine breakdown."

"Or a showdown with the cops," Wavy Hair countered.

"That would've been on TV," Bolan told him. "The airspace over there has got to be crawling with helicopter news crews."

Wavy Hair glared at the tall man. "How come you got out and my brother didn't?" he said.

"Luck of the draw. I turned right, he turned left."

"I thought you said you didn't see him."

"Just a figure of speech. If he'd turned right, we would've come out together."

Wavy Hair looked unconvinced. He looked like he wanted to tear Bolan apart. Butcher Boy restrained him easily.

The Executioner wasn't worried about Wavy Hair. The guy had grounds to suspect him of desertion under fire, not of terminating the rest of the pack, his brother included. As for Butcher Boy, he seemed relieved that the mission was over, and that he had escaped without a scratch. He didn't seem to give a damn about the casualties. Maybe because they weren't his responsibility. He hadn't been the pack leader on this one.

The gate-area loudspeaker crackled. At the counter across from them, a woman in a red-and-black uniform spoke into a hand microphone, announcing last boarding call for a flight to Seattle.

"That's it," Butcher Boy said. "We can't wait any longer. We've got to leave."

He took Wavy Hair by the arm and led him up to the gate. They sat three across over the wing, with Wavy Hair by the window and Bolan on the aisle. Butcher Boy wanted to keep them separated.

After takeoff, Bolan turned to the German and said, "Okay, I know where we're headed, but I don't know why. What's in Seattle?"

"A coming-out party."

The Executioner's ice blue eyes didn't so much as flicker. "Who's coming out?" he asked.

"Legion."

"I thought you'd already done that. Unless killing homicide cops all over the world doesn't count."

"This is different."

"I don't get it."

"You're not expected to. You're new at level five. We've been planning the big night out for a long, long time."

Bolan shifted in his seat. "Aren't we going to be shorthanded for a big job?" he said. "We lost about a dozen people in San Diego."

"Don't worry. We've got more than enough to do the trick. Players are coming in from all over."

"So, are you going to tell me what this big night out is about, or what?"

"Wait and see, Archangel. You'll just have to wait and see."

"You love guessing games, don't you?"

"It's the mark of a superior mind."

The flight attendant interrupted the conversation. She leaned in and asked them what they'd like to drink.

The Executioner knew there was no point in pressing Butcher Boy further. The German wasn't going to give up any more information.

Like the man said, he'd just have to wait and see.

Prison Library, San Quentin, California

HUNCHED OVER the computer keyboard, Bill Willie Pickett scrolled through the latest Legion file one more time, from the beginning. He devoured the first of the series of still images, examining the pale face of an old woman sitting on a couch. She had pendulous, sagging jowls, thin, lipsticked lips, hair like spun cotton and blue eyes as sharp as nail points. She wore a dress made ridiculous by too many bows and too much lace. Beside her on the couch sat a blond woman in her midforties. The younger woman had on a low-cut, sleeveless black dress with a short skirt. She looked blowsy and borderline drunk. In the background of the picture there were other people, out of focus: a party was going on around them. The old woman had just taken a sip of orange drink. The still shot caught her looking over her glass at the younger woman with disapproval, regret, and Pickett thought, a twinge of genuine pain.

Another Kodak moment.

The wisdom of age ignored.

Its hard-earned experience discounted.

Pickett smirked at the video image. He was less than half the old biddy's age, and he already knew that such things were nontransferable. She would never learn; he could see it in her eyes. She would carry her disappointment with her to the grave.

As he moved through the stack of stills, he wondered what the Feds eavesdropping on his computer time were thinking of the show. Could they guess what it all meant? The pictures had obviously been clipped from a videotape. Pictures of people, unnamed. In a place, unnamed. What Pickett knew, and the Feds didn't, was that he was looking at the menu for Legion's big night out.

Among the stills was a picture of a grammar-school building taken from the backside, so the school name wasn't visible. It showed a panorama of kids playing in the schoolyard. Most of the shots were of adults— old, young and in between. He could tell what a few of them did for a living because of what they were wearing; the checker at a grocery store, a mailman, a couple of cops in uniform, and, at the party, a big, hayseed-looking guy with skinny legs and blue-steel .45 who had to be some kind of a cop, too. Most of the menu items were anonymous, bacteria people about to be diced and sliced, and served up on a red gingham tablecloth for all the world to see.

Pickett had known the name of the town for months; recalling that secret made him smile even now. Legion hadn't thrown a dart at a map to pick it out. It'd used the Internet to search out the perfect proving ground for its power. It'd plugged in the requirements, and presto, out popped poor little Port Flattery. It was the kind of place where no one locked their doors at night, where strangers were trusted, or at least always given the benefit of the doubt, an isolated town that was so small it couldn't muster a creditable defense against the forces of Legion. Pickett was proud of the fact that he had helped design the plan for its dissection.

The only pity was, he couldn't be there in person for the festivities, due to a prior long-standing commitment—on death row. Because he knew the Legion attack plan by heart, minute by minute, second by second, he could already see it unfolding in his mind's eye. Legion was sure to provide him with the high points after the fact, a selection of more Kodak moments from the outing.

The final frame of video was the white-on-green population sign at the outskirts of Port Flattery.

It read Population: 1280.

Pickett glanced up at the library clock. Not for long, he thought. Not for long.

FBI Safehouse,
Portland, Oregon

HAL BROGNOLA PUNCHED ON the speakerphone, then swiveled his chair back to face the computer monitor, which was linked to Stony Man's computer lab via a separate, scrambled phone line. The latest intercepted Legion communication to Bill Willie Pickett filled his monitor's screen.

"What do you make of this stuff, Bear?" he asked.

Kurtzman's gruff voice crackled through the speakerphone. "To me it looks like they're all freeze-frames lifted off a videotape. It takes a fairly good camcorder to produce that kind of image quality. Other than that, I don't see anything special from a technical point of view."

"Anybody else got anything?" Brognola asked. "Don't stand on ceremony. Fire when ready."

"A lot of it was shot at the same cocktail party," Carmen Delahunt stated. "It reminds me of home movies. You know, cousin Joey's graduation, Grandma's birthday. Some of the people look like they could be related. Maybe it's from a family video album."

"Only Bill Willie doesn't have any family," Brognola said as the series of pictures flipped past.

"Or none that will claim him," Delahunt added.

"What I see," Akira Tokaido said, "is a bunch of really bad vacation snapshots. You can't even tell where they were taken, except for the obvious fact that the place is on the water.''

"If they're trying to hide the location, it could be important," Barbara Price said.

"Let's go over all the pictures of the town again," Kurtzman suggested. "See if we can pick up a name from the background."

Brognola swiveled his chair to check on Ron Diaz. The programmer sat in front of another terminal. Lines of game code scrolled by on its CRT, but Diaz wasn't looking at the screen. So far, his promise of help in return for protection had been worthless. Brognola could see the man's hands shaking in his lap. He was still scared to death. Even though they were a thousand miles from San Diego, Brognola had been unable to convince him that he was safe. Brognola had already sent for a Bureau doctor, hoping a mild sedative might relax the guy enough so he could focus on the problem at hand.

The Stony Man crew spent the next fifteen minutes poring over the series of images on their individual workstation monitors, enlarging, enhancing the visible detail, to no avail.

"Whoever put this sequence together," Delahunt said, "went to a lot of trouble to keep the town and its general location a secret. Makes you wonder why, doesn't it?"

"There's no road signs or license plates," Tokaido stated, "no business signs, either, but there are plenty of trees and plants. If we have a botanist identify them, maybe we can get an idea of the region we're looking at."

"As in, find the latitude?" Price asked, dubiously. "I don't see how that will narrow things down enough to do us any good."

"Who knows," Kurtzman said, "we might get lucky with some rare species. Go ahead, Akira, get on-line with somebody. Let's have the vegetation identified. I'm switching over to the ICID feed now."

Brognola's monitor changed pictures again, this time from a still shot to live motion. It was from the surveillance videocam in Bill Willie Pickett's cell.

"He looks damned pleased with himself, doesn't he?" Delahunt asked. "Like he's just had a good meal or outstanding sex. Of course, he couldn't have had either, or we would have seen it. The only thing that could have put the grin on his face is the fresh download from Legion."

"I shudder to think what would make that man smile like that," Price said.

"Damn, it's so obvious!" Kurtzman groaned. "Right in front of our bloody noses. Think about it. Legion is a game about a make-believe city where the players hunt down and kill cyberconstructs. If at level five they've taken the game into the real world..."

Price finished the thought for him. "Then they intend to do the same thing in Smallville, or whatever this place is called."

"Wait a minute," Tokaido said. "Assuming that what you say is true, and the people in the pictures are Legion's designated targets, how do we know they're connected to any one particular town? The shots could have been taken over a wide area and still have similarities of topography, ambient light, flora and architecture.''

"What about the population sign?" Delahunt argued. "Why was it included in the photo stack if the particular town isn't important?"

"It could be a red herring or the key to the whole thing," Tokaido replied. "At this point, we have no way of knowing."

"I agree that the facts are few and far between," Kurtzman said, "but they do give us a starting point. We know the town has 1280 people in it. If we combine that with what else we know, that there's a seacoast and evergreen trees, we can compile a list of possible matches from the northeast and northwest coasts, and proceed from there. Of course, our main thrust will still be breaking the chat-room code."

"Speaking of that, I haven't heard a peep from Hunt," Brognola said. "How's he doing?"

The former Berkeley professor answered for himself. "I think I've made a little progress on the Pickett end. Either that or I've been looking at this stuff so long I'm seeing things."

"Let's have it," Brognola said.

"I took your suggestion and researched Pickett's choice of reading material prior to the date of his filing suit for Internet access. Two months before the motion was entered, he checked out all the nonfiction books on Enigma in the prison library."

"Enigma, the Nazi code machine from World War II?"

"Exactly. If you remember, it used a series of interchangeable alphanumeric wheels to generate an incredibly complex code. I think Pickett has applied the same operating principle to his own situation. I think he's using the equivalent of an Enigma machine to make his code unbreakable.''

''Pickett is stuck in a five-by-ten cell,'' Brognola said. ''And he's under observation twenty-four hours a day. If he's got a code generator, why haven't we seen him using it?''

''First off,'' Wethers said, ''the prison intelligence tests are way off the mark. This guy has got to be a genius, a 160-plus IQ. He devised the code so he can carry most of what he needs in his head. Secondly don't forget that he did all this well in advance of filing suit to go on-line. He anticipated law enforcement's monitoring of his interactions with Legion and the need for an unbreakable code. After he worked it all out, he passed the code key to Legion, probably through his attorney, who may or may not have been aware of what he was carrying. When he got the okay from the court to log on to the Net, he and level five already had a secure channel.''

''As I recall, the Allies couldn't crack the Enigma code until they got hold of a working machine,'' Brognola said. ''If he still has the code generator in his possession, then we have it, too, right?''

''Everything Pickett has inside his cell is spread out in front of me,'' Wethers said. ''The machine is here. The problem is finding it.''

''What about your informant out there, Hal?'' Price asked. ''Has he turned up anything useful?''

''We've run into a snag.'' Brognola looked over his shoulder and saw that Diaz was no longer at his post.

The door to the bathroom, which had been open, was now closed. "The guy's had a pretty rough time of it, and it appears he wasn't that tightly wired to begin with. He's still too shaken up to concentrate on the job. I sent for an M.D. to see if some medication would help."

Something heavy thudded on the other side of the bathroom door.

"Oh, shit!" Brognola said, jumping to his feet. The bathroom door was locked. "Diaz! Diaz! Open up!"

When there was no answer, Brognola stepped back and straight-kicked the door. The wood cracked around the knob, but the lock held. On the second kick, the door splintered and swung in.

There was blood splattered and smeared everywhere.

Ron Diaz had fallen facedown over the edge of the tub. Brognola turned him over. The programmer's eyes were open, the pupils fixed. The kitchen paring knife that he'd cut his throat with was still in his hand.

CHAPTER TWELVE

Port Flattery, Washington

Officer Brian O'Hara sat parked in a cruiser next to the big Welcome To Victorian Port Flattery sign beside the highway on the outskirts of town. He had his radar gun in his lap. In the high season, the speed zone leading into PF could be a real moneymaker. The posted limit went from fifty to twenty-five miles per hour in the space of two hundred feet. This time of year, though, the scant traffic was still mostly locals who knew he was there and slowed down. On a Sunday night, a little after nine, he felt lucky if he got to aim his speed gun at one car every five minutes.

With nothing else to occupy his mind, O'Hara sat there kicking himself over the mess he'd made at the Bamfield house earlier in the day. He had never been any good at crime-scene stuff; he got too excited and forgot procedure. It had cost him his probation on the Seattle force. What O'Hara was good at was traffic stops and community relations—two things of the things that PFPD was renowned for. At least the screw-up hadn't been solely his fault; that twit of a prosecuting attorney had loused up, too.

Though he knew Gummy was major-league pissed off, there was no telling yet how important the chief would consider his mistake. O'Hara figured it all depended on the M.E.'s report. If it turned out the woman was murdered, he was probably dead, too.

One thing was sure; he had to stay on his toes for the forseeable future. No more sneaking off for a cat-nap in Flattery Park. The city park was behind the Welcome sign; its entrance was on a side road that ran parallel to the highway. It wasn't much of a park, just a grove of sickly pecker-pole Douglas fir on a postage stamp of a lot, but it closed at sunset, which meant law enforcement could snooze there undisturbed.

The thought of having to stay awake after midnight made Brian O'Hara cringe. He was used to the on-the-job sack time; his current sleep-wake cycle depended on it. To get through the shift in a fully conscious state he was going to need a big-time sugar lift in about two hours.

A pair of headlights appeared over the top of the rise in the distance. It was either a semitruck or an RV, O'Hara thought, picking up the radar gun and taking aim. The red LCD indicator said 50, then the counter began to drop.

No ticket for the Winnebago.

It was going twenty-three miles per hour when it signaled a left turn and pulled over on the shoulder in front of him, blocking his view of the highway, and vice versa. The driver stuck his head out of the window and said, "Can you help me, Officer? I'm looking for Calhoun Street." The guy had a dense black beard and a happy expression on his face. There was another guy in the front passenger's seat, also smiling.

"Sure." O'Hara enjoyed giving directions to tourists almost as much as he enjoyed writing them tickets. He opened the car door and got out, then hooked a thumb toward town. "At the second light, turn left, then go five blocks and take a right up the hill. That's Birch Street, we call it 'B and B row.' Calhoun is the third cross street."

"Thanks, officer."

"No problem," O'Hara said as he turned away.

"Oh, there's one more thing...."

"Sure."

Because it was dark and the sound suppressor tube was flat black, O'Hara didn't see the .22 pistol the driver had in his hand. He did see the muzzle-flash an instant before the high-velocity hollowpoint slug slammed into his right eye. Then he saw nothing. The .22 slug rattled around inside his skull like a pea in a tin cup, bouncing back and forth off the hard bone, in the process cutting a half-dozen zigzag tracks through the soft tissue before it came to a stop.

Blood leaking from both nostrils, O'Hara clutched at the inside of the door, but his hands had no strength. He slid down to the ground.

Aga Karkanian slipped the gun back into the door's map pocket. "Let's get that sucker out of his uniform before he bleeds all over it," the serial killer said.

The front and side doors of the Winnebago popped open, and Karkanian and five of his Legion pack-mates hopped out. They knew what they were doing. Inside of a half a minute they had Brian O'Hara stripped of his uniform shirt and dumped into the trunk of the squad car.

The player known as "Clown" in the killer network put on the dead officer's shirt. He was a rough match in size, had the same short cut, sandy brown hair as O'Hara. His nom de guerre was a tribute to a serial murderer who had died at the hands of the state of Illinois: John Wayne Gacy.

Karkanian and the others jumped back in the Winnebago, leaving Clown to button up his new shirt. They drove up the steep hill that overlooked the town and the bay. On the shoreline on the right, the gray concrete oblong of the pulp mill was lit up as bright as day. White smoke poured from its twin stacks, rising three hundred feet into the black sky. The PF mill turned wood chips into toilet paper around the clock, seven days a week.

This night, the mill would sleep. And, like its workers, perhaps never wake again.

Karkanian chuckled to himself as he looked at the warm, golden lights of the houses sprinkled over the dark hillside below. Legion's big night out was going to turn Port Flattery into a ghost town. Purified of all bacterial life-forms, the city's infrastructure would remain—the mill, the streets, the houses, the waterfront.

Who would ever want to live here after tonight?

No one.

Like the McDonald's restaurant in San Ysidro, site of the Huberty massacre, Port Flattery would be desecrated ground, suitable only as a monument to the memory of the fallen.

Karkanian followed the cop's excellent directions,

driving down the row of turn-of-the-century bed and breakfast inns to Calhoun Street. He had no trouble finding Byrum House, what with all the vehicles parked on the street around it. The Victorian home was brightly lit, inside and out; all the shades were drawn. He pulled past a pair of vans and parked behind another Winnebago.

As Karkanian and crew hurried up the walk, the front door opened a crack. It opened the rest of the way as they trooped up onto the porch. A tall, blond woman dressed in a blacksuit and holding a silenced machine pistol greeted them.

"Welcome, Mr. Mudgett," Della Gridley said to Karkanian. Herman Mudgett was his game handle, a homage to the Victorian mass murderer of the same name. "We were starting to worry about you. You're almost the last to arrive." She stepped aside so they could enter.

The living room of Byrum House was packed with people, ninety-five percent of which were men. All of them were dressed as Della was, in black covert-ops suits. Some had already donned bulletproof vests and combat harnesses. Karkanian guessed they were close to their full fighting complement of fifty. Some of the faces he recognized from previous, smaller-scale, combined-pack hunts; others he knew only by their Legion pseudonyms. He had never encountered them outside of cyberspace.

"Who's still missing?" he asked Spence, one of the few players he knew by sight.

"Butcher Boy and what's left of his pack. They arrived in Seattle three hours ago. They should be here any minute.''

"They hit some trouble, I gather," Karkanian said. "The radio's only been giving up bits and pieces."

In one corner of the room, the big-screen TV was on with the sound muted. CNN was running a special report on the trouble in San Diego earlier in the day.

"We've been following the bulletins since midafternoon," Spence told him, "but there hasn't been much information. When Butcher Boy phoned in from the airport, he said all he knew for sure was that Lizzie and the others didn't make it to the rendezvous point. Evidently they had Diaz cornered in a canyon when a wildfire broke out and separated everybody. He didn't know if the others managed to whack Diaz or not."

"We don't need Lizzie's bunch," Karkanian said.

"No, we've got plenty of troops to handle tonight's work," Spence agreed. "I was just about to go over the assignments one last time before we pick up our weapons."

"Let's hear it," Karkanian prompted.

Spence referred to a blowup map of Port Flattery taped to the climbing roses of the floral-print wallpaper. "As you can see, we've divided the town into three sections. The first is the waterfront. It's the least populated of the bunch, but it covers the most ground. The X's on Main Street indicate the commercial buildings that have apartments upstairs. We don't know which of the boats in the marina have live-aboards on them— whoever draws this assignment is going to have to figure that out on-site. And at the far end of the bay, is the pulp mill with its swing shift. Soon to be a skeleton shift.

"The second section takes in the town's main residential area. That includes the B and Bs and the smaller Victorians, as well as the more recently constructed homes. There are several hundred individual houses to sweep in this part. We'll be going door to door, room by room. I anticipate that this area will take the most time to clean out.

"The last section covers the trailer park on the back side of town and the few minifarms within the city limits. Everyone, be sure and position your support vehicles as indicated on the maps you've already been given. Otherwise you'll run out of ammo."

"We can always use these," one of the male players said. He whipped out a twelve-inch parkerized Recon Tanto knife.

"Which reminds me," Spence said. "We don't have time for the taking of individual trophies tonight. In order to finish the job on schedule, each of us has to account for twenty-six lives. So, kill them quick and move on. Remember, Legion's trophy is the whole town. When we leave, we're going to cross out the 1280 on the population sign and write in a big, fat zero.

"We're holding back one of the two Winnebagos," he went on. "Its crew doesn't have a section assignment after it knocks out the power substation. It'll cruise the streets for stragglers and provide reinforcements if any of the other three groups needs them. Are there any questions?"

There was none.

"Our gear is waiting in the garage," Spence told them.

"Hey, wait a minute," Della said, pointing at the big TV. "Turn on the sound. They've got something new on the San Diego hit."

OUT THE REAR passenger's-side window of the rental car, Mack Bolan got occasional glimpses of starlit water between the stands of tall trees. Puget Sound appeared and disappeared as the two-lane highway twisted west, past a jigsaw puzzle of islands, inlets and bays. Wavy Hair drove the sedan at the speed limit, no faster. Still furious about his missing and potentially dead brother, he hadn't said two words since the airport in San Diego. Butcher Boy had done all the talking. He sat in the front passenger's seat with a map and a penlight, giving directions.

"Take the next right," the German told Wavy Hair. "That's the turnoff we want."

The crossroad was much narrower than the state highway, little more than a gully between walls of black trees. Bolan read the road sign as it flashed past. There was only one destination listed on it: Port Flattery, and the distance was eighteen miles.

The Executioner leaned between the sedan's front seats, far enough forward to get a look at the map Butcher Boy was holding. Beside the German's index finger was the name Port Flattery. The map showed the town at the end of a long, skinny peninsula that stuck out into the sound.

It was an isolated place, for sure, the ideal spot for a serial-killer convention.

In at least one way, it was ideal for his purposes, too. An isolated fire zone gave him the chance to contain Legion and destroy it.

As Bolan sat back, he felt a twinge of unease. Confining Legion to the tip of a remote peninsula worked for his mission, but it didn't necessarily work for the people of Port Flattery. They would be the ones to bear the brunt of the killers' concentrated rage. If and when the league of murderers rearmed him, or when he rearmed himself, he would become a lone predator again. And Legion, to the last man or woman, would become his prey. The problem was, the Executioner couldn't protect the innocent and still do his job.

The road snaked through some low hills, past widely separated small farms. After a gas station at another crossroads, it was pretty much a straight shot into Port Flattery. At the entrance to the city was a welcome sign that read Home Of Victorian Hospitality. A police car was parked beside the sign, and it was occupied by a single officer. Bolan could see a head and shoulders behind the steering wheel.

Wavy Hair clicked his brights on and off, once.

The cop car's headlights flashed on, then off.

If it was a recognition signal, Bolan thought, it meant the local police were already out of the game.

Bolan watched the town of Port Flattery glide by. So small. So vulnerable. He no longer had any lingering doubts about what Legion had in store for the place. The killers had come here in force to make it the jewel in the crown of their terror campaign.

Following a set of printed directions, they drove to Calhoun Street and took the last parking space on the corner. "It looks like we're the last ones to arrive at the party," Butcher Boy said.

"Come on, Archangel," the German said as they exited the vehicle and started up the walk to Byrum House. "There are some people inside you're going to want to meet." The two-story Victorian glowed before them; every light in the place was on.

Wavy Hair entered the front door without knocking, with Butcher Boy and Bolan bringing up the rear. They stepped into the front room, which was crammed full of people, suffocatingly hot and reeked of tobacco and gun oil. All the level-five players wore blacksuits. Some wore night observation devices—NODs— pushed up on top of their heads. The infrared goggles were Russian made. Every one of them had a submachine gun and a side arm. Stacks of full magazines sat on the floor at their feet, as did cans of loose ammo.

Legion was going to turn "the home of Victorian hospitality" into a slaughterhouse.

"We're glad you made it," a tall, blond woman told the German. "Sorry about Lizzie and the others."

"Yeah, we took some lumps, Della."

Bolan scanned the crowd. He recognized only one face. The killer of SAC Lawrence Deeds stepped forward.

"Butcher Boy, why don't you introduce us to your new friend?" Aga Karkanian suggested.

The Executioner looked straight into the eyes of the bearded monster and realized that Karkanian was laughing at him.

"This is Archangel," the German said.

"He's famous already."

"From the game?" Butcher Boy asked.

An autopistol appeared in Karkanian's hand like magic. It was the first of many to pop out in the next second or two. A dozen cocked handguns, pointed at the Executioner.

"Whoa!" Butcher Boy said, stepping out of the line of fire. "What's this for?"

"First, why don't you make sure he's unarmed," Karkanian stated.

While Bolan stood with his hands raised, the German patted him down, quickly but professionally. "He's clean," Butcher Boy announced. "Now, what's with the guns?"

"Have a look," Della said. "Show him, Spence."

A muscular blond guy turned on the VCR. A CNN update of the San Diego attack popped onto the screen. The newswoman announced a breakthrough in the mysterious fire and reported gun battle in the canyon near downtown. Which, she said, authorities suspected were connected to the bomb threat and forced evacuation a short distance away. The cable news network had obtained exclusive rights to a videotape shot by a home owner along the canyon rim.

At gunpoint, Bolan watched the grainy tape. It showed a tall man running across a hillside, firing a machine pistol at a kneeling figure with a rifle. The figure with the rifle dropped to the grass. The tall man picked up the rifle and sighted across the canyon, toward the camera, and fired.

Spence hit the freeze-frame.

There was no doubt whom they were all looking at.

"Why, you dirty son of a bitch!" Wavy Hair shoved aside the others and threw himself at Bolan.

The Executioner shifted his weight on the balls of his feet. He moved just enough to make Wavy Hair miss his lunge and, as the guy rushed past, he punched, striking him with the edge of his hand in the side of the throat. The blow sent Wavy Hair sprawling on the floor. Struggling up to his knees, he clutched his neck, gasping for air.

"Any more of that," Della warned Bolan, "and you die where you stand."

"If he killed the snipers, he must've killed Lizzie and all the others, too," Butcher Boy said. "What the hell is he, a rogue player?"

"No, he's a fucking Fed," Spence snarled. "He's got to be an undercover Fed."

"You were supposed to screen for that, Butcher Boy," Karkanian declared.

"I thought I had. I watched him shoot a pair of federal agents. He must've faked it somehow."

Karkanian faced Bolan again. "What we have here is a dirty Justice Department spy, an assassin who infiltrated our ranks so he could kill us when our backs were turned. The blood of our revered fellow players is on his hands. The question on the table isn't what're we going to do with him, but how're we going to do it. Are there any suggestions from the floor?" He looked down at Wavy Hair, who immediately scrambled to his feet.

"Yeah," the man croaked, "let me handle it. I know just what to do." He picked up a backpack that held loaded magazines and dumped them out on the floor. "Somebody get me some duct tape."

AT A QUARTER TO TEN, Bobbie Marie Potts got in her car and started out for her Calhoun Street rental house. After stewing over the pros and cons of a confrontation all day, she'd decided that she had no choice. She had to apologize to Spence Gridley for her outrageous behavior at the party. She couldn't afford to make an enemy of him. Or of Della, either.

Potts was truly embarrassed over the way she'd come on to her tenant. She'd been driven to it by her frustration with Gummy. Miss Gonerman had been right about him. History was repeating itself. Their relationship had broken up years earlier over a string of infidelities. Gummy just couldn't leave it alone. Why had she thought he'd changed? Because he'd said so? How could she be that gullible?

When Potts couldn't find a parking place near Byrum House, she had to leave her car around the corner. She knew all the strange vehicles had to belong to people visiting the Gridleys. The house on the opposite corner was owned by snowbirds who were out of town until the middle of June. It occurred to her that if the strangers were guests of the Gridleys, they might be some of their friends from Hollywood.

Potts put aside her resolve to apologize. She couldn't do it in front of strangers, not to mention potential clients. She would have to act like it had never happened and hope for the best.

As she stepped up on the porch, she saw that the front door was open. She looked through the screen and saw people dressed in funny get-ups and carrying guns. There were guns all over the place. Spencer Gridley had his camcorder out and was videotaping his guests.

Whatever they were up to, Bobbie Marie Potts didn't want any part of it. Before she could turn away, Della opened the screen.

"Well, if it isn't our favorite landlady," the blonde said. "Come by to check up on us?"

"Uh, no, I—"

Della reached out and grabbed the woman as she tried to back away. She squeezed her arm so hard it hurt, then she pulled her inside the house.

There had to have been fifty people packed into the living room. A half-dozen of them had a tall, dark-haired guy on his knees in the middle of the floor. He was the only person in the place who wasn't dressed for a funeral. Four of them held him down while the other two tied his wrists behind his back with wraps of duct tape. The kneeling man had the straps of an empty backpack over his shoulders. Directing the activity was a wild-eyed man with wavy hair. He was so angry he was actually spitting.

"Everybody," Della said as she pushed Potts forward into the room, "I'd like you to meet our landlady. How about passing that tape over here when you're through."

Potts summoned her courage and said, "What's going on here? Who are all these people?"

"They're not from Hollywood," Spence told her, "and you're not going to sell them any real estate."

"We sent our friends here some video of your little

town, and they thought it was so damned cute they had to come up and kill it," Della said.

Potts didn't understand exactly what that meant, but she'd seen more than enough to be afraid. "If this is some kind of joke," she said, "it isn't very funny."

"A joke? Does this look like a joke?" Della stuck the barrel of a pistol under her nose. "You're dead meat, Bobbie Marie. And so is everybody else in this stupid hick town. Tell you what, though, as a special favor, because you've been so nice, you can be the last to die. Number 1280 out of 1280."

Spence held her arms pinned at her sides while Della tightly taped her wrists together. Then Della tore off a strip of tape and stuck it over her mouth. "In case you were thinking about screaming," the blonde explained.

Then they pulled the tall man to his feet. He wasn't scared; Potts could see it in his ice blue eyes. That surprised her.

The bearded guy led the entire bunch of them out the front door. Potts and the other captive made their exit surrounded by people with guns. The bearded man opened the side door of a Winnebago parked at the curb, and she and the tall man were shoved in and forced to sit side by side on an upholstered bench built into the far wall.

Five others got in with them; as the man with wavy hair was the last, he shut the door. "I know just the place to take him," he said as the bearded man climbed into the Winnebago's driver's seat. "I saw it on the video. Head down toward the waterfront. I'll tell you where to stop."

The bearded man pulled away from the curb. All the other vehicles followed.

As they turned the corner and started down the hill to the water, the tall man leaned close to Potts and whispered, "When it all starts to happen, get on the floor and stay there."

CHAPTER THIRTEEN

Gummy Nordland lay on his back in the dark, staring up at the ceiling of the beachfront cottage. The red-headed ex-wife of the mill manager nestled against the side of his chest, snoring softly. They were both naked under the quilt on her bed. Even though he had his hand on her bare bottom, Nordland wasn't thinking about sex; for the time being, he was all sexed out. He was thinking about Lyla Bamfield. The medical examiner's report would take at least another seventy-two hours to complete, long enough for the perpetrator or perpetrators, if there were any, to be on the other side of the world. The facts surrounding her death kept bouncing around inside his head like lottery balls on a Saturday night. Insufficient facts, unless he just wasn't seeing them right.

Nothing had been stolen from the house, and no attempt had been made to break in. A routine check had shown she didn't owe anyone any money locally. The cliff house had been bought and paid for with the sale of some California real estate. Nobody in town owed her money, either. He tried to think of someone with a grudge against Bamfield big enough to want kill her.

Though he racked his brain, he could come up with no solid suspects.

Sure, some people were jealous over her "stardom." Port Flattery was home to a lot of artistic eccentrics, the former divas of local culture—the unsold painters and self-published poets—who had been replaced by a much bigger fish. But they were toothless, except in Letters to the Editor; even there, it was all petty stuff. There was no real, underlying passion, therefore no motive. If there was cause for someone to kill her, it had to have come from outside PF, from before she'd moved here.

Which brought Nordland back to the Gridleys.

All he knew about them was what they'd told him, or what he'd heard secondhand from Bobbie Marie. Was it a simple coincidence that the night Lyla Bamfield met the only other Hollywood people in town she took a four-hundred-foot plunge to her death? Maybe. Maybe not. He checked the clock on the nightstand. It was just a quarter to ten. Not too late to ask the Gridleys a couple of more questions.

"Are you okay?" the redhead asked, her hand slipping across his bare chest, her smooth leg sliding over his.

"Huh? Yeah, sure." Nordland took her arm off him and sat up in bed.

"What's wrong?"

"Nothing," he told her, reaching for his pants on the bedpost. "I have to go out. Police business."

"Come back when you're done," she said, pulling the covers up to her chin. "I'll keep it nice and warm for you."

Nordland knew she didn't mean the bed. Looking down at her in the half light, he felt some small sympathy for the mill manager. The man's ex-wife was a handful. A couple of handfuls. Rumor around town was they had broken up because her husband couldn't keep her satisfied in the sack. Nordland could see why. Even though the chief was a man who liked sex, and lots of it, now that he was fully sober, he could see there was something wrong with the redhead. Sex was a one-on-one competition to her. As such, it became a grueling sport in a hurry. Like the Daytona 500, only with fewer pit stops.

"I'll drop back by when I can," he said, knowing that he wouldn't.

He got out of there as quickly as he could.

Back in his squad car, the chief headed straight for Calhoun Street. As he ticked off all the information he should have gotten from the Gridleys but hadn't, he had to wonder if the sight and proximity of Della's muscular behind had put him right out of investigative mode. Things like that had distracted him before, though never in an important case. He hadn't even bothered to get their permanent address in Hollywood. And he should have pressed Spence for the names and phone numbers of some of his business associates in California. While he waited for the M.E.'s autopsy results, Nordland could use those names and numbers to double-check the facts the Gridleys had already given him: that they didn't know Bamfield, and that the people they knew didn't know her, either.

If it came down to an out-of-town motive, there were several possibilities, the most prominent being a professional hit. Payback for some prior nasty business dealings down in Tinseltown. The chief had no idea who or what Bamfield had been connected to in the entertainment industry. For all he knew, she could have had dealings with the Mob that had gone sour.

When he turned down the block to Byrum House, Nordland saw a whole caravan of vehicles starting to pull away from the curb out front. He immediately killed his headlights and slowed to a stop. The Gridleys had company. Lots and lots of company. His curiosity aroused, he followed the pack of outsiders with his lights off. Before they reached Main Street and the waterfront, two of the sedans peeled off from the rest. The chief stuck with the larger group, keeping far enough back to stay out of sight.

Nordland pulled the cruiser into an empty lot and watched as the Winnebago in the lead parked at the foot of Flattery Pier. Brake lights flared as the other vehicles followed suit. Like the rest of downtown, Flattery Pier was a relic of the Victorian era. Once it had supported various maritime businesses, ship chandlers, a cannery; now it was just pilings and a railed deck that extended out into the bay.

Under the streetlight, Nordland saw the side door of the Winnebago swing open and men in black start piling out, with automatic weapons showing. For a second, he couldn't believe his eyes. They had submachine guns on shoulder slings, like a SWAT team, only there were too many of them. Similarly dressed, equipped people poured out of the other vehicles, as well. It was more like a terrorist army, he decided, which explained absolutely nothing, unless the Hollywood people were making an action movie.

Two of the black-clad strangers pushed a tall, well-built guy out of the Winnebago. He had his hands tied behind his back. Was he the hero of the flick? Nordland groaned when he saw a tall blond woman pull a shorter one out of the RV's side door. It was Della Gridley and Bobbie Marie. His ex had her hands tied behind her back, too. He could see that her mouth was taped.

The chief drew his Government Model .45 pistol from its holster and spit out a curse. He knew next to nothing about filmmaking, but he knew there had to be equipment, booms, dollies, a director and support crew. It was no movie. What he was watching was a nightmare come to life. His town had been invaded, and a loved one's life was being threatened. Whoever these outsiders were, whatever they wanted, they had the odds on their side, as in at least forty to one. There was no way Nordland could intervene with his 7-shot Colt, not if he hoped to survive.

The mass of blacksuits didn't go anywhere with their captives. They just sort of milled around at the edge of the pier entrance.

Then the crowd parted a bit and he saw what was happening. One of the guys in black had opened up the pack on the back of the tied-up guy and was putting heavy beach rocks in it.

WAVY HAIR DROPPED another ten-pound rock into the almost full pack on Bolan's back. With the water lapping at the shore not fifty feet away, with his arms tied together behind his back so there was no way he could

get out of the shoulder straps, it didn't take a genius
to figure out what the bereaved brother had in mind for
him. The backpack was already carrying about ninety
pounds of stone, more than enough to keep him down.

"Think you can swim to shore with that load on
your back?" Wavy Hair asked his captive.

"Maybe you should put in another real big one, just
to make sure," the Executioner suggested.

"You got it, sucker. One more big rock coming up."

The player known as Spence shoved his video camera and floodlight into Bolan's face, taping his reaction
to the sudden addition of twenty pounds of beach rock.
Spence was recording the entire evening's festivities so
the level-fivers could relive it over and over again, like
Super Bowl highlights.

"Hurry up and finish this!" Karkanian snapped.
"We've got more-important things to do tonight."

Wavy Hair laced the top of the pack closed and tied
it securely. "All done," he said, then he booted his
captive once in the behind. "The plank is that way,
dead man. Move it."

Before the others grabbed his shoulders and pulled
him away, Bolan turned and gave his tormentor a look
that promised a gravestone. Soon. As if touched by a
finger of ice, Wavy Hair instinctively recoiled. Then,
catching himself, he laughed a forced little laugh. The
Legion players marched the Executioner ahead of
them, down the lighted pier, but Wavy Hair didn't kick
him again.

The pier, like the rest of the downtown waterfront,
was deserted. There was no one around to see what

was going on or to try to stop it. On the other side of the wooden rail, the water looked black, deep, and cold.

When they came to the rail at the end of the pier, someone shoved Bolan from behind, slamming him against it.

"Wait. Not yet," Wavy Hair said. He knelt down and quickly duct-taped Bolan's ankles together.

"Unless you're a Harry fucking Houdini, you aren't going anywhere but down," he said, pushing the Executioner's stomach back against the rail. "This is for what you did to my brother."

"Let's do it," Butcher Boy said.

Wavy Hair and the German grabbed Bolan by the ankles and arms and lifted, sliding him headfirst over the rail. As he went over, somewhere behind him, Bolan heard the tape-gagged woman's bleat of terror.

It was twenty-five feet to the water, which translated into a couple of seconds of free fall. The Executioner inhaled as deeply as he could before he hit. The fifty-degree water was an explosive jolt to his system. Cold fire. People had died from the shock of just falling in Puget Sound, but instant death wasn't what Wavy Hair had in mind. He wanted Bolan to drown while struggling in the frigid darkness on the bottom of the bay.

As Bolan plummeted, the rock-loaded backpack acted like a keel weight, pulling him over onto his back. He didn't know how deep the water was, but the quicker he hit bottom, the better, which was the reason he'd baited Wavy Hair into topping off the pack.

His fall through the dark went on and on, then he hit bottom with bone-jarring suddenness, landing with his arms trapped beneath the heavy pack.

He could see nothing underwater, but he didn't need to. The escape act was a matter of touch. Twisting onto his side on the bay bottom, he dug his fingertips into the back pocket of his pants, fishing out a two-by-three-inch square of black plastic. Butcher Boy had over-looked it during the pat-down. Inside his pocket, it felt about as lethal as a credit card. Actually it was a Tekna knife, concealed in a skinny plastic case.

He pushed the button on the side of the case with his thumb, and out popped a two-inch-wide, but ex-tremely thin, double-edged blade. Two slashes, and the wrist restraints were history. He shrugged out of the backpack's shoulder straps and quickly cut through the duct tape around his ankles. Kicking off from the bot-tom, Bolan swam back toward the pier.

When he touched the pilings, he let himself glide to the surface under the overhang of the decking. Tread-ing water, he could hear the sounds of the Legion cars starting up and pulling away. The wave surge pushed him against the sharp barnacles on the pilings, so he swam away from them, around the end of the pier and toward the beach.

When the toes of his shoes hit sand, he stood and walked the rest of the way in. The air felt warm, and it was, compared to the water. As he approached the foot of the pier, a figure stepped out of the shadows to block his path. Bolan kept walking right at the guy. Another couple of yards was all he needed to bring him into kick range.

"Stop there," the man said. He raised a .45 auto-matic in a two-handed grip. "I'm the police chief around here, and I'm in kind of a hurry. The bastards who pitched you over the rail have taken my ex-wife hostage. I need an explanation from you, and I need it fast, or I'm going to drop you like a bad habit.''

Bolan sized up the head cop of Port Flattery. Though his voice was a little quavery with excitement, he held the big blue-steel Colt rock-steady in his hands. ''Your ex-wife's in big trouble, Chief,'' he said. ''So's everybody else in town. The guys in black are terrorists.''

''Terrorists? What the hell do they want with us?''

''They want you dead.''

''Come with me,'' the cop said, lowering the hammer on the automatic with his thumb. ''I've got a blanket in my car.''

Bolan used the blanket to dry off as best he could while the chief got on his squad car's radio. Only one of his on-duty officers responded to the urgent call for assistance.

''Teddy,'' the chief said, ''we've got an A-number-one emergency on our hands. This is no joke. It's a goddamned invasion. About four dozen heavily armed terrorists just tried to drown a guy down at the pier, and they've got Bobbie Marie as a hostage. I can't get Brian to answer my radio call. The lazy jerk's probably down in the park, sleeping in the back seat again. Wake him up and set up a roadblock on the highway. Don't let anyone leave town. The terrorists are driving sedans, vans and two Winnebagos. If you confront these guys, shoot to kill. They've got automatic weapons.''

''The bad guys aren't going anywhere,'' Bolan said, ''not until they've finished what they came here to do.''

The chief lowered his mike. "Who the hell are they? Who the hell are you?"

"There's no time to explain it all," the Executioner said. "These people are stone killers. Right now they're dividing up into extermination teams. I know because I saw their battle plan stuck up on a wall. They mean to wipe out this whole town tonight, every man, woman, and child."

"Why?"

"To make a point."

"Which is?"

"That they have the power to do it. And that people like you and me don't have the power to stop them. Look, Chief, all you really need to know is that they're armed and intent on mass murder. If we're going to stop them, we need weapons and backup."

"The station's just a block down the street," the cop told him. "We've got guns there." As Bolan jumped into the passenger's seat, he added, "They call me Gummy. You got a name?"

"It's not important."

"Whatever you say, bud."

"How many officers do you have?"

"Two on duty, though one of them isn't worth a shit. And three more off duty."

"No reserves?"

"No, but there's a volunteer fire department."

"We're going to need them to help us evacuate the town."

"Christ almighty," Nordland groaned.

A few seconds later, the chief swerved to a stop in front of the little brick police station. There were no lights on inside, and a spare cruiser sat parked by the side door. It was Nordland's entrance of choice. As soon as he got the door open, the chief flicked on the lights and led Bolan to the weapons locker, which stood in one corner of his tiny, windowless office.

"We don't have much in the way of an arsenal," the chief said, unlocking the padlock and swinging back the metal door.

It was an understatement.

The Port Flattery police department's armory consisted of three Smith & Wesson shotguns, 12-gauge riot pumps with pistol grips and folding rear stocks, and one high-powered rifle, a 10-shot Remington semiauto designed for deer hunting in brushy cover. Along with the quartet of low-tech long guns was a pair of .38-caliber revolvers so battered they looked like they had to have been retired from service.

"That's it?"

"Afraid so, except for some odds and ends of gear the previous chief collected."

"Let's see."

Nordland pulled open the big drawer beneath the gun compartment. Inside were paper boxes of ammunition, a couple of armored vests and a few riot-control hand grenades. Bolan recognized their model numbers. The M-492 A was a Thunderflash stunner. The others were standard CS gas.

Way too little.

Perhaps way too late.

The Executioner grimaced.

The task he and the chief faced was looking more and more impossible by the minute, and the lives of more than twelve hundred innocent people hung in the balance. Bolan knew the time had come to forget about mission parameters, about state secrets and political repercussions. "Get on the horn," he told Nordland. "Call the state patrol and the National Guard. Get them down here on the double and in force."

The chief picked up the phone and hit the autodial button for the state patrol. About half the necessary digits had beeped when the office lights went out and the room plunged into darkness.

"I got a flashlight here in my desk," Nordland said. Then he cursed. "The phone's out, too. Stone dead."

"They cut the lines. We're on our own."

The chief's flashlight cut a white path through the gloom.

"Over here with that," Bolan said.

The Executioner handed the chief the Remington 7400 semiauto, a box of .30-06 soft-nose bullets, one of the vests and two grenades. For himself, he took one of the riot pump guns, a box of high brass, Number One buckshot shells and a couple of Thunderflashes. He stuck one of the beat-up .38s in his waistband, then pulled on the remaining piece of body armor. There was an extra flashlight in a corner of the drawer. He tested it to make sure it worked before slipping it in his pocket.

"You've still got the radio in your squad car," Bolan reminded Nordland as they went out the way they'd come in. "Call your officers again. We're going to need them with us."

Outside, all the lights in town were off. The turrets of the Victorian waterfront buildings were dimly visible, spiky silhouettes against the starry night sky. Beyond them, the hillsides where the townsfolk lived were impenetrably black. The only place with power was the pulp mill way down the bay. Its emergency generator had kicked in, and it was still lit up.

This time, when Nordland tried to raise his officers, neither answered. "Somebody's left a mike open," he stated. "I can't get through. It looks like it's down to you and me, bud. What are we going to do?"

"If we're going to save the most people," Bolan said, "we've got to split up. From the map I saw, they've divided the town into three parts. You take the area along the water from here to the mill. When you find honest citizens, help them to take solid cover. When you find the bad guys, don't try to arrest them. Kill them. Do it as quick as you can. And keep close to cover yourself. They've got night-vision goggles. They can see in the dark."

"What're you going to do?"

"The rest of the town is my responsibility."

"That doesn't seem right. I mean, I'm the chief here. I still don't know who you are."

"I'm a guy who's done this kind of work before."

They both knew he had assigned Nordland the easiest duty, if any of it could be called that. By handing him the waterfront, Bolan had given the chief the best odds of survival. *Best* didn't mean much, though. His chances were still slim to none.

"When you get to the mill and clear it of bad guys," the Executioner said, "come back this way and look for me. Have you got the keys to that other squad car?"

Nordland reached in his pocket and tossed them to him.

"Nice knowing you, bud."

"Same here."

CHAPTER FOURTEEN

Officer Ted Ramsey fishtailed the cruiser away from the pumps of Port Flattery's only gas station and slashed a squealing left turn onto the street. With emergency lights flashing, but no siren on, he barreled up the hill toward the city limits. Driving with one hand along the steep straightaway, Ramsey tried his radio again. He pressed the Send button on the microphone and said, "Come on, Brian, answer me. We've got trouble. Repeat. Big trouble. Answer me. Over." He released the transmit button and waited.

There was no reply.

"Man, oh man," Ramsey muttered, tossing the mike onto the floor, "did you ever pick the wrong night to screw up." He floored the accelerator, making the Ford's fuel-injected V-8 howl. What the chief had told him was starting to sink in.

Four dozen gunmen.

Hostages.

Roadblock.

Shoot to kill.

Ramsey never expected to be confronted by anything of the sort in dinky little Port Flattery. That was one of the reasons he'd decided to try to get on the force here. Unlike O'Hara, who had screwed up on the job elsewhere, Ramsey had a perfect service record with the Tacoma department. He'd come to PF because he wanted to live long enough to see his retirement.

And now this.

Two men trying to hold a roadblock against fifty sounded a whole lot like an assisted double suicide to him. And the "two" part assumed he could find O'Hara before the shit hit the fan. It occurred to Ramsey as he highballed along the back road to Flattery Park that he could just keep going, straight out of town, and never look back. When questioned afterward, he could plead momentary insanity, irresistible impulse or attention deficit disorder—at least he'd still be alive. He could have bailed out on the good people Port Flattery, but he didn't. He'd sworn a solemn oath to protect them, and he took that kind of thing very seriously.

Because the back road was unlit and the houses along it few and far between, he didn't realize the power was out until he nearly missed the entrance to Flattery Park in the dark. Slamming on his brakes, he slowed enough to make the turn onto the gravel driveway. The streetlight above the rustic, chiseled burl sign was off, and through the stands of toothpick park trees he couldn't see the glow of the mercury-vapor lamp over the highway, by the welcome to PF sign.

Panic started to creep up on Ramsey as he drove through the open gate, down the bright tunnel his headlights made. If the town was blacked out, they were beyond screwed. How was a six-person local PD going to find and stop an army of terrorists in the pitch-dark? As he rounded the drive, his headlights lit up the rear of the other squad car, which was parked in front of the park's concrete-block toilets.

He could see a head sticking up above the driver's headrest. It looked like Brian was awake, anyway, which didn't explain what he was doing, sitting there in the dark. Ramsey pulled in behind the cruiser and, leaving his lights on, got out. "Brian, you asshole!" he shouted as he trotted for the driver's door. "Why did you shut off your radio?"

As he stepped up to the open window, he saw his fellow officer had something strange on top of his head. It looked like electronic equipment, held on with straps.

"What are you playing at?" Ramsey asked.

When the man in the driver's seat half turned toward him, he realized it wasn't Brian. Ramsey backed up, and as he did so, reached for his side arm.

The guy who wasn't Brian casually leaned out the window and fired a silenced pistol at him.

A searing pain ripped into Ramsey's right shoulder and spun him against the side of the patrol car. As he bounced off, his 9 mm service automatic slipped from his hand. He couldn't hold on to the Beretta, his whole arm had gone dead down to his fingertips. His legs still worked, though.

Ramsey could hear the patrol car door opening behind him as he raced back into the lights of his own cruiser. Something whizzed by his hip, and the left headlight crashed out. He managed another two steps before a bullet caught him in the middle of the back. It drove him facedown in the gravel. For a second, he couldn't move; he couldn't even breathe. Then he heard the crunch of footsteps coming up behind him.

Ramsey tried to crawl the last ten feet to his squad car's open door. The pistol coughed again. The bullet missed his cheek by a quarter inch, snapping shards of rock into his face. He wasn't going to make it.

"Oh shit, oh shit," Ramsey groaned into the dirt.

"You guessed it, pal," said the voice behind him.

Ramsey didn't hear the final cough of the pistol. By the time the sound reached his ears, he had no brain left to interpret it.

The mass killer known as Clown stared at the newly made corpse, drinking in the moment, then returned to O'Hara's patrol car. As he backed out of the parking lot, he made sure he drove over the fallen officer's body.

HUDDLED ON THE BENCH in the back of the Winnebago, Bobbie Marie Potts couldn't get the sound of the splash out of her head. The tall man hadn't yelled, hadn't screamed, even though he could have. He wasn't gagged like her. He had gone quietly to his death, except for the splash.

Sitting around her were men in black. They'd killed without a second thought, killed and taken pleasure from it. What kind of people could do a thing like that? Monsters, devils in human form.

Potts tried to retreat into herself, to find a tiny place where she could feel safe. Her fondest memories were of no help. Images from her childhood, of her parents—none of it offered protection from the terror, the certain knowledge that this night she would die a violent death.

The bearded man drove them back up the hill, into

the main residential area of Port Flattery. He drove them past houses that Potts had sold and resold. She knew the people who lived in them. She knew their politics and their hobbies and their children's first names, and she couldn't warn them what was coming. Not that a warning would do any good. How could regular folks fight an enemy like this, an enemy without human feeling?

The Winnebago rolled on to the outer edge of Port Flattery's "affordable housing" development, Marwood Creek. She was staring out the side window when the lights went out in every house on the street. All at once. In the glow of the RV's dashboard, she saw the men in black pull the electronic gizmos down over their eyes. Soon devils would be running loose in the streets of Port Flattery.

Where was the law? Where was Gummy? she asked herself. The answer came to her at once. He was in some married woman's bed, no doubt. Would the police chief sleep through the attack? she wondered. Would he wake up dead beside the last of his many one-night stands?

The bearded man stopped the Winnebago at the curb, then all the monsters got out, leaving her alone in the back.

Remembering what the tall man had said, Potts slipped down off the bench to the floor of the RV. She rested her cheek on the rough carpet and began to pray.

For herself.

For her town.

CHAPTER FIFTEEN

Fatso, the Flattery Inn Bed and Breakfast's calico cat, purred softly as Nathan Barber carried her down the foyer and out the narrow double doors to the wrap-around front porch. When he put her down, the cat shot off, tail held high, down the steps, around the topiary shrubs and into the side yard. The Flattery Inn had eight bedrooms but just three guests tonight: a middle-aged couple from Victoria, British Columbia, and a single man from Seattle, which was about par for a pre-season Sunday night.

Between them, Barber and his wife, Carla, had cracked a half-dozen certificates of deposit to update the hulking mansion; in the process, they had put a large dent in their trust-fund income. The Flattery Inn, also known as Hutton House, after its original owners, had to be rebuilt from the ground up. The foundation had been constructed of inferior, locally made red brick, which turned to a fine powder after seventy-five years of exposure to the elements. Because of the failed foundation, the entire structure sagged inward. The upstairs floors visibly canted one way or another, and none of the doors would stay shut. It had taken the

Barbers close to three years to get the place in its current, top-notch shape.

After two years of running their dream business, a historic Victorian B and B, the Barbers were hugely sick of it. They'd discovered that being a gracious host seven days a week was a royal pain in the ass: they were tired of the routine of cleaning house, of making the same special Victorian breakfast, of listening to the same inane comments and questions while they bussed the dishes.

Maybe it would have been bearable if he and Carla hadn't been chained, hand and foot, to the business. Their money, the CDs, the stocks, all came from their respective families. They had grandparents, parents, aunts and uncles to answer to if the place didn't run in the black. The profits were so marginal and so irregular that they couldn't afford to hire someone to take over the B and B a few days a month. The Barbers had to stay there and do it all themselves. They were prisoners of their own dream.

Though there was no sign out front, Hutton House was listed for sale, had been for eighteen months without so much as a nibble. The blush was off the rose as far as getting big money for Port Flattery bed and breakfasts. Only well-established businesses were drawing any buyer interest, which was another reason the Barbers had to stay home—they needed to show potential buyers that the place made money.

Barber sat on the front steps. The night was mild and moonless. There was no wind for a change. He tried to remember how much he used to enjoy living here. The air. The water. The peace and quiet. Those memories felt like they belonged to someone else.

A block away, car headlights turned onto Birch Street. For a second he got his hopes up that it was another guest for the inn, another seventy-five bucks in the kitty. The car pulled in front of the Rectory B and B, and the headlights winked out.

So much for the kitty.

He turned at the sound of the front door opening behind him.

"Evening," said the single guy from Seattle. He was wearing a light windbreaker and a Mariners baseball cap. "Thought I might go for a bit of a walk. Can't do that where I live in the city. Take your life in your hands to go out after dark."

"Only thing you've got to worry about around here are the potholes," Barber said. "If some asphalt falls off the back of the city maintenance truck, we call it a 'road repair.'"

"This place is what America must've been like in the fifties."

They always said that, sooner or later.

"Time warp," Barber agreed.

He always said that, too.

"Do I need a key to get back in?"

"No, the door will be open. Enjoy yourself."

The single guy walked down the wooden steps to the brick path that connected to the sidewalk. He got about halfway there when the lights failed—street-lights, house lights. Everything on Birch Street went black.

"Whoa!" the guest said, stopping in the middle of the path. He turned to Barber. "Hey, what's up?"

"Power outage. It's nothing to worry about. It happens sometimes when a tree falls on the lines." He stood up on the steps, steadying himself on the rail.

Barber's eyes were still adjusting to the dark when he sensed a scurry of movement from the side yard to his left. He turned and his jaw fell open. He was so startled by the human silhouettes running toward him that he froze on the steps. Muzzle-flashes, starbursts of yellow orange, underlit the faces of the attackers charging out of the night. Their silenced weapons didn't roar, but clattered like sewing machines gone amok. Bullets screamed across the lawn, thwacking into the guy from Seattle, chopping him down before he could run.

This can't be happening! Barber told himself, even as the ornately turned porch post splintered beside his head. He dived for the front doors, silenced bullets pursuing him, blasting out the frosted-glass panes.

"Carla!" he cried as he sprinted down the dark foyer. "Carla!" He didn't know what else to yell. His wife was upstairs, in their third-floor bedroom. They didn't own a gun. Where was he going? What was he going to do when he got there? Barber didn't know. He was in full panic mode.

As he vaulted up the narrow wooden staircase, he could hear the tramp of heavy feet on the porch steps. He took the stairs four at a time. When he reached the second floor, he saw a weak light in front of him. The Moyers from Victoria stood in the hall outside their room. Mr. Moyer had a small flashlight. Mrs. Moyer put out her hand to Barber as he rushed past.

"Mr. Barber," she said, "we heard glass breaking. What on earth's wrong?"

He didn't stop. "Guns!" he shouted over his shoulder as he dashed up the staircase to the top floor. "They've got guns!"

And *they* were already coming up the stairs.

Carla, flashlight in hand, met him at the third-floor landing. "My God, Nate—"

Her words were cut off by a metallic clattering and a horrible shriek of pain from the floor below.

Barber grabbed his wife by the arm and half dragged her around the newel post of the Flattery Inn's final flight of stairs. "Come on, it's our only chance," he said.

The stairs ended abruptly, in a trapdoor in the ceiling. Carla held the light for him while he got it open. The door didn't lead to the attic, but through it. When Barber pushed back the door, the night sky appeared overhead. He pulled his wife up on the roof, then slammed the door shut.

They stood on a small platform, a ten-by-ten-foot rectangle bounded by a waist-high fence of wrought-iron spikes. It was called a widow's walk, a place where the wife of a Victorian sea captain could search the horizon for a glimpse of sail and pray for the return of a missing husband. On three sides around them, the stately mansions of Birch Street stood in layers of shadow. Then footfalls hammered the stairs below.

"They're coming!" Barber said.

The trapdoor to the roof had no outside latch. There was no way to keep the killers from following them up.

"We can't lock it, Nate," Carla said.

There was only one thing to do. Barber stepped onto the door and sat down. Almost at once, someone lunged against it from the other side. The door rose, opening a crack, then slammed shut. Barber bounced, but he held on to the iron ring in the door's center.

From across the street, they heard the sounds of breaking glass and bloodcurdling screams.

"Oh, God," Carla said, moving closer to him.

"Stand back," Barber warned her. He knew what was coming, ready or not.

The trapdoor rattled beneath him as gunfire from below blasted up through it. The volley of slugs raised a cloud of dust on the rooftop. Dust and blood, aerosolized. Bullets tore Nathan Barber apart, but somehow he managed to hang on to the ring, like a bronc rider to the grave.

When the shooting stopped, the men below tried to shoulder the door open, but the weight of his body blocked it. After a minute or two of effort, they gave up.

"Nathan? Nathan?" she whispered.

There was no answer.

It was so dark on the roof that she could hardly see him, hunched there over the iron ring, but Carla knew he was dead. She wanted to touch him, but she didn't. She was too afraid of what her trembling fingers would find. Without an instant's hesitation, he'd given up his life for her. Though they'd been married for ten years, it was something she'd never expected.

Then she heard the intruders come out onto the front

porch below. They were laughing. After what they'd done to Nathan, they were laughing.

Carla couldn't help herself. "Bastards!" she screamed into the night, her eyes blinded by tears, her face sticky with her husband's misted blood. "Dirty murdering bastards!"

THROUGH THE SQUAD CAR'S open window, Bolan heard a woman cry out, her voice full of pain and fury. As her shrill curse echoed down the dark hillside, it was joined by other cries. The killing had begun. He accelerated up the hill, and with his headlights shut off, turned down Birch Street, moving toward the screams.

With its assault under way and the town blacked out, Legion clearly was no longer concerned about keeping its presence a secret. Infectious terror was part of the plan. It kept the intended victims off balance, vulnerable. The murderers were attempting to annihilate a population twenty-five times bigger than their own. They could succeed only if that population was too scared, too disoriented to fight back. Because their numbers were relatively small, Legion had to concentrate on the town a block at a time, clearing one street before moving on to the next. The concentration of forces meant just one thing to the Executioner: a target-rich environment.

A short way down Birch Street, Bolan slowed the patrol car to a stop. In the darkness ahead, he saw strobe-light muzzle-flashes. They were coming from the sidewalk on both sides of the mansion-lined street. For an instant, brake lights flared in the middle of the road, then they winked out. Bolan saw a sedan with its lights off pulling away down the street. It was crawling along, keeping up with the house-to-house slaughter.

The ammo wagon.

Not just ammo. Replacement SMGs, too.

Legion planned to wear out some gun barrels tonight.

Bolan grabbed the riot pump gun from the passenger's seat. As he exited the cruiser, he pulled the flashlight out of his pocket. He ran around the front of the car and onto the sidewalk, closing on the Legion mobile extermination team from the rear. As they had already swept that end of the street, he figured they wouldn't be expecting trouble from behind. Because they were NOD-equipped and he wasn't, the Executioner had to keep tight to cover as he advanced, and it slowed him.

As he darted from a hedge to a tree trunk, he heard a woman weeping on the rooftop high above him. The great house's doors stood open and a body lay sprawled on the brick walk. Now that his eyes had adjusted to the dark, Bolan could make out the mansion across the street. Its front door was open, too.

A slow-motion whirlwind was sweeping up the street, breaking in the doors, breaking out the windows.

Yellow lights flickered inside the ground floor of the B and B two doors up the street. The whirlwind was breaking people, too. That's what it had come here to do.

The Executioner cut right, along the side of a mansion. He followed a crushed-cinder path through the back garden, then hurdled a low wire-hoop fence into the adjoining yard. As he passed close by the gabled back porch of the house, he saw a dead man lying in a crumpled heap at the bottom of the steps. The guy had almost escaped with his life.

Almost didn't count.

Bolan vaulted the next fence and turned left, down the side yard for the street. As he ran, he heard shouts and screams coming from inside the three-story, multiturreted home. Yellow-orange lights strobed behind the windows of the upper floor. The screams stopped before he reached the corner of the wide front porch. Whoever they were, it was too late to save them.

The Executioner climbed the porch's side rail and got into position alongside a wooden bench swing. With the 12-gauge in his right hand and the flashlight in his left, he waited for the Legion crew to make its exit.

He didn't have to wait long. The killing was done upstairs. Heavy boots thudded on hardwood, then a cluster of dark shapes emerged from the front door.

"Hey!" Bolan shouted. He paused a beat, just long enough to let them turn their heads his way, then he flicked on the high-power flashlight. The three men in black recoiled from the sudden glare of the flashlight. The Russian NODs they wore amplified the intense burst of light thirty-five thousand times.

It was like he'd driven ice picks into their eyes.

The Legion players yelped and staggered back, clawing at their goggles. One of them opened up with his SMG, shooting blind. Bullets sprayed into the porch floor and ceiling.

Bolan fired the 12-gauge from the hip, taking out the shooter first. Then he dropped the flashlight and pumped the slide, firing and pumping, firing and pumping. He only took head shots, to avoid the body armor he knew they were wearing. The close-range blasts of Number One buckshot lifted the mass murderers off their feet and sent them crashing to their backs on the porch.

As the Executioner retrieved the flashlight, something stirred on the floor, thrashing and gurgling in the dark. Ready to fire again, he swept the white beam over the trio for a fraction of an instant, then shut it off. The man closest to him was unlucky enough to still be alive. Burning gunpowder had crisped his hair and left it smoking like a pile of leaves. The remains of his face and the night-vision goggles mingled in the same gory crater. Bolan had neither the time nor the inclination to deliver a mercy bullet. He slipped out the way he'd come, via the porch rail.

Bullets clipped wood shingles as he rounded the side of the house. Pursuit had picked him up. Bolan sprinted for the backyard, and when he reached it, he jumped the rear fence and cut right, retracing his original route through the neighboring yards. He ran as fast as he could, knowing that Legion would be sweeping that side of the street for him.

When he figured he was close to the squad car, he cut right again, turning along the side of a mansion and heading back for Birch. As he passed the doors of a root cellar, a figure rushed out at him from the deep shadow. He was moving so fast and the attacker was so close that he couldn't get the shotgun up and aimed. A knife blade flashed in the weak starlight, then a stunning impact knocked him off his feet.

Bolan went down hard on the grass on his back. His attacker landed on top of him, stabbing in a frenzy until the knife point caught in the fabric of the Kevlar vest, just over his heart. The attacker threw her full weight against the handle trying to drive it through and into him.

He easily broke her grip on the knife and rolled her off. She came up on the balls of her feet like a cat. She wore jeans and a gray sweatshirt.

She wasn't Legion.

She was local.

"Back off," Bolan told her. "I'm not one of them."

The woman clawed her shoulder-length hair out of her face as she started to circle him.

"You can't fight these guys with a knife," Bolan said, tossing the kitchen carver into the darkness. "They're wearing body armor, just like me."

"They killed my husband."

"If you stay out here, you're going to get yourself killed, too."

"Maybe I want to die."

"You don't want to die. You want them dead. And, lady, that's my job, not yours. You've got to get back in the house and hide until this is over."

She didn't move.

The Executioner reached under his armored vest. "Here, take this," he said, handing the service revolver over to her, butt first. "The gun's loaded. If they come in after you, aim for their heads. Now, do like I told you, get in there and hide."

He watched her retreat into the deep shadow beside the mansion, then took off for the street. Before he reached the front corner of the house, a pistol shot rang out behind him. Bolan turned and ran back.

A violent struggle was under way on the ground in front of the root cellar. A man wearing a NOD had the long-haired woman pinned to the earth and was choking her with both hands.

"Try and shoot me in the back, you fucking bitch," the killer snarled into her face.

The Executioner closed the gap in a heartbeat. He moved so quickly and so quietly that the Legion player sensed his presence only when he felt the warm muzzle of the 12-gauge pressed against the side of his throat. The murderer released his grip on the woman's neck and started to raise his hands.

In this case, surrender wasn't an option.

The riot gun boomed, point-blank. The effect was like a guillotine: instant decapitation. The killer's body toppled onto its side in the grass; the detached head arced away, thunking on the root-cellar door then rolling down its slope and coming to a stop at Bolan's feet. He bent down and removed the NOD. When he held it up to his eyes, he glimpsed a yellow-green world. The device still worked.

"Don't make me tie you up. I don't have the time," he told the woman as he helped her to her feet. "Get in the house and stay there."

She was staring at the dark head shape on the grass. He had to shake her shoulder to get her attention. "Did you hear what I said?"

"No...I mean, yes. I'm going. I'll hide."

He didn't move until she closed the root-cellar door behind her. At the corner of the mansion, before he crossed Birch Street, he pulled on the night-vision goggles. They peeled back the blackness with an infrared scalpel, revealing details of a double row of ghostly Victorian houses, sculptured shrubs, picket fences, old-fashioned light poles.

Bolan crossed the street on a dead run. As he advanced up the sidewalk, he saw what the darkness had hidden: fresh corpses bright as lemon drops against the dark green of the grass. In the middle of the street ahead, the brake lights of the ammo car winked off as it moved up another ten feet.

With the NOD pulled down over his face, Bolan had a perfect disguise. The night-vision goggles were what separated the Legion players from their victims. He stepped into the street and trotted for the ammo wagon, holding the riot gun by the pistol grip, low along the side of his leg. The car was creeping ahead in spurts, a few feet at a time. The Executioner stepped up to the driver's window without being challenged.

The guy behind the wheel wore a NOD, and under it was a communication headset. Before he took a good look at his new customer, he automatically held out a handful of 30-round mags. When the driver saw the business end of the 12-gauge pointed at him, he knew something was wrong—Legion wasn't using scatter-guns. If he wore an expression of surprise or fear at that moment, the NOD concealed it.

Bolan pushed the muzzle of the riot gun through the window and fired. The blast rocked the car on its springs, and in the same instant, bright yellow splashed the inside of the windshield, the dashboard and the side windows.

The now driverless sedan continued its slow creep down Birch Street. Bolan jacked a live round into the shotgun and moved with the car, using it as rolling cover.

A spray of autofire crashed through the car windows from the other side of the street. A second burst thunked into the door panels. The pursuit had finally caught up with him. Yellow-green insect men in NODs charged across neatly manicured lawns, on a beeline course for the ammo wagon.

Bolan yanked the pin on a stun grenade and tossed it over the roof of the car. It skittered across the asphalt and bounced back from the curb. As the Legion players reached the sidewalk, the Thunderflash began to scream.

THE POWER OUTAGE caught Fred Ferguson alone in the windowless production room of the weekly *Bugle*. He was working late at the downtown office, laying out the front page of the next issue. When the lights failed, he was trying to make a decision about the banner headline, whether to go with Ex-Actress Takes Cliff Plunge, or the more titillating Suspicious Fall Kills TV Star.

Right away, Ferguson knew something weird was going on. Whenever the power failed in the small town, it was always due to a windstorm. The lights always flickered a few times, or dimmed alarmingly, so you got a clue that a blackout was on the way. This time was different. There was no wind, and there was no warning. It was like someone just pulled the plug.

The production room was so dark that Ferguson

couldn't see his hands in front of his face. Between him and the nearest exit stood an obstacle course of drafting tables, desks, chairs, water coolers, wastebaskets. He managed to feel his way around those hazards, only to stumble over a knee-high stack of the previous week's unsold copies. He hit the floor cursing. Pushing up to his hands and knees, he crawled across the indoor-outdoor carpet until he reached the paper's front door.

Outside he found the town completely blacked out. Again this was strange. Usually only a section of Port Flattery lost its power.

Ferguson decided it had the makings of a story, so he locked the door and walked over to his 1958 Chevy Bel-Air two-door. For reasons that no one fully understood or questioned, in PF it was considered hip and "local" to drive a classic American gas-guzzler. The cherrier the better. He started up the Bel-Air and headed down pitch-black Main Street. That there was nobody on duty at the police station didn't surprise him. It was never manned at night. On an impulse, he stopped his car at the curb and got out.

Right off, he saw what looked like two pairs of brake lights flare way down at the other end of the waterfront street. But he found the funny sounds coming from up the hill, along B and B row, far more interesting. People were yelling up there in the dark, and there were crashes, like glass breaking. It sounded like nothing he'd ever heard before. He scratched his head, damned if he could figure out what was going on. But it occurred to him that whatever it was, with all that screaming, it was going to knock Lyla Bamfield off the top of the front page.

Ferguson jumped back in his Chevy and motored up the hill. He was about halfway up when a string of single gunshots rang out behind him, down on Main. Before he could make the left turn onto Birch Street or a U-turn back to the waterfront, headlights appeared out of nowhere behind him. First headlights, then red-and-blue flashing lights. It was a patrol car.

The squad car gave its siren a little goose, but Ferguson was already pulling over. He put the Powerglide in Park, leaving the engine running, and reached for his notepad and his 35 mm camera.

As he got out of the car, he was hit in the face by a spotlight.

"Hey!" he cried. "Brian! Teddy! It's me. Shut that fool thing off." Shielding his eyes with his trusty notepad, he kept walking toward the light, walking and talking nonstop. "What's all the ruckus about?" he asked. "I thought I just heard shots."

Ferguson got no answer, but as he neared the cop car's front bumper the spotlight went off, then the driver's door swung open. In the glow of the Bel-Air's taillights, Ferguson saw a weird gizmo strapped on top of the officer's head. It stopped the editor in his tracks. Squinting, he saw the guy in front of him wasn't Ted or Brian or anybody else he knew. But whoever it was had on a PFPD uniform shirt. Otherwise, the guy was out of uniform. Instead of the regulation beige polyester trousers with the brown pinstripe down the side, he was wearing black, loose-fitting slacks cut like BDU pants.

Then Ferguson heard a cough, and the right side of his chest went numb. Like it was instantly frozen. Stunned, he staggered back a step. He didn't have a clue what had just happened. When he tried to suck in a breath, the pain began, right in the center of the numb spot, a searing pain that cut right through him. He thought for sure he was having a heart attack. He clutched at his chest and his fingers came away wet.

Blood?

When he looked up, he saw the gun.

So many questions occurred to him then, newspaperman's questions. Who? What? And most important of all, why? But there were no answers forthcoming. Only more terrible pain as the gun coughed again.

Ferguson's legs buckled, and he fell onto his butt in the street. He didn't want to roll onto his back, but he was suddenly too weak to stop it from happening. He stared up at the night sky, at stars made blurry by his flowing tears.

Then there was nothing.

Not even pain.

BEFORE THE THUNDERFLASH started to whistle, Bolan ducked behind the car and closed his eyes. The shrill squeak lasted a fraction of a second. It was meant to draw an enemy's attention.

Then came the "gotcha."

The stun grenade detonated in a blaze of arc light thousands of times brighter than the flashlight beam, bright enough to blind the NOD-equipped players for hours. But they didn't have hours to get better. They didn't even have minutes.

The Executioner let the ammo car roll on ahead of him. Along the parking strip, three pack members were down. Like sideswiped dogs, they twisted on the grass, howling. All they could see was white on white on white. They ripped off their NODs, but that changed nothing. They were still blind, and death was still coming. Faces in the gutter, they howled louder.

Mack Bolan stepped up on the curb and circled around behind them.

No court would ever hear their cases.

No jury would deliberate their fates.

No appeal would save their lives.

The 12-gauge bellowed, and lemon yellow skull shards skittered across the asphalt. The shotgun's slide went snick-snick as Bolan ejected the smoking hull.

Suddenly it got real quiet on Birch Street. Peppered by the contents of their pack-mate's head, the remaining two players realized there were far worse things than being struck blind.

The sole of the Executioner's shoe scraped softly on the sidewalk as he moved over to the man next in line. Bolan pulled the trigger before he could cry out. The riot gun boomed, and more fragments of skull scattered across the asphalt, blown by a 12-gauge wind.

The last guy raised his face from the gutter. "Who the fuck are you?" he growled.

"A public servant," Bolan replied.

Again the riot gun roared.

Bolan picked up one of the silenced SMGs from the lawn, slipped his arm through the shoulder sling, then started to feed the pump gun more shells. A crash from

down the street made him look up. The ammo car had
rolled up over the curb and slammed into a tree.

In a stone mansion a little farther on, bright lights
wheeled behind dark second-floor windows. The Executioner tipped the NOD up over his forehead. They
weren't gun flashes. They were moving, but they were
steady.

Camera lights.

Bolan knew firsthand what that meant. Pulling the
NOD back down, he broke into a dead run. A beauti-
fully lettered sign on the mansion's lawn read Scarborough Manor, A Bed And Breakfast. Cutting across
the wet grass, he jumped the stone steps to the porch.
The front door gaped open. Inside, someone screamed,
then there was laughter.

The devil's own.

CHAPTER SIXTEEN

With the Remington Brushmaster in his hand and his holstered .45 slapping his hip, Gummy Nordland ran down Port Flattery's blacked-out Main Street, a six-block-long canyon of Victoriana. Hundred-year-old commercial buildings faced each other along the narrow waterfront avenue. Some were clad with stone, some with brick. The tallest was five stories, not counting turrets. All the ground floors had shops and restaurants in them catering to the tourist trade. In some cases, the upstairs had been made into apartments. In other cases, the topmost floors were gutted down to the framing and had been that way as long as the police chief could remember.

The only lights on the street came from the back ends of two vehicles, a sedan and a van that were stopped in the middle of the road ahead. In the red-orange glow the chief saw figures in black running along the sidewalk in front of the Guemes Tower. Glass shattered, and the figures disappeared inside.

Nordland picked up the pace as best he could. He didn't run much anymore. There just wasn't any call for it. After jogging a couple of blocks, he could already feel a burn in his knees and shins. He would've taken the squad car, except he was afraid it would act like a bullet magnet.

As he neared the ground-floor entrance of the old Pffeifer building, the van's brake lights winked off and it pulled away up the street, toward the marina.

The chief was glad to see it go.

His odds of survival had just doubled.

The front door of the Pffeifer building stood ajar, a gaping hole where its beveled-glass pane had been. The odor of cordite smoke wafted out onto the street, mixing with the smell of salt water and rotting seaweed. Nordland knew the people who lived up there: a retired couple, originally from Olympia, and a divorced man who worked for the city parks as a gardener. If they were home this night, they were already dead.

Their blood was on his hands. Innocent blood. If he'd taken the trouble to dig a little deeper into the Gridleys' background, the blackout, the killings, none of it might have happened. As a faithful born-here, he'd been playing by Port Flattery rules, the first of which said "No hurry, it can wait." Now he was like the Dutch boy with his finger stuck in the dike, trying to hold back the flood. At least he wasn't alone in the fight. Although he had to admit it irked him more than a little that he was surrendering part of his authority to the tall stranger with the cold eyes. But what choice did he have? The town was under siege. His officers weren't worth a shit ninety percent of the time, and the guy looked like he knew what he was doing. The chief had lots of questions about him, such as who was he and why had the people in black thrown him off the pier, questions he intended to answer if he lived long enough.

Nordland hurried on, keeping tight to the fronts of the buildings, hoping that whoever was driving the sedan wasn't looking in his rearview mirror. When he got within fifty feet of the car and the last entry point of the hit team, the Guemes Tower, he stopped at the corner of a shop entrance, out of breath. His heart pounding, he flicked off the Remington's safety.

The chief had hunted big game in the Olympic Mountains since he was a boy. He'd shot deer, elk, cougar and black bear, but he'd never tried to put a hole in a human being before. In fact no police officer in Port Flattery had taken a life in the line of duty for more than thirty years.

That was about to change.

Nordland put his arm through the rifle's sling, braced himself against the mitered stone facade and lined up his shot. It was good that the range was so close because it was pitch-dark on the street. He knew if he missed, if he gave them a chance to shoot back, he would be dead in a hurry. There was too much firepower on the other side.

He told himself to aim for the heads as he snuggled into the sling.

The front stairs of the Guemes Tower were steep, long and made of wood. Even out on the street Nordland could hear the tramp of boots coming down them. He didn't shoot when the first guy stepped out. He had to let them all get out on the sidewalk before he opened fire. He watched, his finger curled around the Brushmaster's trigger, as the four killers turned away from him, heading for the entrance to the next set of upstairs apartments. After what he figured they'd already done to the folks living on Main Street, the chief didn't feel bad about shooting them in the back.

He aimed the stubby-barreled rifle at the guy on the left and squeezed the trigger. The rifle barked and bucked, the gun shot thunderclapping in the canyon. Before the first echo, Nordland fired again. He kept on firing without pause, as fast as he could, knocking the murderers down like bowling pins. After the sixth shot he realized that two were down but not out. They'd struggled to their knees, facing him. The chief fired frantically, emptying the rest of the magazine into their heads.

Whether they were dead when he was done, he didn't know, and there was no time to check. One thing was for sure: they were sorely messed up.

Shifting the rifle to his left hand, the chief drew his .45 and raced for the sedan.

Whatever the driver was thinking, whether he was contemplating getting out and returning fire or speeding away, he didn't do either. As Nordland rounded the back bumper he shot at him through the car's rear window, shattering it. On the run, he fired three times through the side rear and driver's windows. The car horn sounded as the Government Model Colt locked back, empty.

Nordland opened the driver's door, grabbed the dead guy by the collar and jerked him off the steering wheel and out onto the street. The front of the car was littered with broken glass, the dash spattered with blood, the back seat's cargo of 30-round magazines and spare

H&K machine pistols buried under glittering chunks of the rear window. The chief set his rifle on the passenger's seat and got in. He slapped a fresh clip into his pistol, then dropped the sedan into gear. Stomping the gas, he sped for the marina.

By himself, he had taken out five bad guys. He was so pumped he wanted to shout. His elation lasted about a minute, then his hands started to shake on the sticky steering wheel. They were covered in blood. Between his shoulder blades he could feel the springs poking through the holes he'd put in the driver seat. The dead guy's seat. Everything started to spin. Nordland stuck his head out the window and let the wind whip against his face.

"Don't hurl," he ordered himself. "Don't fucking hurl."

As he roared past the last of the commercial buildings, he saw a cluster of faint lights high over the water.

Red, green, white.

Sailboat running lights.

As he closed in on them, the jagged black hump of the marina jetty appeared, jutting into the bay on his left. On the other side of the heaped boulders, flashlight beams stabbed crazily into the night, sweeping over the tops of the rows of masts. The 150-slip boat haven was only half-full this time of year, but there were quite a few live-aboards down there—commercial fishermen, as well as recreational sailors. They normally got their power from lines strung along the docks. With the electricity cut off, the live-aboards would switch to their batteries or be out on deck with emergency lanterns, wondering what had happened.

A connected row of single-story, sheet-metal buildings zoomed past on his right. They housed the marina's businesses: Flattery Bait and Tackle, Port Marine Repair and Prop Shop, Stacy's Boat Haven Café and the twenty-four-hour coin-operated laundry and rest room. On the other side of the laundry was the boat-repair yard.

Nordland hit the brakes when he saw the van he was looking for. It was nosed into a parking space in front of the ramp that led down to the docks. The driver's door stood wide open; the courtesy light was on and he could see there was no driver inside.

The chief pulled in behind the van, blocking it in with the rear quarter of the sedan. For a second he thought about taking one of the submachine guns from the back seat, but decided against it. He'd never fired one before, and he was afraid he couldn't control it on full-auto. Given the close quarters of the marina, there was a very real possibility of hitting one of the live-aboards with a stray bullet. He picked up the Brush-master and racked a fresh 10-round clip into it. Armed with pistol and long gun, he crossed the gravel to the top of the steel ramp.

The complex of interconnected docks was bathed in a dismal glow, a sickly, battery-powered half light. He could see to the end of the gas dock, and the channel that led out into the bay, but only just barely. And there were broad patches of impenetrable shadow between. Shipboard dogs yapped; people shouted; running feet thudded on the floating wooden docks.

As he started down the steep ramp, silenced machine guns stuttered, a woman screamed, and then there were splashes.

Man-overboard splashes.

In clusters.

The sailors had been hit and had fallen in, or they'd jumped in to escape being shot.

On the dock ahead of Nordland, a figure knelt, struggling to untie a line from a mooring cleat. The stern of the thirty-foot Bayliner was already free and swinging away from the gas dock. The chief could see a guy in the boat's cockpit, working over the controls. The twin 100-horse Mercs bellowed as they roared to life, churning the water to foam. The kneeling man had the line loose, but now the boat was drifting away from him. He made a suicide jump for the bow rail. He caught it with one hand, then managed to grip it with the other. Before he could pull himself up, the boat captain threw the Mercs in gear.

So much for the No Wake sign.

The Bayliner's bow angled up at sixty degrees, the Mercs spit a double rooster tail and the guy clinging to the rail hung on for dear life as the boat surged forward.

Three dark figures appeared in the dim light at the end of the dock. As the Bayliner's captain started to cut a radical left turn into the channel, they blistered it from bow to stern with autofire.

The wooden hut that protected the gas pumps blocked Nordland's view of the action. He couldn't see whether the captain had been hit, or whether he had just ducked to avoid the fusillade. Either way, the effect was the same: the Bayliner missed the turn. Its fiber-

glass hull shrieked as it plowed headlong into the side
of the jetty. After a fraction of a second, the Bayliner
and its built-in gas tanks parted company. With a rock-
ing boom and a ball of orange flame, the boat exploded.
Burning gas rained on the docks, on the decks of the
moored boats; it hissed as it spattered the surface of
the water.

The liquid fire was still falling as Nordland ran for
the cover of the gas pumps. He knew he stood no
chance if he tried to slug it out toe to toe on the narrow
docks. He needed a diversion. A big one. When he tried
to lift one of the pump handles, he found it was locked.
The other one had a padlock on it, too. The effort was
pointless, anyway. He'd forgotten that the pumps were
powered by electricity.

From the center of the dock complex came a sustained burst of suppressed autofire. Three or four submachine guns were unloading at once. The racket was
punctuated by a series of very loud, very rapid single
shots. Some commercial fisherman was returning fire,
probably with a semiautomatic that served as his seal
gun when the fish-and-game boys weren't looking.
Bullets from good guys and bad sparked off steel masts
and hulls, ricocheting wildly.

Nordland kept low as he peeked into the powerboats
tied up along the edge of the dock. He found what he
was looking for in a battered aluminum skiff: two six-
gallon gas cans. The chief shoulder slung his rifle and
pulled the cans onto the dock. Both were nearly full.

As he unscrewed the gas caps, the rifle stopped bark-
ing. It had run out of ammo, or its shooter had run out
of luck. Either way, Nordland knew he had to hurry.

He held one tank under each arm and splashed gas over a wide section of dock. Then he poured a narrow stream all the way back to the foot of the access ramp. When he put down the cans, he saw what a mess he'd made of himself. He'd spilled fuel all over his shoes and pants cuffs. There was no time to worry about that.

The chief unslung the Brushmaster. From the shouts and splashes, he knew about where the killers were, but he couldn't pick out targets because of all the hulls and superstructures in the way. He needed some altitude. He jumped aboard a nearby sportfisher and climbed the ladder to the flybridge. That vantage point gave him a better angle. He could see muzzle-flashes two docks over. Then he saw a man in black firing from behind a storage box.

Resting the stock on the top of the windshield, Nordland put the bead on the guy's head and fired. The .30-06 announced its presence with a gut-rattling boom. Before the smoking hull hit the deck, the chief had the sights back on target. The gunman moved around behind the wooden box. He wasn't hit. Nordland fired again, just to make sure they knew where he was. His second shot blew the door off the storage locker, and the soft-nose bullet sailed on, whining off the jetty rocks beyond.

When a bunch of guys in black started to move back toward the gas dock, the chief scrambled down from the flybridge and sprinted for the foot of the ramp. As he turned and knelt, three of them came around the corner at the end of the dock. They were really high-kicking, charging him. This was the part of the plan where things got loose. The chief had never lit a gasoline fuse before. He had no idea how long it would take for it to reach and ignite the soaked part of the dock.

Better too soon than too late, he told himself as he flicked his lighter.

A blue flame leaped up from the dock at his feet, then shot toward the onrushing killers. His timing was perfect. With a whoosh, a fifteen-foot section of dock burst into flame right in front of the guys in black. They couldn't stop. They could either run through the fire or take a swim.

Maybe they were afraid of water.

Maybe the sudden flare of light blinded them.

They came flying through the wall of flame. Nordland had the Brushmaster snugged tight against his shoulder. The deer rifle boomed, and like a giant invisible finger, the .30-06 sent the Legion players flying off the dock and into the water.

The chief was reaching for another clip when a hail of slugs peppered his position, chipping the dock, zipping into the water behind him. He turned to run and took a round in the back of the right calf. The impact made him stumble, and he dropped the Remington.

As he pushed up from his belly, more bullets rained around him. He could feel the tramp of boots on the dock through the palms of his hands. They were coming after him. Nordland scrambled to his feet and hobbled up the metal ramp. Bullets clanged at his heels as he stepped onto the street.

He headed for the sedan, hip-hopping on the bum leg. Before he could reach it, a spray of gunfire from behind kicked up the dirt alongside the van. At that instant he made a choice. He knew if he forgot about the car and went for the dark outline of the connected businesses, they'd hunt him down like a wounded animal. The car was the only real chance he had.

With bullets zinging past him on all sides, he made it around the rear of the van and into the sedan's front seat. The engine turned over on the first try. In a spray of dust and gravel, he swerved out onto the street. Right away he realized he had a problem. Because of the bullet hole in his calf, it hurt like hell to push down on the gas pedal. The car slowed for a second while he switched feet on the gas.

When he looked up in his rearview mirror, he saw the van's headlights flash on. They were coming after him.

Nordland stomped the pedal flat, only letting up as he neared the dogleg right that would take him back to the highway. The street ended in a wide fan of gravel in front of the boat-launch ramp. He feathered the brakes with his left foot, then punched the gas, squirting around the bend.

In the rearview mirror, the van's lights emerged from the cloud of dust.

It was gaining on him.

The chief had another hard decision to make, a choice between survival and duty. He had three seconds to think it over.

When Nordland reached the highway, he cut left, heading out of town. He mashed the pedal against the firewall, trying to pick up speed before he hit the big hill to the bluffs. He was doing close to seventy-five when the grade started. By the time he got to the top, it had slowed him down to forty-five.

When Nordland checked his rearview, it was nothing but headlights.

CHAPTER SEVENTEEN

Inside the wide foyer of Scarborough Manor, everything was green on green. The walls, the plank floors, the hall tree and coatrack, they all radiated the same cool temperature, which Bolan's NOD translated into shades of kelly, of olive, of emerald, edged with lime. Before he saw it, the Executioner smelled blood, coppery sweet, death's rank perfume.

Down the foyer on the right, half the wall was splattered with lemon yellow. The corona of droplets started at head height and reached the ceiling. In the open doorway, Bolan saw the corpse of a man. He was lying across the threshold, his face resting on its cheek in a yellow pool.

The room was empty.

As Bolan turned up the stairs, he saw more yellow droplets sprinkled over the green treads. Someone wounded had climbed up them, and recently, too, or the drops would have cooled and lost their bright color. The flight of steps stopped at a landing in front of a six-foot-high stained-glass window before branching in two and continuing up to meet the next floor. Under the dark, arched window lay another body. It was the owner of the dripping blood. It looked like she had been finished off with a heavy-bladed knife, like a machete or a hatchet. Messy work. The polished wood floor was smeared with yellow. Yellow footprints led up the steps to the second story.

Again he heard the laughter, then a silenced subgun stuttered a half-dozen times.

Bolan climbed the steps, pausing at the top to peer down the hall. At the end of it a door stood ajar. A light swirled from inside the open room, painting the hallway opposite a painfully brilliant yellow white. The Executioner flipped up the NOD. He could see just fine in the light coming from the doorway.

There were closed doors on both sides of the hall, doors that could conceal enemies. Then he heard another scream. This time much weaker than before.

Remembering what he'd seen on the Deeds video, Bolan forgot about protecting his back, about sweeping the closed rooms before he advanced. Though he moved past the doors on a dead run, his footfalls hardly made a sound. He seemed to glide over the floor.

He stopped at the edge of the open doorway. He could hear people talking inside. He counted three voices, all male.

"How's this?" someone asked.

"Move that one closer."

"This one?"

"No, the old woman. That's it. Got it. Super."

Bolan sucked in a breath and rounded the doorjamb with the pump gun at waist height. He stepped into a scene right out of a horror movie.

The bed that filled most of the room was a huge mahogany four-poster with a tassled canopy and a gold-brocade coverlet. On it were piled the bodies of the newly dead. Six. Seven. Eight. They were so entangled, it was hard to tell at a glance. He could see they were all Japanese, though, and all ages. From grandpa to grandson, heaped together on the bloody bed like they were at a gruesome, eternal slumber party. And in the middle of the corpses, sitting with his back against the headboard, was a man in black. His arms were folded proudly across his chest, and he was grinning for Spence Gridley, the Legion photographer, whose camera-mounted floodlight starkly illuminated the entire room.

Gridley was looking through the camcorder's lens, trying to frame the shot, so he didn't see Bolan appear in the doorway. He would have seen the expression change on the face of the guy in the bed. It went from glee to terror in the blink of an eye.

On the other side of the cameraman was another player. His right hand held a machine pistol to the head of the woman he forced to kneel in front of him. His left hand clutched a mass of her shiny black hair.

She was the screamer, and with good reason.

The killers had made her watch while they liquidated every member of her family.

Before the guy on the bed could shout a warning, Bolan touched off the 12-gauge. In the small room, the three-inch Magnum round's report was earsplitting. Number One buck splintered the headboard and hammered the head of the killer into it. A dozen lead pills found his face, shattering teeth, cheekbones, eye sockets, ripping through his tongue, palate, eyes and brain.

Cordite smoke billowed over the corpse-heaped four-poster.

On the move, the Executioner pumped the riot gun's slide. He'd intended to take down the cameraman next, but the guy pivoted away at the last second, opening up the other killer to a frontal attack.

In the military and intel communities, they always taught first-timers never to look directly into the eyes of a human target because they might empathize with the fear they saw there, empathy that could weaken their resolve to do the deed. This wasn't Bolan's first time, not his hundredth time. He had no empathy whatsoever for creatures like these. And his resolve was harder than vanadium steel.

As he one-handed the shotgun by its pistol grip, holding it out in front of him like a dueling pistol, Bolan locked eyes with the killer. The guy could have shot the Japanese woman then and there, and maybe he would've done her a favor if he had, but what he saw in the Executioner's face turned him to stone for a split second.

What he saw was the end of the line.

The 12-gauge roared in his face, snapping his head back. An arm gone suddenly limp swung wildly, flinging his machine pistol against the wall, even as his body followed his head, jerking violently backward. His fingers tangled in the woman's long black hair, dragging her with him, dragging her down on top of him. As the boom died away, Bolan realized she was still screaming, like a banshee. The sound raised the short hairs on the back of his neck.

Then something crashed and the room went dark.

Gridley had thrown down his camera and broken the floodlight. Bolan pumped the slide as he turned and fired blind from the hip, aiming for the sound of the cameraman's movement. The shotgun's blast obliterated the noise of running feet.

The Executioner quickly pulled the NOD over his eyes so he could see. The cameraman was gone. A fist-sized chunk was missing from the door frame. When he looked back at the room, there was yellow everywhere: floor, walls, ceiling, windowpanes, bedposts. Only one heat source was moving: the woman struggled to free herself from the dead murderer's hand.

Bolan had given her back her life, or what was left of it; there was nothing more he could do for her. There was something the dead guy could do for him, though, while his body was still registering a lively yellow in the NOD. The Executioner switched the shotgun to his weak hand and grabbed the killer by the arm, dragging him to the door. Then he muscled the limp body to its feet, holding it up by pinning it face-first against the wall.

The question was, had Legion abandoned the mansion or were the killers waiting for him around the corner?

With a grunt of effort, Bolan pitched the corpse into the hall.

Before it hit the floor, he had his answer. A barrage of pops from silenced machine guns scorched the hallway, shattering decorative vases, dropping framed pictures from the walls, blasting great rips in the polished wood floor.

Bolan waited until the shooting stopped, then he

waited a little more. The Legion players could see a body on the floor out there, but at a distance of more than a few yards they couldn't tell who it belonged to. The resolution of the Russian NODs left much to be desired.

When he heard the planking creak, he knew someone was coming forward to check on the corpse. The Executioner rounded the door low and fast, with the scattergun in his left hand and the borrowed SMG in his right. There were a lot of available targets. Yellow forms crouched in doorways on both sides of the hall, and at the foot of the stairs leading to the third floor. The closest man, the body checker, was the first to die. Bolan's sudden appearance caught him flat-footed in the middle of the hall. The shotgun boomed, bowling the killer onto his back.

Even as Bolan dumped the riot gun, he brought the machine pistol into play, pinning the trigger. It stuttered in his fist, spewing a stream of smoking brass out its ejection port, spewing white-hot death from its muzzle. The man in the doorway on his right took multiple hits in the face and throat, and went down without returning fire. The guy on the other side of the hall managed to get off a poorly aimed burst before the Executioner walked the line of slugs across his head. He crashed against the door frame and pitched forward into the hall on his face.

At the end of the corridor, three more yellow men were in full retreat. The rest of the pack had taken a silent vote and decided they wanted no part of what he was offering. They couldn't go down the stairs, because that would've put them square in his sights, so they went up.

Bolan bent over one of the dead guys, picking up a spare full magazine from his combat harness, then hurried to the foot of the staircase. A quick peek up told him it was unprotected. When he neared the top of the steps, he got down on his belly, poked his head up and peered along the floor.

Three yellow figures knelt in doorways, waiting for him.

As he ducked, a volley of autofire gouged the planks above his head, skipping off the top step and slapping into the wall behind him.

Someone shouted at him from the far end of the hall.

"We've got hostages up here! Back off, or they all die!"

AGA KARKANIAN KNEW things weren't going to go exactly as planned shortly after his pack hit the recently built residential section of Port Flattery. It was Bacteria Land at its most virulent, Breeder City, also known as "affordable housing." It was the kind of place where nobody wanted to live for long, where, from the moment they moved in, everybody was thinking about selling and moving out. And what did these first-time buyers get for their down payment? A tract house that was the mirror image of the one next door. Other than that, and a slight difference in color, the homes in the Marwood Creek development were indistinguishable. Their driveways were side by side, ending in matching "two-car" garages that really held a car-and-a-half.

Six-foot-high wooden fences separated identical twenty-five-by-fifty-foot backyards.

Under Karkanian's direction, the Legion players had cleaned out the first couple of houses with no trouble, shooting the surprised and terrified occupants in their beds, but after that, they encountered resistance.

Furious resistance.

Keeping his head below the level of the windowsill, Karkanian leaned into the boxwood hedge, shoved his SMG through the broken-out pane and fired off a withering burst. As he withdrew his weapon, a chorus of pistol shots rang out, too many for it to be from just one gun. A hail of slugs clipped chunks of wood-grained plastic from the window frame. Karkanian ducked and brushed the sharp fragments out of his hair.

He and the other level-five strategists hadn't taken into account that many of the bacteria people of Port Flattery were armed and dangerous. Legion had expected that an attack with automatic weapons in total darkness would render their victims paralyzed with fear and therefore helpless, allowing them to move through the lesser beings like wolves through sheep.

Not so.

In the distance, he could hear unsilenced gun shots popping off all over town. If the rest of the Legion force was having the same difficulty he was, and it appeared that it was, a change in tactics was probably in order. It might be more effective to further concentrate the attack teams, to move them all into a single area, so they could overrun and destroy pockets of resistance more easily. The links between Karkanian and the hunting packs were supposed to be the ammo-car drivers, who each wore communication headsets. The bearded killer pulled his own minimicrophone closer to his mouth and tried to make contact with the pack assigned to the bed and breakfasts. "Ripper," he said, "give me a status report."

Ripper didn't answer.

He would never answer. He and his ammo wagon were halfway up a tree on Birch Street.

But Karkanian didn't know that yet.

He tried several more times to get a response, and when he failed, he broke off with a curse. Something had either gone wrong with the communication gear or the B and B team was in worse shape than he feared.

"Red Rover," he said, "where are you?"

The reply came back immediately from the other Winnebago. "We're cruising the north side of town, looking for refugees."

"Head over to Birch Street on the double and find out what's happened to our people. They're not answering anymore. They may be in trouble."

"We're on our way."

"Mudgett?" a new voice said through his earpiece. "This is Butcher Boy with the waterfront team."

"What's up?"

"We ran into some trouble at the marina. We had most of the targets cornered, but before we could finish the job, some guy started shooting back. He took out three of our players before he turned tail. I'm chasing him now. I'm right on his back bumper. He's headed for the pulp mill in one of our cars."

"Our car? How'd he get it?"

"Damned if I know. But the guys we left in the

commercial district never showed up, and it's their car.''

"He killed them and took it,'' Karkanian said.

"Looks like.''

"Well, get the bastard. And when you've done that, call me back. Keep me informed.''

"Understood.''

More gunfire erupted in the house above his head. Karkanian scuttled around the corner and watched his people withdraw from the tiny concrete front porch. For the third time, his pack had been turned back by a flurry of gun shots. Karkanian tired of the delay, of the effrontery of these two-legged bacteria. Legion would have its due.

"Stop this nonsense,'' he said into his mike. "Get some gasoline and burn the house. That'll bring the scum out.''

BOLAN PAUSED on the stairs while he considered the Legion players' shouted threat. He didn't have to think on it long. He knew if they did, in fact, have hostages, they were going to kill them no matter what he did. He took the last Thunderflash from under his vest, stuck his thumb through the pull ring and yanked the safety pin. He let the spoon flip off on the stairs, counted to three, then arced the stun grenade over his head, down the middle of the hall. It hit the floor with a clunk, then rolled.

Bolan covered the lenses of his NOD with his palms as the grenade issued a piercing whistle. The explosion shook the big house to its foundation. Grabbing up the machine pistol, the Executioner mounted the last three steps. As had happened before in the street, the super-intense flash of light had put down his opposition. Two of the three men he'd seen in the hall were thrashing on the floor, clawing at their NODs. The third guy was nowhere in sight, which didn't bode well for the hostages, if they existed.

Bolan raced down the hall, shooting first one, then the other player without stopping. He hit them both in the head with 3-round bursts at extreme close range. They wouldn't get up again.

When the Executioner neared the end of the hall, he saw an open doorway on his left. He knew if the third killer had been looking down the hall when the Thunderflash went off, then he, too, was blinded. He could be on his back inside the open room, helpless.

No such luck.

A bright yellow head and shoulders appeared around the door frame, and a machine gun clattered. Two of the dozen bullets fired slammed into the center of Bolan's chest protector. The impacts knocked him sideways, but he didn't lose his balance. He hardly lost a step. As he fired back and charged the door, the head and shoulders retreated.

When Bolan took a deep breath, it hurt bad. It felt like the bullets had cracked a rib. He gritted his teeth and took the doorway in a diving roll, coming up in a fighting crouch with the subgun in both hands.

The lower sash of the window in front of him was partway up, open wide enough for someone to slip through. Two long steps brought Bolan to the glass. An iron drainpipe ran all the way to the ground. It looked strong enough to hold a man's weight, but no man was visible, either on the pipe or the grass below.

Bolan surveyed the room. The hostages were for real. There were five of them on the king-size bed, a man, a woman and three kids. They were still very much alive, although they didn't look particularly grateful for the rescue. They lay shoulder to shoulder on their backs, and the bedsprings were squeaking because they were shaking so hard.

Maybe they didn't know they were rescued, he thought. Or maybe they weren't rescued.

At the same instant the realization hit him, Bolan reacted, broad-jumping for the bed.

A burst of machine-gun fire ripped from under the bedframe, at ankle height.

The Executioner landed on the mattress with both feet, straddling the woman and one of her children. Screaming, the hostages melted away from around his legs, scattering off the bed, which allowed him to open fire through the top of the mattress.

The H&K coughed twice, then nothing.

As he dumped the empty mag and reached behind his back for the spare, the killer scrambled out from under the bed.

Bolan had no time to finish the reload; he barely had time to jump.

Dropping the gun, the Executioner dived as the player brought up his weapon. Bullets sprayed the ceiling as they hit the floor together.

Bolan pinned the muzzle to the ground and ripped the NOD off his opponent's face. He recognized the guy. It was the cameraman. He hit Spence on the chin with a solid right cross that made him loosen his grip on the machine gun. Before the Executioner could get control of the weapon, Spence snatched his NOD off, as well. With a smooth, powerful move, he rolled and flipped Bolan off.

The Executioner regained his feet in a room as dark as pitch. "Stay along the walls and in the corners," he warned the hostages. With one hand out in front of him, he felt for the enemy.

Something whooshed past his face. If it was a knife, it was a big one.

Bolan circled; away from the blade, he hoped. He strained to hear the floor creak, the sounds of breath, anything that would give away the killer's position.

The edge of his hand hit the bedpost. It made a soft thunk, and he was the one in trouble.

The machete hissed out of the blackness, chunking into the knurled post. Bolan pivoted in the direction of the blow. His eyes were shut tight, both hands extended, his fingers outstretched. Now he could feel where Spence was, feel his body heat, feel his heart beating. An invisible tether connected them. The Executioner's hands grazed the cameraman's elbow and shoulder, gripping with sudden force, and, continuing to twist from the soles of his feet, he hurled the man over his hip.

Flung headlong, Spence hit the nightstand, crashing it over.

Bolan was on him before he could recover, turning him over onto his side, powerful fingertips seeking the pressure points that would stop the flow of blood to his brain.

Spence had no intention of going quietly into the night. He slung an elbow into the middle of Bolan's chest, striking the area that had been hit by bullets. When Bolan groaned, Spence repeated the strike, again and again, blow laid over blow. The pain made the Executioner forget where he was and what he was doing, which allowed Spence to wriggle free.

As Bolan rose, he heard the sound of scrambling feet along the wall, then a shrill squeal.

"I've got a kid," Spence said, his voice tight with fear. "I'll twist his head off if you come near me again."

"Do as he says!" a woman pleaded from somewhere against the wall. "Please do as he says."

Bolan didn't reply. He had dropped to his hands and knees and felt around on the floor for one of the dropped NODs. On the second sweep of his arm he found one. He quickly put it on, and the room came into view, if not perfect focus.

Spence had a child, all right. He gripped the boy by the back of the neck with one hand, while with the other he fumbled along the wall behind him. He was trying to find the window.

Bolan advanced without a sound, on the balls of his feet, angling his path so he'd reach the window at about the same time as Spence. He was three feet away when the guy found the open window. The man looked profoundly relieved. He thought he was going to get out of there. At that instant he relaxed his grip on the boy.

That was the moment when Bolan struck with a rock-hard fist to the side of the head. Before the man could recover, he pulled the boy free and pushed him out of the way. There would be no respite now, no trading of punches, no escape. Bolan weighed in on the stunned killer, alternating blows to the face and body.

His grunts of effort were matched by Spence's grunts of pain.

The Executioner pounded the man to his knees, then snap-kicked him in the face. Spence slumped to the floor, but Bolan didn't leave him there for the count. He grabbed the guy by the back of the collar and twisted him toward the half-open window.

"You wanted out," the Executioner said, catching hold of the seat of the man's pants, "you're going to get your wish."

Bolan jerked Spence up like a rag doll and pitched him headfirst through the window glass.

Spence screamed as he dropped through the dark, screamed all the way to the ground. His cry of terror ended with a soft thump somewhere down in the side yard.

Bolan turned to find the family now huddled together in a corner. "That guy won't be bothering anyone, ever again," he said. "Is everyone okay? Is the boy okay?"

"Yes, thanks to you," the woman said.

"We thought we were dead," her husband told him. "You saved our lives. I wish we could see your face."

The sound of a heavy vehicle pulling up outside sent Bolan hurrying back to the window. It was a Winnebago. The RV stopped in the middle of the street, the side doors opened and guys wearing NODs came pouring out.

The battle wasn't over, not by a long shot.

He didn't want to panic these people any more than

they already were, so he didn't give them the ugly details. Instead he said, "I want you to stay put right here until help arrives. Don't go downstairs, and don't go out on the street for any reason."

"Don't worry," the woman said. "We aren't going anywhere until the lights come back on."

"Or the sun comes up," her husband added.

Bolan located his machine pistol and fed it a full magazine. Slipping the shoulder sling over his arm, he opened the window wider. He stepped over the sill, ducked out the window and grabbed hold of the drainpipe.

"THIS IS RED ROVER," said a voice in Karkanian's earpiece. "We're on Birch Street, and it doesn't look good."

"Go on."

"There are seven of our guys down over here, including Ripper. We found a flash grenade casing in the street next to three bodies. It looks like whoever killed them used the grenade to blind them, then blew them all to hell with a shotgun. We haven't located the rest of our people yet. They could be in one of the mansions."

"Find them," Karkanian ordered. "And if they're alive, bring them over here to me. We need to adjust our game plan."

"Roger."

A small-caliber round, probably a .22, whined over Karkanian's head like an angry bee. Once again he had to change position to stay out of the line of fire. Burning the tract house turned out to be a bad idea. Oh, they had routed the bacteria people inside, right enough, then mowed them down on their back lawn, but it took too much time. To torch and clean this one section of town could take all night.

And there was another serious downside to setting fires. The light from the blaze made the Legion players visible to the natives.

And the natives in Marwood Creek were armed and restless.

"Mudgett?" a woman's voice said in his headset. "What the hell's going on over there? It sounds like a shooting gallery."

"Della? Where are you?"

"We just finished off the farms on the outskirts of town. We're right on schedule. We had no trouble with the targets. Nailed them clean. Only casualty was Chainsaw. He got bit in the ass by a German shepherd, but he's okay. I'm looking at the entrance to the trailer park right now."

"I need you over here to back us up."

"Back you up? You've got to be kidding."

Karkanian hadn't expected an argument from her. He realized he should have. "I'm not kidding."

"Look, I've already deployed my team," she said. "We're in position to take down the park. Should be a piece of cake. When we're done, we'll come over and help you out of your little jam."

Karkanian hated the tone in her voice. He hated that he couldn't make her obey him. "Do us both a favor," he told her, "and watch yourselves. We've lost some people already." He didn't think it was wise to let her know how many of their side had gone down. He was afraid she might decide to bag the op. If there was going to be a retreat, it had to be in force or lots more level-fivers were going to die.

"I'll check back when we've mopped up," she said.

"You do that."

Karkanian hoped the concern he felt wasn't starting to show in his voice. The way things were going, he was beginning to worry that the battle would soon be completely out of control, the game plan damaged beyond repair. It was one thing to abandon the founding concept of Legion's big night out, the murder of an entire American town; it was another to be defeated by the very beings you claimed superiority over.

He couldn't let that happen.

Defeat was out of the question.

BOLAN CLIMBED DOWN the three-story drainpipe, stepping off it into a flower bed. On the ground on the other side of the concrete walk lay the body of the cameraman, Spence. He could tell from the angle of the man's head that his neck was broken. The Executioner moved quickly to the front corner of the mansion and took cover behind a shrub.

The Winnebago still stood in the middle of the street. As he watched, yellow figures darted across lawns, ran up steps and entered the great houses that had already been hit. It didn't take a brain trust to figure out why they were backtracking all of a sudden.

They were looking for the rest of their people. And when they found them, they weren't going to be pleased.

The turn of events was something Bolan hadn't considered. It looked like the people who had survived the first wave of the Legion attack were going to have to endure a second. They might even think the bad guys were the cavalry come to save them and step out of hiding with cheers for their liberators.

He had to put a stop to it, and quick, which meant stepping further into harm's way.

He unscrewed the sound suppressor from the Heckler & Koch's muzzle and tossed the fat cylinder away. Then he trotted out to the front of Scarborough Manor, raised the machine pistol and opened fire on the Winnebago. He raked it front to rear with lead, breaking out the side windows, and pocking its sheet-metal skin with 9 mm holes.

Without a suppressor, the machine gun was plenty loud, and it drew answering fire almost at once.

Bullets were already sailing over Bolan's head as he turned to run.

"He's down here," somebody behind him shouted. "This way!"

The Executioner sprinted down the concrete walk that bordered the mansion. In the back, beyond the formal flower garden, was a smaller guest house. The stone cottage was plenty big enough for a family of six. He jumped the front stairs, kicked in the front door and rushed in.

He found out right away that the place was occupied. A light hit him in the side of the face. Somebody stepped out from beside the wall and stuck a snub-nosed revolver behind his ear.

"Drop the gun," said a man in a terry-cloth bathrobe.

A brave thing to do.

But dumb.

Bolan ducked and shot an elbow hard into the shorter guy's stomach. The snub-nose boomed up at the ceiling, shooting two feet of flame out the barrel. The flashlight dropped and went out when it hit the floor.

As the guy doubled over, gasping for breath, Bolan wrenched the pistol from his hand.

A burst of autofire skipped through the open door, shattering a mirror over the mantelpiece.

The Executioner jerked the man out of the line of fire and pushed him to the floor. "Stay down," he said. "I'm one of the good guys."

More slugs pelted the cottage's living room, sparking off the round stones of the fireplace, hacking a china hutch to shards and splinters and thumping into the back of an upholstered chair. A wide fan of fire. Bolan could tell it was coming from steep angles outside, the bullet tracks crisscrossing in the doorway. Then came the sound of cracking wood—the back door was in the process of being kicked in.

"Is there anyone else in the house?" Bolan asked the man on the floor.

"No, just me. The wife and kids are in Seattle, thank God. This is unbelievable. The town's a war zone."

"Time to pull back," Bolan said, grabbing the guy by the shoulder. He guided them to the staircase and they retreated to the second floor.

"That thingamajig on your head, " the man said, "it helps you see in the dark?"

Bolan didn't answer. He was too busy surveying the

terrain. In a minute or two, the upper floor of the cottage was going to be crawling with Legion. He stripped off his armored vest and handed it to the guy. "Put this on," he said. "You're going to need it."

"But what about you?"

"I'll make do." Bolan's NOD-assisted gaze returned to an inset square in the ceiling. "Where does that trapdoor go?"

"To the attic, but its just rafters and insulation."

"What kind?"

"Huh?"

"What kind of insulation? Roll or blown in?"

"Blown in. There's tons of it up there."

"Okay, what I want you to do is to get in the deepest darkest closet you've got," the Executioner said. He put the revolver back in the man's hand. "Get down on the floor with your back to the wall. If somebody sticks their head in the closet, blow it off."

"Where are you going?"

"Up. Now, beat it." Bolan slipped the SMG's sling over his shoulder and pulled an antique washstand away from the wall and under the trapdoor. He jumped up on the marble top, pushed the trap out of its frame and pulled himself up and into the attic.

There was no way out.

The ceiling joists were buried somewhere under the knee-deep drift of insulation. In Bolan's NOD, the fiberglass fill was all the same color—a uniform olive green.

Feeling under the stuff with the toe of his shoe, he located a joist and walked along it. He needed to put some space between himself and the trapdoor, space that would allow the Legion players to get well inside the attic before he showed himself.

To his left, a brick chimney ran up through the roof. It was the most likely hiding place because it provided solid cover. Bolan stepped over to it, then immediately backtracked to the attic's midline. His real hide would be on the opposite side. As he crossed the joists, he smoothed out the holes he made in the loose insulation, leaving no telltale footprints behind.

Before he sat he shoveled the fiberglass out of the way, then he tore a wide strip out of the bottom of his still-damp T-shirt and used it to cover his nose and mouth. Taking a seat on the joist, he heaped the loose insulation around and over him, making sure to cover the top of his head. Then he pulled his arms into the heap and picked the machine pistol out of his lap. Only the lens tubes of his NOD goggles and the stubby gun barrel protruded from the pile.

It didn't take long for a head to appear above the frame of the trapdoor. Bolan was glad because it was starting to get warm under the fiberglass, and it itched.

The Legion player looked around, and seeing nothing but green, waved up his three buddies, who quickly joined him around the trap.

Bolan could tell from their body language that they thought they were going to have some fun.

Fish-in-a-barrel fun.

The first guy pointed over at the chimney, and the rest spread out. Then they all began to advance with weapons at the ready.

Bolan let them get into position before he made his move. They were lined up between him and the chimney like dominoes. The nearest man was only four feet away. When Bolan touched the H&K's trigger, the insulation began to fly, as did the bodies.

The first guy fell away with bullets to the neck and head, and when he hit, he raised a cloud of fiberglass fluff. The next man in line never got his gun around. Bolan caught him under the chin with a 9 mm uppercut that crashed him onto his back, sending more fluff flying. The last two killers fired blind, sweeping the drifts of insulation in the hope of finding their attacker before he found them.

Hope died as the Executioner stitched their heads with lead, slamming them into the roof rafters. They pitched, headfirst, into the waist-high drifts of insulation.

Bolan stood up and promptly sneezed.

He was caught in the middle of a snowstorm. A scratchy snowstorm.

Pushing aside the insulation, he found the machine pistol the closest guy had dropped. He checked the mag to make sure it was full, then got out of there.

"WHAT HAPPENED TO YOU?" the Winnebago's driver asked.

He was looking down at Bolan, who was covered, head to foot, with tufts of fiberglass. He thought it was one of his players, met with an accident. It didn't occur to him that this was the guy his team had been sent out to kill. "Man, you are a mess!"

"Mess is relative," the Executioner said. He fired the machine pistol through the sheet-metal side of the

RV, punching through it, through the driver and into the ceiling.

Inside the Winnebago, Bolan brushed himself off with a hand towel, then turned on the interior light. In a duffel bag, he found some black fatigues that fit nice and loose. After he quickly exchanged his damp clothes for dry ones, he searched the RV's dashboard. He had just put his hand on Legion's battle maps when the dead driver's headset made a crackling sound.

Bolan picked it up and put it on.

"Red Rover?" a concerned voice said.

The Executioner recognized the voice. It was one he had committed to memory. It was the voice of Aga Karkanian.

"Yeah," he answered.

"Did you find the rest of our people?"

"Yeah."

"Are they alive?"

"Yeah."

"That's great news. Bring them over to the corner of Stanton and Marwood."

Bolan located the two streets on his map.

"Be right there," he said as he dropped the RV into gear.

CHAPTER EIGHTEEN

When Gummy Nordland's borrowed sedan cleared the crest of the hill, the load came off the engine and the car shot ahead with a sudden surge of speed. The chief watched the van's lights shrink in the rearview mirror. Even as the pursuit fell back, orange strobe lights flickered at him. Bullets started zipping into the sedan's trunk lid and skimming off the roof.

He couldn't make the car go any faster. At ninety miles per hour, the gas pedal became a volume knob: the engine roared louder, but that didn't translate into forward momentum. It was probably just as well. The steering had gone all soft, like the tires were floating a fraction of an inch above the roadway. Behind him, the headlights had started to grow larger again. No longer hobbled by the hill, the van was gaining.

Nordland was running out of breathing room, but he still had a slight edge. After all, he'd been born here. He'd lived his whole life here. And more to the point, he'd spent years as a beat cop driving up and down Port Flattery's side streets and back roads. He knew shortcuts that didn't appear on any map, and wouldn't occur to the bastards chasing him until it was too late for them to do anything about it.

When he figured the van was close enough to his back bumper, he started looking for a turnoff from the highway. Or more accurately, a veer-off. He was going too fast to take a sharp corner without rolling the car a few dozen times.

The old Texaco station screamed up at him on the left. He cut the wheel over, slashing up the wide driveway. The sedan went airborne for thirty feet, came down with a crash beside the door to the station's service bay and roared onto the empty lot beyond. Veering some more, Nordland just managed to clear the gap between a pair of creosote-soaked logs that served as a parking barrier. Then he touched his brakes. Just a little, so he could drive over the edge of the Beckmans' lawn and not through their living room.

As he bounded onto a narrow paved street, he put some pressure on the brakes. The sedan's rear end swung wide and loose, back wheels skidding, before he got it under control.

In the rearview mirror, there was only black.

Flicking on his high beams, Nordland put the pedal down again. He'd ditched the killers, but only briefly. He had gained precious seconds, and he was going to need every one of them.

The chief hogged the middle of the street, racing past woodlots and fenced pastures, prefabricated sheet-metal barns and abandoned, moss-covered farmhouses. He headed toward the sickly glow in the sky and the underlit pillars of rising steam. The street climbed and fell over a series of low hills. Because the road was straight, he could keep the engine redlined. Because it was so narrow, he couldn't keep his eye on the rearview. He had to steal quick peeks every now and then. When the black hilltop behind him became suddenly visible, lit by the high beams of another vehicle, Nordland knew the van was on his tail again. In front of him, the mill's smokestacks appeared over the treetops: gray concrete towers decorated with aircraft warning lights.

It was going to be close.

He had to slow down to make the entrance to the mill road. Hammering the brakes, he screeched around the turn. The road angled steeply to the brightly lit plant. He could see acres of wood chips, steaming in the preliminary-treatment pits. From the pit area, a covered conveyor belt led up at a seventy-degree angle to the tenth story of a building sided with corrugated sheet steel. Beyond that were the smokestacks, and beyond them, the mill's loading pier, which stuck out into the bay.

Nordland cut off the corners of the turns as he slalomed down the mill road. At the foot of the hill was a guardhouse, a glassed-in hut barely big enough for one guy. There was no one in it, as the mill didn't have a security staff. It did, however, have a swing-shift crew of fifteen who helped keep the machinery running twenty-four hours a day. The skeleton crew couldn't produce as much paper as the day shift, but it was cheaper to keep the plant running at a low output than to stop and start the system every day. Nordland had plans for those fifteen guys. He had a back seat full of weapons and ammunition, and intended to arm them and lead them back to town to fight.

At gunpoint if necessary.

As he shot past the little guardhouse, he looked back. The van was speeding down the hill behind him. He passed the neat, low building that housed the mill's administrative staff and the cafeteria. At that time of night, nobody was in either place. Ahead was the parking lot for the mill workers, which had about a dozen cars in it. In the daylight-bright floodlights, Nordland could see the double hangar-size doors in the side of the metal plant were closed. He'd hoped to be able to drive right in; that wasn't going to happen. But the big sliding door on the right had a smaller, man-size door cut into it, and that was open.

As Nordland roared up, a guy in a blaze orange hard hat and a plaid flannel shirt stepped over the threshold and looked out. He had hearing protectors clamped around his neck. Another guy in an orange hard hat appeared beside him.

The chief slammed on his brakes, skidding to a bone-jarring stop fifteen feet from the plant door.

The guy in the red-and-gray flannel shirt and suspenders blinked at him in amazement. The other man, who wore denim bib-fronts, did the same. Nordland knew them both. He'd gone to school with Larry and Gilbert.

"Goddammit, don't just stand there!" the chief shouted as he shoved open the driver door. "Give me a hand, you two!"

Gilbert stepped through the doorway and stopped.

By the time Larry rounded the front of the car, Nordland had already lifted his bad leg out the door. He used the windowframe to pull himself to his feet. His wounded leg had stiffened so much that he could hardly bend his knee, and it hurt like hell to put weight on the foot.

"What happened to you?" Larry asked, looking down at his bloody pant leg and shoe.

"What happened to the car?" Gilbert asked, gesturing at the crashed-out windows and bullet holes.

Up by the guardhouse, an engine roared and tires screeched on asphalt. The van full of killers bore down on them fast.

"No time to explain," Nordland said. "Help me with the guns."

"Guns?" Larry repeated. "What guns?"

As the van whipped by the administrative building, a guy leaned way out of the front passenger's window and opened fire. Machine-gun bullets thudded into the side of the sedan, clipping off the side mirror and popping rear and front tires, dropping it abruptly onto its wheel rims. The slugs hit the front windshield and ricocheted, spanging into the corrugated hangar doors.

And into Gilbert.

He clutched his chest with both hands and sat down hard. His mouth opened and shut as if he were trying to say something important, but couldn't spit it out. Then blood shot from his throat in a bright stream, splattering the front fender.

"Oh, God," Larry said, beating a rapid retreat.

"Come back here, you idiot!" the chief cried.

But Larry had other ideas. As he made a beeline for the open door, a spray of slugs rattled the steel wall all around him. Nordland had no choice. He had to give the guy some covering fire or he was going to get killed. The chief drew his pistol, braced his wrist against the top of the car door and sighted on the speeding van.

He knew it was a lost cause even before he started to fire. The van was coming too fast, and the shooting angle was lousy. He didn't have a hope in hell of hitting the guy with the machine gun. If he was lucky, he could make him duck, though.

Nordland punched out seven quick shots as the van rushed at him. The first pair hit high in center of the windshield, close enough to the ten-ring to make the driver flinch and suddenly swerve, which caused the chief's next three rapid-fire shots to miss the target completely. The sixth bullet blasted out the van's left headlight, and the final shot drilled the windshield, this time closer to the bottom—the whole center of it went suddenly opaque as the safety glass spiderwebbed and caved inward. The driver swerved again, this time much more violently, and stomped his brakes, sending the van in a looping, 360-degree skid.

The chief seized the opportunity to hop around the front of the sedan and make a break for the open door. Ahead of him, Larry disappeared through the entryway. Nordland moved at half speed across the gap. More bullets zipped over his shoulder, clanging the corrugated steel, spitting sparks into his face. With a final, desperate lunge, the chief hopped over the threshold.

"Help me close the door!" he shouted at Larry's departing back. The guy didn't even turn to look. He hightailed it around a huge metal tank and disappeared.

With slugs raining around him, The chief unhooked the door and slammed it shut. Then he dropped the wooden crossbar that served as a lock. The shooting abruptly stopped. He knew the barred entry wouldn't keep the killers out for long.

There were any number of ways into the mill, which was basically a cavernous processing shed. The concrete floor supported the weight of massive pressing and rolling machines, vats, boilers and tiers of fifty-five-gallon drums of corrosive chemicals. Steel catwalks and thick bundles of pipe were all that marked the sixth, eighth and tenth stories. From the mill floor, you could look up and see the underside of the roof almost 150 feet above.

Nordland dumped the Colt's empty clip on the concrete and replaced it with a full one. His last. He had just seven rounds left. Holstering the handgun, he started hopping for the plant office as fast as he could. He had to warn the swing shift what was coming.

THE FRONT DOOR of the double-wide trailer splintered off its hinges under the sole of Della's boot. With the Russian NOD on her head and the German machine pistol in her hands, she felt invincible, like the Terminator. As the door crashed down inside, she stepped in on it.

From the narrow hallway to her right, a nasty little yapper of a dog charged at her. Della let the angry fluffball get within ten feet of her before she blasted it. Full-auto fire kicked it back the way it'd come, but in several distinct pieces.

Her Legion pack-mates entered behind her and fanned out.

"I've never been in a manufactured home before," she said. "I've always wondered about the quality."

With that, she sent a full-power snap-kick into the facing interior wall. The plasterboard yielded with a crunch, and her boot went through it up to the ankle.

"Guess it won't stop bullets, then," she said, pulling her foot out of the hole.

Della braced her legs and opened up on the place, shooting through the flimsy walls at random. She emptied the 30-round mag and cracked in another. She was trying to get the home owners to run. Unlike their late pooch, they were too scared to give her sport.

The tall blonde strode down the trailer's hall. One by one, she kicked in the doors: closet, bathroom, then the bedrooms and found nobody home. The door at the end of the hall yielded to her boot with a shriek. Through her NOD she saw a wiry little man trying to help his overweight wife out a very narrow sliding window. He had her boosted up high enough, but she didn't have the strength to pull herself through. When the door came down, both of them jerked their heads toward the doorway, looking right at Della, but unable to see her in the dark.

She shot the man first, three rounds at the base of the skull, and watched as the large woman crashed down on top of him. His ribs snapped like breadsticks, crisp and quick. Seated on her dead husband's chest, the woman opened her mouth wide to scream.

Della filled it with lead.

The job done, she led her pack out the front door.

The Belle Vista trailer park attracted manufactured-home enthusiasts of all stripes and income levels. Some of the trailers actually looked like houses, of a rudimentary sort, with bay windows, front porches and cedar decks. Others made no pretense about being houses; they were just rectangular metal boxes on wheels.

The next trailer in line was a gleaming silver bullet, its wheels hidden behind short pieces of white picket fence. It looked like a spaceship from the 1940s, with a striped-canvas awning on the side and folding chairs set out around a picnic table.

Della reared back and tried to kick the Airstream's door in. All she managed to do was to put a huge dent in the metal skin. Miffed, she fired a short burst point-blank into the lock, blowing it and the doorknob away. Her SMG came up empty.

"Go on," she told the others as she dumped the mag on the ground.

While she fumbled for a fresh clip, her pack-mates charged through the door. Della slapped the full mag home and flipped the H&K's cocking handle to chamber the first round. She paused for a second, listening for the sounds of silenced autoweapons dishing out red murder. Instead what she heard was cannon fire.

Booming reports shook the trailer. Suppressed sub-guns clattered madly, then another pair of booms rang out.

Della could see the muzzle-flashes of the single shots. They winked at her through the miniblinds that covered the windows at the trailer's aerodynamically rounded rear. In a single bound, she leaped on top of the picnic table. Holding her weapon against her hip, she opened fire. She shot through the back end of the Airstream, fanning her muzzle back and forth to saturate the area. By the time her gun again ran out of bullets, she had turned the shiny skin into a mass of ragged holes. She thought it looked vaguely like the teeth of a giant cheese grater.

Almost at once, her pack-mates came out of the trailer's door. Between them, they dragged a limp figure by the arms. They set the man down beside a picket fence wheel cover.

"Well?" Della said, pitching the spent clip aside.

"You really fucked him up," one of the players said.

"Hamburger," another added. "Take a look for yourself."

She jumped down from the table. Her ravening volley had practically cut the guy in two. Yellow blobs hung out from under the tail of his shirt. His insides were on the outside.

Della reloaded again. This was a piece of cake. Just like she'd told Karkanian. She was beginning to wonder about the guy, to wonder whether half the stuff he claimed to have done was real. Or maybe he just wasn't any good at this kind of operation. Maybe he lacked the necessary stones to be an exterminator.

It took a woman to do a man's work, she thought.

"Let's split up," Della told the others. "We can cover more ground that way. Watch your background, though. We don't want to shoot each other by accident."

As Della moved on, she saw someone peeking out around the corner of a curtain in the trailer across the lane. A yellow half head quickly ducked back. She touched off a quick burst that stitched up the exterior wall and blew in the window. She couldn't tell if she'd hit anybody.

But she didn't like being spied on by bacterial life-forms.

She ran up the steps to the little porch, shot off the door lock and charged into the living room, ready to fire.

Something bright yellow vanished behind the kitchen counter. Then, from the other side of the living room, at the entrance to a hall, a gun cracked and flashed. The slug creased the side of her neck. It felt like she'd been touched by a branding iron, and that angered her.

"Why you dirty..." she said, turning her weapon at the hall and pinning the trigger. The subgun bucked in her hands, spitting lead and hot hulls. Della angled her shots through two walls, paper-thin walls that provided no cover. Somebody moaned and fell, hitting the floor with a thud.

"Okay, you, behind the counter," she said, stepping to the side. "Come on out, or I'll shoot."

Yellow hands slowly appeared above the countertop, then arms, then a man's head.

Della shot him once in the face. Before turning down the hall, she rounded the counter and looked down at him. She saw the grip of a revolver sticking out of his trouser's waistband. He'd waited too long to pull it. Maybe he thought he could catch her off guard as he came around the counter.

Wrong.

Dead wrong.

Through the trailer's open door, she could hear a few, unsilenced gun shots that had to be of bacterial origin. They made her smile. What was it that the aliens from Mars always said after they landed their saucer on the White House lawn?

Resistance is futile.

When Della looked around the living room, she knew there were more targets in this trailer. The place was crawling with kiddie toys. She hadn't the chance to blast any real young ones yet, the opportunity to nip future breeders in the bud, and that was something she'd been looking forward to for weeks.

She stormed down the hallway, stepping over the body of a woman and the small-caliber automatic pistol she had dropped. She booted in doors until she came to what had to be a kid's bedroom. Kids, plural. There were two single beds. Girls, from the dolls and ruffles on the pillows. The covers were turned back. Della put a hand to the sheet. Still warm.

They couldn't be far.

Crossing the hall, she kicked down the door opposite. Boys' room. Bunk beds. Model airplanes hanging from strings thumbtacked to the ceiling. Toys in a heap in one corner. No one in sight.

The window was open, and the curtain pushed outside.

When Della looked out, she saw four little yellow figures dashing for the trailer across the lane.

"You can run, but you can't hide," she said as she headed for the front door.

By the time she got outside, the children were gone. The trailer they'd been running for was skinned with aluminum siding painted two-tone, and it had a two-tone metal awning along the side held up by metal pipes. Della noticed the car under the awning. It was a Plymouth Duster. The license-plate holder read Happiness Is Hugging Your Teacher.

The icing on the cake, Della thought as she climbed the three little steps to the trailer's side door, steps decorated with a pair of concrete elves and a plastic squirrel.

WHEN THE SEDAN suddenly veered off the highway in front of him, Butcher Boy thought the chase was over. He thought for sure the driver was going to lose it, either rolling the car or crashing it into the front of the old gas station. The German watched in disbelief as the sedan flew over the concrete pad where the gas pumps had once stood, past the low building, traveling parallel to him for a fraction of a second before it angled out into the empty lot, raising a furious cloud of dust.

"Scheisse!" he cried, reverting to his mother tongue as he stomped on the brakes. As he tried to keep the van from sliding sideways, out of the corner of his eye he tracked his escaping quarry.

The sedan's brake lights flashed once, then disappeared into the blackness.

"Where'd he go?" Wavy Hair said from the passenger's seat. "We've lost him!"

"He's still heading for the mill," Butcher Boy assured his pack-mate. "He's just taking an alternate route to get there."

Butcher Boy skidded around the next left turn on two wheels. The road was barely wide enough for one car and there were deep ditches on either side of it. He steered down the center, straddling the crown. His high beams lit up a long, straight stretch of road. In the far distance, he could see a stop sign, which had to mark a major crossroad.

"Which street is he taking?" Wavy Hair asked. "We could get lost out here in a hurry."

Butcher Boy responded to the question by reaching down and turning off his headlights.

"Oh, fuck," Wavy Hair groaned as the world went black.

"There!" the German said, pointing to the right. He caught a rosy glow, a glimpse of taillights before they vanished over a hilltop.

Flipping his lights back on, Butcher Boy cranked a wheel-spinning turn at the stop sign, then mashed the gas pedal down.

"We've got him now," he said.

The van rapidly picked up speed. Though loaded down with battle gear and eight large men, its engine had a lot more power than the sedan's. The German wasn't shy about pushing the mill to the limit, either. Accustomed to the wide-open, no-speed-limit driving in his native country, he wasn't intimidated by speeds in excess of one hundred miles per hour, even on a supernarrow, unfamiliar, unlit street.

The other players weren't so sanguine. The back road was full of dips and bumps that sent them and their gear bouncing all over the inside of the cargo compartment. They didn't complain, though. They didn't want to break Butcher Boy's concentration. One slip of the wheel, and they'd be spread like broken trash bags, over one hundred yards of roadside.

"There he is!" Wavy Hair said as the back end of the sedan appeared a half mile in front of them. No sooner than he got the words out, then the taillights vanished.

Butcher Boy slowed as the entrance to the mill road loomed on the left. It occurred to him that the driver of the sedan could have changed his mind about the mill and remained on the back road, which S-curved back to the highway. The German decided it didn't matter; they had business at the mill, either way. He whipped a hard turn, down the road to the plant, which came into view immediately.

The place was lit up like Christmas.

At least there'd be no more running around with cumbersome night-vision devices strapped to their heads, he thought. The fumes rising from the vast wood-chip piles smelled like brimstone. An appropriate aroma, considering what Legion was about to turn the mill into.

As they rushed by the unoccupied guard shack and shot the gradual slope toward the plant building, the sedan came into view again. Butcher Boy could see three men standing beside the car. Two of them wore orange hats.

"I'll get the bastards," Wavy Hair said, unfastening his seat belt and picking up his Heckler & Koch MP-5 A-3 from the floor. "Try to hold it steady, if you can."

Wavy Hair leaned out the window and sprayed the car and the three men with a sustained burst of autofire. He emptied half the 30-round magazine in a little more than a second. The hail of barely aimed bullets kicked sparks and puffs of dust from the side of the metal building. One of the men went down behind the car.

Another started to run around the front bumper toward the open doorway. The third drew a pistol.

"Look out!" Butcher Boy shouted.

The top of the windshield imploded, spraying the players in the cargo area with bits of glass. Heavy bullets swept over their heads, through the length of the compartment and exited through ragged holes in the back doors.

Butcher Boy reacted to the near miss and the sting of flecks of glass against his cheek by flinching at the wheel. The sudden swerve put Wavy Hair well off his aim.

Just as the German recovered control of the van, another large-caliber bullet struck the windshield at the base. Butcher Boy felt the breeze as the bullet whipped between the front bucket seats. The combined effect of three hits caved the windshield in like a wet paper bag. Crazed with cracks, its center collapsed onto the dashboard. Butcher Boy reacted again, stamping the brakes and cutting the wheel hard over.

The van wasn't going fast enough to flip over in the parking lot. It skidded in a complete circle, a gut-wrenching 360 degrees.

Half-hanging out the passenger's-side window, Wavy Hair held on to the side mirror strut for dear life. He recovered in time to empty the rest of his magazine into the hangar door.

The door to the mill slammed shut.

"It's all right," Butcher Boy said. "They aren't going anywhere."

Thanks to Gridley, who had wheedled a tour of the plant and videotaped the experience, Legion had a complete floor plan of the place. They knew all the access points, all the strategically important areas. They had used this information to construct their plan of attack. Although the team that had been assigned to hit the mill was missing nearly half its personnel, thanks to the guy driving the sedan, the job was still doable. It just meant that they had to lug around more ammo.

"Take as many full magazines as you can carry," the German told the others. "We won't be coming back here until we're finished."

As they bundled up the 30-round clips and stowed them in knapsacks, an overamplified voice boomed through the sheet-metal building. Butcher Boy couldn't make out all the words because of the echo and the squeal of feedback, but it sounded like somebody was putting out a warning.

Not that it would change things.

After securing his own ammo stash, Butcher Boy opened a footlocker near the back doors and pulled from it a length of hardened steel chain with a heavy padlock attached. The chain had been prepared in advance, based on measurements Gridley had provided. It had been prepared for just one purpose: to seal off the parking-lot entrance to the plant. He fitted the looped end of the chain over the doorknob in the normal-size door, then stretched the rest through the U-shaped handles of the huge sliding doors. Pulling it taut, he fastened the chain back on itself with a padlock.

When he returned to the back of the van, Wavy Hair was passing out similar chain sets to the other players. They had enough to lock every exit from the mill. Their plan was to enter the mill, seal the workers in, then wipe them out.

When Wavy Hair was done, Butcher Boy said, "Go ahead. You know the drill."

Wavy Hair took two players and led them along the side of the building, toward the north entrance of the plant, which bordered the wood-chip holding areas. Butcher Boy ordered the other four to follow him, in the opposite direction.

As they rounded the corner of the mill, they came upon another set of hangar doors, and farther down, toward the water, a single, regular-size door set in a two-story section of the building. Butcher Boy waved for two of the players to take the single door, while he and the remaining pair entered via the hangar.

At his direction, they pulled back the right-hand slider a couple of feet, enough for them to slip inside. One hundred feet in front of them, at the end of a machine as big as a freight car, a guy in a hard hat and hearing protectors was running a forklift. The machine wound ten-foot-wide sheets of brown paper around steel spindles. The hard-hat guy slid one of the lift's prongs into the core of a huge roll of paper. He was so engrossed that he didn't see them and he couldn't hear them because his ears were covered. The forklift strained to raise the roll from the machine. Once it was clear, however, the little vehicle moved with surprising agility.

When the operator turned his side toward them, Butcher Boy and his pals cut loose with their machine pistols. The shock of bullets whanging into the fork-lift's roll cage got his attention. He looked at them, but he didn't have a clue what was happening, why the air was full of steel-jacketed hornets.

Bullets ripped into the paper roll and banged off the concrete floor. The millworker got the picture, quick. He was in a no-win situation. The forklift was speedy, but it wasn't faster than a bullet. If he turned to run away from them, he opened his unprotected back to their fire. If he drove it toward them, he only made their job easier. If he stayed on the lift, they would shoot him off of it. If he bailed and took to his heels, they would blast him down.

In the end, he decided to trust his feet more than the forklift. He jumped out the far side of the vehicle and tried to reach the corner of the rolling machine.

Butcher Boy led him perfectly and touched off a 3-round burst. It cut a diagonal line across the guy's back from right hip to left shoulder, sending him whirling to the concrete. His hard hat skittered across the floor.

From the paper-storage area on their left came the sounds of running feet, stuttering subguns and richochets.

"Hey, we've got a couple over here!" one of the players called out. "They're coming your way!"

Butcher Boy paused long enough to padlock the hangar doors, then spread out his men and waved them forward.

The storage shed consisted of a series of massive cradles set in rows along the walls and down the center of the floor. The cradles held the huge rolls of paper horizontally, with one end sticking out into the aisle, and they were stacked one on top of another, nearly reaching the ceiling. There was enough space between the rows in the middle of the storage area for a forklift to maneuver in and out.

Butcher Boy saw the other two players at the end of the long aisle. They waved him toward the wall. The bacteria had fled that way.

When he reached the wall, no one was in sight on the floor. Looking at the ends of the rolls of paper, the German realized it was possible to climb up them, using the spindle holes and the gaps where curving edges touched as foot- and handholds.

He slung his H&K and started climbing up the stack in the center aisle. When he reached the top, he pulled himself onto the back of the nearest roll. It was slick as glass. From the new vantage point, he could see the top of the rolls across the aisle.

He saw two workers cowering, hiding against the wall, and they could see him, too. They were only fifty feet away.

When he swung his machine gun around and pointed it at them, they raised their hands and slowly straightened. Butcher Boy let them have a short burst of nines, just to see what they'd do. The gunfire rattled the sheet metal behind and above their heads.

The two workers looked at each other, then they took off across the broad humps of the paper rolls, slipping, sliding, falling, getting up, falling again. Over the sights of the machine pistol, it looked most comical, like a Three Stooges routine.

If it was a comedy, it was a black one.

Butcher Boy shot the legs out from under the guy on the right. He fell over the top of a roll and slid down into the valley between it and its neighbor. The other worker looked over his shoulder to see what happened to his friend, and it caused him to miss his footing. Arms flailing, he slid off the end of the roll and fell twenty feet to the concrete. He was still alive when the other players reached him.

That didn't last long.

They fired their machine guns point-blank into him.

"Hey!" Butcher Boy shouted down at them. "The other one is still up there. He's just wounded."

While the German climbed down from his perch, two of the players climbed up the wall of rolls on the other side. A staccato clattering signaled they had dispatched him, as well.

After he'd reassembled his pack, Butcher Boy again took the lead, moving them back to the main plant area. When they arrived at the hangar doors, they scanned the place for targets. High on the wall on the other side of the building, something caught the German's keen eye. A man was moving, very slowly up a ladder to the first of the towering catwalks. He was favoring one leg, as if he was hurt.

"How about a little contest?" Butcher Boy said. "See that guy over there on the ladder? Let's all set our guns on single shot and see who can pick him off the wall."

Four players lined up behind him, and as they did, they all dropped to one knee like a firing squad.

"We shoot one at a time, and in order," he told the others, "or we won't be able to tell which one of us hits him."

The German took the first shot. He held his gun in

an offhand position, corrected the elevation for an eighty-yard shot and squeezed off a round. The 9 mm bullet zipped across the cavernous plant.

A miss!

It sparked off a steel pipe three feet to the right of the man's head.

"Batter up," Butcher Boy said. "Who's next?"

CHAPTER NINETEEN

A half hour before the power went out, Mary Louise Gonerman had nodded off in front of the TV. She was sound asleep when, like a bug in the hands of inquisitive small boys, her little town began to be pulled apart.

She was dreaming about her best friend, Lill, who had died years earlier. In her dream, she pulled up in front of Lill's A-frame out on Beach Road in her little gold Duster when there was a jolting boom. It rattled the windows in their frames and made her ceramic statuettes—a dancing seventeenth-century English nobleman and his gracious lady—dance for real on top of her bookcase.

Gonerman's brain tried to integrate the external input into the dream sequence, but it was impossible.

She stirred from sleep in time to hear a second bang. This one made her jerk in surprise. Clutching the arms of her recliner, she blinked in the dark. For a second, she thought she'd had a stroke in her sleep and gone blind. She thought that the sound she'd heard had been made by a blood clot as it shut off the blood supply to part of her brain. Straining, she could make out the radium-painted hands of her electric alarm clock, and she realized that the power was off, which was why it was so dark. That didn't explain the noises, of course.

She always kept a flashlight in the bookcase by her TV chair, just in case something like that happened. She picked up the flashlight, started to turn it on, but caught herself. Gonerman shut her eyes and listened as hard as she could. Her hearing was still excellent, the last of her senses to remain pretty much intact.

In the distance, there were more pops.

It sounded like Fourth of July or New Year's Eve, when local idiots fired guns in the air.

Only it wasn't.

She wondered if the government had installed a new national holiday and failed to properly notify her. There'd been nothing in the local paper about it, but of course that was no test. The *Bugle* had gone from bad to worse after Fred Ferguson took it over.

It was hard for Gonerman to get her mind around the possibility that her life might actually be in jeopardy from some outside, malevolent force. Things like that didn't happen in Port Flattery, not even in a trailer park like Belle Vista. Her experience told that if her life was at risk, it was because she was eighty-four years old and everything she'd been born with was starting to fail.

A third and fourth gun shot and the sound of breaking glass made her sit up straight in her chair. Something was definitely not right. Something bad was happening. Clamping her hand over the lens of the flashlight to minimize its glare against her windows, she turned it on and walked through the little kitchenette to her bedroom at the rear of the trailer.

She heard people running outside, and there were screams.

Once in her bedroom, the old woman turned off the flashlight. She didn't need it to find her way around. She knew where everything was. She opened the door to her closet, pushed aside her collection of mail-order-catalog dresses and reached into the back corner. Her hand closed around the oiled wooden forestock of her old deer rifle. She'd had it since she was sixteen. She lifted out the Winchester 94 carbine and set it on the bed. It still weighed the same six pounds it always had, but nowadays six pounds felt like sixty to her. She kept the shells for it in a shoebox on the floor of the closet. It took her a moment more to find the right one and dig out the box of twenty rounds.

She didn't dare turn the flashlight on to put in the bullets. As long as it was dark in her trailer, she figured whoever was running around outside wouldn't know there was anyone at home.

It was an easy gun to load, even in the dark.

She pushed six .30-caliber shells into the side loading port, then cycled the lever action, sending the last one into the firing chamber. That done, she shoved a final bullet in the side. Very carefully, she held the external hammer with her thumb and squeezed the trigger. She lowered the hammer all the way down, then raised it back up to half-cock.

The last time she'd fired the weapon had been in the late fall of 1985. The father of one of her students had invited her to accompany the family on a deer hunt over in Okanagan County. She'd dropped her buck with one shot at seventy-five yards. She'd never forget the way it fell over, like it'd been poleaxed. It didn't take another step. Something inside told her that she'd never top that shot, and even though she never made a formal decision to quit deer hunting, somehow she never got around to going again. She always had something more important to do when the time came.

More shots snapped her to full alert. These were close. They came from across the road at the Pinkleys'. She thought she saw the gun flashes through her bedroom curtain. Good Lord, she thought, pulling the carbine closer.

Then came a soft tapping at the window behind her.

The old woman twisted around on her bed, but kept the rifle lying across her lap.

The tapping continued, insistent.

"Who's there?" she demanded.

"Miss Gonerman?" a reedy voice said. "It's me, Shane."

"Shane Pinkley?"

"Yes, ma'am."

Gonerman pulled back the corner of the curtain. The whole Pinkley brood stared up at her—Shane, Amber, Dylan and Tiffany in their flannel pajamas.

"Come to the door," Miss Gonerman said. "Hurry."

She risked the flashlight so she could let them in and still banged her shin on the telephone stand. When she opened the door, the children rushed into the trailer. She closed the door and locked it and slid across the safety chain. Then she turned out the flashlight.

"Oh, could we *please* have the light, Miss Gonerman?" Amber asked.

"Do you want them to see us?" Dylan said. "Do you want them to get us?"

"Tell me, quickly, children," the old woman said. "What's happening out there?"

Shane, who was eight and the oldest, replied, "First the power went out, then people starting shooting. Somebody broke into our trailer. My mom said to go out the window so we did."

"We heard guns," Tiffany added. "In our house."

"Mom and Dad had guns," Dylan said. "Maybe they shot the bad people."

Gonerman felt suddenly light-headed, as if she were going to faint. She caught herself, though, and forced herself to concentrate. The children were in danger. She was in danger, too.

"All right, we're going to move back to my bedroom now," she said. "We'll be safe there. Take my hand, Shane, and Dylan take his, and Amber take Dylan's, and Tiffany take Amber's so we don't get separated in the dark."

She led the living chain through the pitch-black trailer. When they reached the bedroom, she said, "Sit on the floor by the edge of the bed. And if anything happens—"

"You mean, like if the bad people try to come in and get us?" Amber asked.

Gonerman didn't want to scare them with the fine print. "When I tell you," she said, "just wriggle in under the bed and stay there quietly until I tell you to come out."

Outside, something made a sound near her car.

"Shh," she told the kids.

A foot scraped on the gravel, then someone stepped up on her little side porch. The doorknob rattled as someone tested it.

The old woman picked up the Winchester and rested the butt on top of her thigh. She didn't lift the hammer to full cock, but her thumb was on it.

PORT FLATTERY'S prosecuting attorney, Hughie Pearson, was practicing his tai chi when the power failed. As was his nightly routine, he was performing a series of *chi kung* breathing exercises. They required him to stand in a bent-thigh position while holding his arms in various attitudes and inhaling and exhaling as completely as possible. Pearson had picked up the soft martial art as a stress reliever and joint loosener. Nobody in town knew he practiced it, he'd made sure of that. Secrets were hard to come by in a place like PF, where everybody's business was everybody's business.

Also, in PF, things that ran counter to expectation were soundly dismissed. Pearson had had a reputation since grade school as a wimp and a toady. For the longest time, he'd organized his life around disproving that opinion, to no avail. You couldn't change people's minds; you could only look pathetic trying.

When the lights went out in Port Flattery, he was holding the imaginary tai chi ball in front of him, his arms curled around it, his palms cupped it, his fingers pressed it. The blackout didn't startle him—his *chi* was flowing. He finished his deep exhale, then straightened from the horseman's stance.

Pearson walked over to his window and looked out. He lived in the upper story of Ewing House, a big

Victorian that had been converted to flats many years earlier. Once a farmhouse, it was on the north and least-populated side of town. From his window, he could normally see the edge of Marwood Creek development and the grotesquely clear-cut slopes of the new Victorian View Estates. Tonight he couldn't see diddly.

He picked up his phone and got no dial tone. It was dead, which set off alarm bells in his head.

Pearson was a volunteer fireman. He'd joined the fire department for the wrong reason, to show everyone he'd grown up with that he was brave enough to put his skin on the line for the sake of their lives and property. Of course, he had impressed none of the people who had already made up their minds about him. To them, he was still a wimp. But that was okay because he liked the job. It usually gave him more satisfaction than being prosecutor. He got a real kick out of wearing the gear, too. He also liked carrying it around in the trunk of his luxury car.

When the power went out, as it usually did during winter storms, the PF fire department often had a busy time of it. Fires during blackouts weren't uncommon. People suddenly got it into their heads to try to cook Thanksgiving turkeys on their wood stoves. Half-asleep, they kicked over kerosene lanterns on the way to the bathroom. Sometimes old folks got overexcited at the prospect of going to bed without their electric blankets and had heart attacks. Of course, in a case like tonight, if any of those things happened, no one would be able to call the fire department for help.

Which meant that certain firemen, like Pearson, with

radio-equipped cars, were automatically assigned to street patrol.

Pearson found his vest-pocket flashlight. He turned it on and held it in his teeth while he put on some jogging shoes and an old chamois shirt. Then he walked down the three steep flights of stairs to his car, which was parked in the Victorian's carport.

He'd just gotten in the car and shut off the flashlight when a van turned down his street. Before the van got very far, two people waving flashlights walked out from the darkness onto the side of the road. The van stopped in the middle of the street, and the people with flashlights stepped in front of the headlights. Pearson recognized them as the couple who lived on the corner. They raised dahlias commercially on some leased acreage west of town.

He was about to get out to see what the trouble was when something metallic clattered, an orange flame licked out and, presto, his neighbors were down on their backs in the middle of the street. A guy in a black ninja suit with what looked like an automatic weapon stepped into the headlights' glare, looked over the bodies, then retreated into the darkness.

As the van started rolling again, Pearson dropped below the level of the dash and stayed there until it had moved on around the corner. Then he got out of his car and ran across the street to see if he could help the Hurlburtons.

He swept the flashlight beam over their bodies and knew at once that they were beyond help. Both had multiple bullet holes in the chest and head.

It was a goddamned crime scene, right on his own corner.

Whether there was a connection between the power outage, the phones being down and the killers in the van, Pearson had no way of knowing. What he did know was that streets of Port Flattery were no longer safe.

He turned on his heel and sprinted back up to his apartment. He was getting his pistol out of the sock drawer when some movement out the window caught his attention. As he moved toward the glass, he put the Walther PPK inside his waistband. Flames were leaping into the sky on the edge of the Marwood Creek development.

He snatched a pair of binoculars from the top of his bureau so he could get a better look.

A corner house was engulfed in fire, and there was a Winnebago parked across the street. He tightened down the focus. He could see people running around in the firelight, but they were too far away to make out.

He hurried back to his car. Instead of driving the eight blocks straight to Marwood Creek and the fire, he went completely around the development and came in from the other side. What he saw in his headlights looked like a scene from a disaster movie: women and children rushing across the identical, postage-stamp front lawns wrapped in blankets ripped from their beds. They all were hurrying away from the fire, even though it was at least one hundred yards off.

When Pearson got out of the Lexus, he heard gun shots crackle from up the street.

"Come on, Pearson," said a gruff voice behind him, "we've got work to do."

It was the fire chief, Max Benn. He didn't have his fire gear on. He had a battery-powered, high-intensity spotlight in one hand and a scoped deer rifle in the other.

"Max, for Christ's sake, I just saw these guys in a van kill two people across the street from my apartment."

"Yeah, well, they also set fire to the Delongs' house and then killed them in their backyard when they ran out. Shot them down like dogs. Follow me, son. We've got a barricade set up at the end of Sullivan Street."

"Where are the police?"

"Nobody knows," Benn said. "They're either off hiding somewhere or dead."

Firelight from the Delongs' tract home lit the tops of two pickups and an Escort that were parked nose to tail across the middle of the intersection. Behind the vehicles were ten or so men and boys, all of them armed, all of them shooting at will.

"I hope you brought some rocks to throw," Benn said as they approached the barricade.

Pearson pulled out his .380-caliber autopistol. "Never fired it in anger before," he said as he bellied up to the Escort. "But I can tell you, I'm plenty angry now."

"We've got them pinned down between the Delongs' and the Sizemores'," said a breathless voice beside him.

Pearson looked down and saw that the speaker was a teenage boy he didn't recognize. The kid was frantically pumping up an air rifle so he could take another shot.

One guy in the firing line had brought a wicked-looking compound bow. He was shooting arrows tipped with broad-head, big-game points. He arced his shots high over the roof of the Sizemores' place, dropping the arrows almost straight down into the gap between it and the burning house, where the killers were thought to be.

Pearson thumbed off his pistol's safety, rested the heel of his gun hand on the Escort's roof and searched the edge of the flickering light for one of the men in black.

"UNDER THE BED, now," Mary Louise Gonerman whispered.

Quickly and quietly, the Pinkley children did what they were told.

The retired schoolteacher used the Winchester as a crutch to help her rise soundlessly from the end of the bed. Reaching out into the darkness, she caught hold of the edge of the bedroom door and slowly closed it.

As the latch clicked shut, there came a splintering crash from her living room.

Pulse pounding, Gonerman sat back on the end of the bed. She raised the carbine's hammer to full cock, and jammed the point of the steel-shod butt into her chenille bedspread. She knew it was pointless for her to try to hold the rifle steady at her shoulder. It was too heavy. With her fingers wrapped around the stock and through the action lever's steel loop, she aimed the gun at the center of the door.

There didn't seem to be any point in keeping her eyes open. She couldn't see her nose in front of her face, and she thought she could hear better with her eyes shut. It helped her to concentrate.

Gonerman knew every sound inside her little trailer. The most distracting ones—the noise of the refrigerator motor turning on, the whir of the clock on her electric stove, the ticking of her electric baseboard heater— were gone because the power was out. The sounds that remained were easy to identify: the whisk-whisk, whisk-whisk of her heart beating, the soft breathing of the children under the bed, the widely spaced creak of footsteps moving over the vinyl tile floor of her kitchenette.

Whoever it was, was coming her way.

AFTER SHE KICKED IN the trailer door, Della Gridley held her fire. Flushing out her new quarry with bullets seemed too easy, like overkill in the small trailer. She decided that it might be more fun to play hide-and-seek. Using the considerable advantage of her NOD, she would search out the little buggers in the dark and when she tagged them, they would stay tagged.

Della stepped inside the cramped living room. The smell of the place hit her like a kick in the stomach, a mixture of mothballs and corned beef, overlaced with the cloying sweetness of a spring-meadow-scent, plug-in air freshener.

Ghastly.

As were the furnishings.

She scanned the room with her NOD. In shades of green, the Early American decor looked positively scabrous, from the hooked rag rugs to the Colonial-style sofa with its vile pleated dust skirt. Whichever people lived in the midst of this accumulation of unbelievable crap, Della knew she was doing them a favor by putting them out of their misery.

With careful steps she advanced, checking behind the recliner and under the dust skirt for signs of bacterial life and finding none. There was no place to hide in the living room.

She opened a closet door and discovered the source of the mothball odor. A selection of cloth coats hung on plastic hangers, and on a shelf behind them were stacks of neatly folded linens.

Della moved on to the kitchenette. It was really just a nook in the living room with a vinyl floor. It had a tiny stove and one of those half-size refrigerators. Though the counter was clear and there was nothing in the sink, this was clearly where the corned-beef smell came from: pickling spices, bay leaf, clove, peppercorn and the aroma of slow-simmered animal fat.

Like a witch in a fairy story, she looked in all the cupboards for children and found none.

Which left two doors at the end of the living room.

Della tried the one on the right first. It turned out to be a tiny bathroom, swimming in spring-meadow scent. She pulled back the shower curtain. The tub had a little metal stool in it, which fit with everything else she'd seen and smelled. The stool was supposed to make it easier for a geriatric to get in and out of the tub.

Backing out of the bathroom, Della faced the final door. They had to be behind it, she told herself. She was a bit disappointed. Where was the surprise in that?

She hefted the machine pistol in her right hand. Maybe she should just shoot through it and end the boring nonsuspense. No, she would play the game to the finish.

Della reached out for the doorknob.

AS SHE HEARD THE DOOR to the bathroom open, Gonerman considered shouting out a warning that she was armed and prepared to shoot. Then she thought better of it. Her only advantage lay in the fact that the intruder didn't know exactly where she was. And she couldn't count on whoever was searching her trailer being intimidated by a shaky old woman's voice on the other side of a flimsy door. If she'd been by herself, she might have tried it, but she had the safety of the children to think of. And when it came to kids, Mary Louise Gonerman, the spinster, was a mother bear.

The floorboards groaned as the person stepped out of the bathroom. The old woman concentrated as hard as she could, listening for the rasp of the brass door latch. When she heard the mechanism turn, she pulled the Winchester's trigger.

The noise of the gun shot shook the trailer's walls.

Over the ringing in her ears, Gonerman could hear a gasping, choking sound coming from the living room. She stood and, levering the carbine's action, chambered another .30-caliber round. Her hand felt for and found the flat surface of the door. Her fingertips touched the ragged little hole on her side of it. It was much higher up than she'd thought it would be. It would have creased the top of her head, or passed right over it, if she'd been the one on the other side.

She pulled the door open and braced herself against the jamb.

Gurgling, strangling noises came from the middle of the living room. Her eyes still closed, Gonerman shouldered the rifle and fired at the sounds. The report didn't seem as loud the second time—her ears were still in shock from the first. She felt the familiar, painful jolt of the recoil. She didn't remember it hurting that much.

Automatically she flipped the Model 94's lever, reloading and recocking in one smooth movement.

She heard a rustle and fired again, right into its center.

Someone moaned in the dark.

She fired again, and, determined to have the thing over with, levered and fired, levered and fired into the same narrow space, until the hammer finally clicked on an empty chamber.

Gonerman let the muzzle of the rifle rest against the floor. She listened for more sounds of movement, but heard nothing. There was no more labored breathing, no desperate moans.

She turned back for her bedroom. Setting the gun on her bed, she fumbled around on the spread for the box of shells and, finding it, managed to get two rounds into the carbine's loading slot. Then she picked up the rifle and her flashlight.

"Everything's okay," she told the children as she stepped into the living room. "Stay where you are, and I'll be back in a minute." Then she closed the bedroom door.

When she shone her flashlight around the small room, she saw the intruder curled up on the floor beside the recliner. It was a blond woman, dressed all in black. And she had a strange-looking contraption over her eyes.

Unlike Mary Louise Gonerman's last-ever buck deer, this wasn't a clean kill.

Not a clean kill at all.

Gonerman shouldered and fired her gun once more.

Then she went to the linen closet and got out an old bedsheet from the bottom of the stack. She used it to cover the body so the children wouldn't see it.

CHAPTER TWENTY

Stony Man Farm, Virginia

Aaron Kurtzman took another sip from a steaming ceramic mug. The coffee was fresh and brewed so strong it took half a cup of milk to turn it from black to brown. On the third swallow, the caffeine rush hit him. He felt a pleasant warmth and a surge of energy that he sorely needed. He and the rest of the cybersquad had logged a lot of high-intensity hours hammering on the Legion problem.

From a paper box beside the coffeemaker, he took a selection of pastries. Caffeine and sugar, he told himself as he wheeled back toward the ramp of his elevated workstation. Brain food.

"Bear, I think we've finally got something solid on the location," Akira Tokaido said, turning in his ergonomic chair.

"Let's hear it." Kurtzman changed course to roll up beside him.

"I ran frames from the video past a botanist friend on the Net," the young man said. "From his review of the plant life, he says the place we're looking for is north of the forty-fifth parallel, which would make it either northern New York State or Maine on the East Coast or Washington State on the west. Because of the physical characteristics of the landscape, he favors Washington as the location.''

"We checked on road signs in those three states," Carmen Delahunt chimed in, "and the green color of the population sign matches Washington's."

"What about the population itself?" Kurtzman asked. "The number 1280?"

"That's the clincher," Tokaido told him. "We ran down all the small towns bordering on salt water in western Washington, and we came up with just two possible matches. When I called the police department in Skynomish, near Olympia, I got the 911 dispatcher, who told me everything was copacetic, no reports of unusual criminal activity. When I called Port Flattery, up on the Strait of Juan de Fuca, I was informed by an automated operator that all lines were temporarily out of service."

"Like the place just dropped off the face of the earth," Delahunt added.

"Which doesn't bode well for the 1280 people who live there," Barbara Price said.

"The signs and portents get worse," Hunt Wethers explained. "Pickett's code just gave up the ghost. Turns out he wasn't using a book or a magazine to generate it. Would you believe W. H. Smith's 'Calendar of British Walks'?" The former cybernetics professor waved three out-of-date calendars in the air, then typed in a keystroke command at his console. Images scanned from the publications appeared on the wall screens. "He's had copies of these calendars in his cell for years, if the printed dates are any guide. There are roughly three hundred words of copy under each monthly landscape picture. The words describe a picturesque hike through the British countryside. The thirty-six months of calendar pages from 1993 through 1995 are the basis for his e-mail code. I think we can assume that a guy with a mind like his would have no trouble memorizing that many snippets of copy.''

''What made the code so hard to break?'' Price asked.

Wethers used a cyberpointer to indicate a line drawing to the right of the hike description. ''See this little diagram of the route? In particular, notice the crudely drawn tree symbols that dot the map. Their number is different in each of the thirty-six months. Pickett always prefaced his coded transmissions with a number, from one to thirty-six, which indicated the month's copy the code was based on. If you don't know what the number means, you're up the creek without a paddle.''

''But, Hunt,'' Delahunt said, ''there are more than thirty-six trees in the drawing on screen.''

''When there are more than thirty-six trees, he automatically subtracts thirty-six and comes up with a number within the range.''

''Have we figured out how he got the key to the code to his pals in Legion?'' Kurtzman said.

''He wasn't under surveillance when he developed it,'' Wethers replied. ''My guess is, he got his lawyer to carry it out of prison, knowingly or unknowingly. Likewise, he might have passed on the key without knowing what it was." The ex-academic typed in a new command and the picture on the screen changed.

"What you're looking at now is the close of Pickett's last transmission," he announced.

The words on the screen said, "Warmest wishes for the picnic. P.S.—thanks for sending me a copy of the menu."

"Picnic? Menu? What is he talking about?" Price asked.

"I think the menu is the home video," Wethers told her. "The people shown in it are some of the victims Legion intends to murder. Their plate of fare, so to speak."

"Gruesome," Kurtzman said, "but it fits."

"Carmen," Price directed, "get Hal on the horn. He needs to hear all this."

FBI Field Office,
Portland, Oregon

HAL BROGNOLA BROKE the secure connection with Stony Man Farm and immediately hit the redial button. The Portland SAC picked up his home phone on the third ring.

"This is Brognola. I've got a hot one on my hands. We've identified a potential mass-hostage situation in an isolated town in Washington State. I need your help, Chuck."

"Name it."

"I've got to have immediate transportation to the site. It's on the Olympic peninsula. It's called Port Flattery."

"I know it," the SAC said. "I've been through the area on vacation. The fastest way to get you there is to jet you to Boeing Field in the Lear and have a helicopter waiting to take you the rest of the way."

"What's the ETA?"

"An hour and a half to get you on-site."

Brognola didn't know if they had that long.

"There's no faster way?"

"Not that I know of. There's no place to land a Lear over there. All the runways are too short for jets. If you take a prop plane from Portland, it'll put you even further behind the time curve."

Brognola took a breath while he chewed over the ramifications, then he said, "I need you to arrange for the Seattle field office to transport a full assault team to Port Flattery ASAP. I want every available agent on the job. They should be prepared to meet heavily armed and determined opposition. When they land, I want status updates every five minutes while I'm en route. And one more thing. Alert the Washington National Guard. In case the situation is out of hand when our people touch down, I want them to be able to immediately call in massive reinforcements."

"This is big time."

"How soon can I get in the air?"

"Hang up and get Agent Ransom to drive you to the airport. The Lear will be ready to take off when you arrive."

"Thanks, Chuck," Hal said.

"Good luck."

Brognola grabbed his shoulder holster and .357 pistol from the coat hook behind the office door. He shrugged into the harness on his way out.

CHAPTER TWENTY-ONE

Port Flattery, Washington

At the sound of gun shots from across the street, Bobbie Marie Potts flinched on the Winnebago's carpet. She knew the house that was under attack and the family who owned it—the Delongs, husband, wife and two small children. He worked for the county assessor. Potts lay there, trembling, imagining the unimaginable. When the orange lights started to flicker and beat against the RV's side window, she steeled herself and rolled up into a sitting position. Then she got to her feet.

Out the window, the Delong house was on fire. Flames were shooting out the tops of the living room's half-open sliding windows. The curtains were burning like oil-soaked torches. Even as she watched, more gunfire rattled and the living-room windows shattered. Bits and pieces of glass tumbled out onto the tiny, neatly kept lawn. Someone was still inside!

Potts looked on as the fire leaped the gutter and took hold on the shake roof. Lines of flame crept up the slope to the ridgeline, up the ridgeline to the peak. Fire absolutely gushed out of the windows, melding with the flames engulfing the roof. It was going to burn to the ground. At the edge of the blaze, men in black scuttled like cockroaches, then all at once, they disappeared down the side yard.

Another brief volley of gunfire erupted from the back of the house, then there was silence.

Potts tried to tell herself that the stillness meant the Delongs had gotten away. But she knew it wasn't possible. She had sold seven houses in Marwood Creek. She knew the layout of the backyard, how the house sat on the lot. There was a six-foot-high cedar fence between the Delongs and a hope of safety.

They were surely lost.

As was she.

A gun shot barked down the street, and a bullet whined, then whacked into the side of the burning house. Then came another shot, and another. Potts watched in amazement as the killers took cover in the Sizemores' side yard.

Her friends and neighbors were fighting back!

Their bravery boosted her spirits. The murderers weren't invincible, after all. Her incapacitating fear was replaced with a sudden fury. Better to go down battling, she told herself.

Potts looked over at the Winnebago's dashboard. The keys still hung in the ignition. Behind her, at the rear of the RV, an arsenal was piled up on the floor. It clicked in her mind that if the killers ran out of bullets, they couldn't hurt anybody else. If they'd didn't have an escape vehicle, they wouldn't get away with the killings they'd already done. If she just drove away, it would leave them stranded, hung out to dry.

Her wrists were taped behind her back. When she tried to pull them apart, twisting her arms, the tape stretched a little, but she was still held fast. She looked around frantically for something to cut it with. The RV had been stripped of its stove, sink and fridge to make room for men and weapons. She found a sharp edge on an exposed wall strut and began sawing the tape against it.

AGA KARKANIAN CROUCHED along the side yard of the tract house, wincing at the heat billowing from the blaze next door. His face and beard were bathed in sweat and oily soot. The fire had been a tactical mistake, and the mistake had been compounded by the layout of the housing development. Because the bacteria's dwellings were jammed so close together, a warning of danger had passed quickly down the rows of identical homes. In a matter of minutes, the intended victims had made a mass exodus. They'd even escaped from the home next door to the fire.

And now the bacteria had turned.

As he and his pack-mates had swept through the deserted houses on that side of the street, the residents of Marwood Creek were busy organizing a defense. They'd pulled together a barricade and, when the hunters showed themselves, opened fire en masse.

With a hiss, a white shaft plummeted from the sky and sank deep into the sod a few feet away. There were already half a dozen arrows sticking out of the lawn. Small-arms fire clipped the edge of the house that Karkanian was hiding behind, splintering away the cedar siding, emptying the windows of their last shards of glass.

An attempt to take the barricade was out of the question. There was too much open ground between it and Legion's position. Even with bulletproof vests, they stood an excellent chance of being hit by massed fire. Karkanian considered using the Winnebago as an armored personnel carrier, driving it right up to the barrier. But he knew if it was disabled by hostile bullets, they might be stuck without a ride out of town.

Given the current mood of the populace, that was the last thing Karkanian wanted.

The arrogance of these inferior and insignificant people infuriated him, but more than that, he was angry with himself for not having foreseen what was happening to them now, for not having devised a countermove.

Another white arrow screamed down from on high.

This one didn't bury itself harmlessly in the grass. It caught one of the players in the neck. The stump of the shaft and fletching stuck almost straight up beside his head. The arrow point cut deep into his torso. The man let out a shriek and reached around, spinning, grabbing hold of the arrow shaft. The more he pulled, the more he turned, the more damage the broad headpoint's razor edges did inside him. He was coring himself, like an apple.

Blood drooling from his lips, the killer stumbled out from the cover of the house, out into the middle of the lawn.

The small arms crackled from down the street. The wounded player was met with a hail of bullets of all sizes. They slapped his vest, plucked at his shirt sleeves and trouser legs and kicked up chunks of grass between his boots. Then a heavy-caliber rifle boomed, and the player's head snapped to one side. His NOD flew off. Pink matter pelted the lawn as he went down.

None of the other players, Karkanian included, had made a move to try to help him.

They were thinking of themselves, of their own skins.

With an arrow wound like that, the guy was dead anyway.

"We can't stay here any longer," said the player kneeling next to Karkanian. "They'll just wear us down. Or trap us. They could be circling around behind us right now."

"Red Rover's supposed to be on the way," Karkanian said. "His crew will back us up."

"Six or seven more guns aren't going to fix this problem."

Karkanian looked behind him. There were nine players left in his pack. Nine or fifteen, what did it matter when the opposition had hundreds on its side?

"Face up to it or we're all going to die on this street," the player told him.

Karkanian growled an oath. The choice was clear. There was no choice. The Winnebago sat parked on the other side of the street. To reach it, they had to cross 150 feet of no-man's-land.

He turned to his pack-mates and said, "Listen up. We're going to retreat to the RV. We'll move in staggered groups of three. The second group in line will provide covering fire for the first. After the first group crosses, it and the third will give cover to the second. Then first and second will protect the third. Let's do it quick. Now!''

He led the first group himself. He was halfway across the lawn before the covering fire began. There was no time to look down the street or consider what was whistling over his head. He kept his eyes on the prize, high-kicking for the protection of the RV. He skidded to a stop behind the rear of the Winnebago. The other two players reached safety, as well. The protective fire had worked. As he prepared to shoot at the barrier, he waved his arm at the second group.

"Come on!" he cried.

Karkanian pinned his machine pistol's trigger and fanned bullets over the length of the barricade. He knew the chances of scoring a hit were slim. He just wanted to keep the shooters' heads down. Despite the bullets Legion was sending downrange, more and more gun shots boomed from behind the barrier. The bacteria had realized what little danger they were in.

As the second group dashed across the road, the middle player in the running file did a sudden, awkward flip and crashed to her side in the street. Her legs were still moving, but she wasn't going anywhere. The other two players reached cover without being hit.

Karkanian dumped his weapon's empty mag and reloaded.

As the third group prepared to make its break, the RV's engine started up.

"Who's in there?" Karkanian shouted, counting heads. Realizing that everyone was accounted for, except their female prisoner, he made a lunge for the side door.

In the heat of battle, he had forgotten about the blond woman. He found her in the driver's seat, frantically trying to get the Winnebago in forward gear. He caught a handful of her hair and tried to pull her out of the driver's seat. She hung on to the steering wheel with both hands.

Karkanian swung his balled fist into the side of her head, once, twice, three times. The third blow made her give up her death grip on the wheel. Grabbing her under the arms, he was able to drag her out of the driver's seat. After he rolled her over onto her stomach on the floor, Karkanian put a knee in the middle of her back and twisted her arms behind her. Pulling a roll of tape from his pocket, he rebound her wrists securely. Then, as an extra bit of security, he likewise fastened her ankles together.

The woman woke up as he turned her onto her back. "Bastard!" she screeched up in his face. "You're going to die tonight!"

Karkanian shut her mouth with another strip of duct tape. She glared at him. He laughed and bent over her, planting a scratchy kiss on her forehead. "Someone's going to die, honey, but it sure isn't me."

BOLAN ROLLED UP on the corner of Stanton and Marwood with headlights blacked out and his borrowed NOD pulled down over his eyes. What he saw made him smile. The forces of Legion were in full retreat, driven back to their RV by a ragtag army of outraged citizens. It seemed that the self-proclaimed superior beings of level five had taken their opponents a bit too lightly. Their entire game plan hinged on the victims being too cowed and too stupid to fight back. It turned out that the killer geniuses suffered from the same frailties as everyone else. Pride goeth before a fall.

As the Executioner watched, one of the running players took what looked like a mortal hit and went down in the street. The others didn't stop to help her up; they just ran by. As the last of the players crossed the street, all of them jumped in the Winnebago. Under concentrated gunfire, it cut a squealing U-turn and exited the development at top speed, turning left in front of him and highballing it up the dark road.

Bolan punched the gas. As he cleared the intersection, the side window spiderwebbed and a slug slapped the passenger's seat. Friendly fire.

Gradually he gained on the other RV. He drew up close to the back bumper and stayed there. He was close enough to see in the rectangular rear window. A yellow head and shoulders stared back at him. He stole a peek in his rearview mirror and was relieved that the Port Flattery irregulars had had the good sense not to follow.

The Legion headset crackled in his ear. "Red Rover, is that you back there?"

It was Aga Karkanian again. "Yeah, I'm on your tail," Bolan said. "What's the plan?"

"We'll pick up Butcher Boy and his team at the mill. Help them finish off there if they need it. Then we'll disappear, like we planned."

"Got it."

"Drop back, Red Rover, you're making me nervous. And turn your lights on."

The Executioner eased back on the gas. Only when he was well behind did he flip up the NOD and hit his lights. As they sped across town, toward the mill, he listened in as Karkanian established contact with a player called Clown and let him know that a full-scale retreat was under way. When Karkanian tried to reach Della and her crew at the trailer park, he got no answer. It appeared that that pack had gone down in flames, too.

Bolan could hear the frustration and anger in Karkanian's voice.

Then his own plans started to unravel a bit at the corners.

"Red Rover," Karkanian said, "give Bluebeard the headset. I need to talk to him."

Whoever Bluebeard was, he was probably dead; he certainly wasn't in Bolan's RV.

"He didn't make it," the Executioner said.

It was a poor answer because it left open a follow-up question. Not that he had many response options.

"Who did?" Karkanian asked.

The Executioner didn't know the names of the players missing in action, so he couldn't fake it. He had no choice but to tell the truth.

"Nobody made it."

"Nobody? You said you picked up the others."

"Yeah, well, I exaggerated a little."

In a sudden flare of brake lights, the RV in front of him slowed. Bolan had to follow suit or rear end the other vehicle. As he locked up his wheels, a head reappeared in the back window. The guy was looking at him, and he wasn't smiling.

In the headset, Bolan heard the man shout, "I only see one guy in there, and it's not Red Rover. It's that fucking guy we drowned."

As the Winnebago pulled away again, the player in the back started to kick the window. The glass flexed and the soles of his boot left smeared prints on it, then the rear window popped out of its frame and shattered on the highway.

Bolan drove over it.

The player stuck a machine pistol out the window opening. A strobe flickered and bullets tracked through the windshield, cutting crusty holes just above the dash. They whizzed to the right and left of the driver's seat and thunked into the rear wall.

The Executioner hit the brakes and picked the submachine gun up from his lap. As the lead RV moved out of range, he jammed the muzzle against the inside of the windshield, popping off three quick single shots around the hole. Then he used the muzzle and front sight to punch out a jagged opening in the glass. He thrust the barrel through his homemade gun port and flattened the gas pedal.

The Winnebago rapidly grew larger in front of him. When he could read the numbers on the license plate, he hit his high beams and squeezed off a couple of ranging rounds.

A tiny hole appeared above the window opening, close to the roof line. The other shot was a clean miss. Adjusting the angle of fire, he shot again. This time high again, but way to the left.

It wasn't going to work.

The bumps in the road kept throwing off his aim.

The guy in the back opened fire again, sending a line of bullets through the Winnebago's grille. It was easier for him to score because he wasn't trying to drive, too.

Bolan thumbed down the fire-selector switch. If subtle wasn't working, try something full-auto.

He flattened the trigger, hosing the back end of the Winnebago with bullets as he roared up on it. For a second, the shooter stood framed in the window hole, then the slugs found him and he dropped out of sight.

Nobody else jumped up to take his place.

Ahead, the lights of the mill loomed; their glow lit up a wide strip of the near horizon. But Bolan was so close to the rear end of the lead RV that he couldn't see the smokestacks, or the turnoff for the plant road.

Karkanian cut a hard turn that caught him by surprise. Bolan had to slow down or lose it on the corner. As the Winnebago barreled down the narrow, curving road, he pulled back up to within spitting distance.

When Karkanian whipped over to the right, Bolan saw the guard hut. It sat on a concrete island that divided the road in two. He stomped the gas and swerved left, around the far side of the hut. As he roared by the other RV, the Executioner saw faces behind the side window. Then he saw Karkanian glaring at him from the driver's seat.

When Bolan got in front by half an RV-length he cut the wheel hard over to the right.

Winnebago met Winnebago with a crash of metal and glass. The Executioner had timed his bump perfectly. Karkanian's rig was driven off the road and onto the landscaped front yard of the mill's administrative building. When its right wheels hit the front steps, it tipped up on the two opposite wheels. Karkanian tried to right it, but the lawn's sod couldn't hold the weight. As the lawn slipped, so did the supporting wheels. The Winnebago toppled over onto its side and skidded seventy feet before coming to a stop on the asphalt in front of the mill cafeteria.

Bolan hit his brakes, putting his RV into a slow, tailfirst slide. The rear end came around 180 degrees before he got it stopped. Out the bullet-hole-laced windshield, he saw the side door of the overturned Winnebago flop open and survivors start to climb out.

Grabbing a pair of Legion's SMGs from the rear, Bolan got out of the RV and into firing position against its front bumper. As he sighted down on the other Winnebago, he saw a woman emerge from the makeshift emergency exit. Gagged and bound, she was passed up and lifted out by two players. It was the landlady.

Bolan waited until she was safely behind the Winnebago before he opened fire.

When the next players appeared, he picked them off as they prepared to jump to the ground. The afterimage lingered in his mind for a second, a silhouette of sprawling arms and legs.

After that, no more targets showed themselves. The level-fivers still in the Winnebago were having second thoughts about trying to make a break for it.

In the mill's floodlights, something glistened on the tarmac. A sheet of liquid flowed from under the back of the overturned RV, and the smell told Bolan it was gasoline. The Winnebago's big tanks had ruptured.

Bolan angled a shot off the asphalt. It sparked, but the fumes didn't ignite.

He tried again.

With a whoosh, the wave of fuel burst into flame. A wall of fire turned into a lake, and in the middle of the lake was the Legion RV. Now the players wanted out, but it was too late.

The Winnebago became their crematorium.

On the other side of the burning wreck, Karkanian and one other player dragged the woman up the walk to the cafeteria's front door. The serial killer seemed to have lost his taste for confrontation, which was understandable. His odds had plummeted in the past few seconds, from way ahead to even money. Maybe it hadn't occurred to him that Bolan had the keys to the only Winnebago still operational. Maybe he planned to call Butcher Boy and Wavy Hair over from the mill and catch him in a squeeze play. So far, there hadn't been a peep through Bolan's headset.

The glass in the cafeteria door shattered.

The Executioner used the burning RV as distant cover, keeping it between him and the fire lane from the cafeteria entrance. With only two guns to hold the cafeteria door, he decided to take his chances. He jumped out into the fire lane and charged, a blazing machine pistol in either fist. At the cafeteria entrance, the player on the left panicked and tried to bail on the position. He went down in an avalanche of glass. Karkanian grabbed the woman off the floor and moved out of range.

Bolan entered the cafeteria on a dead run. Behind him, a string of bullets animated the chairs stacked on the long dining tables. As he slid to a stop below the service counter, Karkanian ducked back into what had to be the kitchen.

"Don't you get it?" Bolan shouted at him. "You're going nowhere. This is the last stop on the tour."

"I've got a hostage. I'll kill her if you don't back off. I'll gut her like a trout."

Bolan stole a peek around the bottom of the counter. Karkanian was backing up. Before he moved out of sight, Bolan saw he had the woman in front of him, as a shield. Her mouth was taped; her hands were tied behind her back. Her ankles were bound, too. Karkanian had one arm around her waist, and he was dragging her along.

As the way was now clear, the Executioner advanced to the kitchen entrance. Hands moving with precision, he paused to check each of his machine pistol's mags. He put the clip with the most ammo back in one of the guns, stuck the other magazine in his waistband and discarded the second SMG.

Then he went through the kitchen door low and quick. By the time Karkanian reacted with a short burst of gunfire, he was behind a stainless-steel cabinet.

The kitchen had three rows of waist-high workstations, the last of which was set against the far wall. Karkanian and his hostage were by the cooking ranges, two rows over.

"Aren't you going to tell me to let her go?" the serial killer asked.

"That would be a waste of breath," Bolan said. "She's dead meat."

"You have an interesting take on things, Archangel."

"How's this for interesting? If she's already dead, I'm free to act. You've got no shield."

"You're bluffing."

Bolan rose up above the edge of the work surface. He was glad Legion had good taste in guns. This one fired from a closed bolt, and was therefore highly accurate. He could see a bit of the woman's blond hair sticking up from behind the countertop. He bore down and fired single shots, five in quick succession. The slugs whacked into the grease shield of the commercial range inches above her head.

He wanted to give Karkanian a little food for thought, and he had. All of a sudden it was *Let's Make a Deal*.

"If you let me go, she can stay here," the mass killer said. "I'll take the tape off her mouth so you know she's okay."

There was a pause as the killer removed the tape gag, then the woman shouted to him, shrill and angry. "Kill the bastard! Forget about me. Kill him!"

A fist smacked against flesh, then there was silence.

Bolan was already in motion, crawling on his belly to the middle row of steel workstations. If the woman was unconscious, she would be even more a load to drag around. It was time to do or die. He raised himself into a crouch, then jumped into the aisle.

There was nothing to shoot at; they were both gone.

As soon as Karkanian punched the blonde on the jaw, he flopped her over his shoulder in a fireman's carry, and moved quickly around the corner of the kitchen. It was a subduing technique he'd often used on solo hunts. Usually he didn't have to carry the victim far, to a waiting van or a car trunk. In this case, he carried her to the door of the refrigerated meat locker. It was a walk-in, and it was set up so the cafeteria cooks could do their butchering on the premises. Not only were there carcasses of whole cows hanging from hooks in the ceiling, but also there were power tools for the dismembering of same.

The band saw caught his eye.

He lugged the woman inside the windowless locker and shut the door behind them softly. It was cold and it smelled good, meaty, like his place on Benton Avenue. Soon it would smell even better.

Karkanian lifted the unconscious woman onto the cutting table, turning her face toward the band saw's cutting loop. It was a formidable-looking machine, capable of cutting through a steer's semifrozen hindquarter in the blink of an eye. It would slice up the middle-aged woman like she was made of room-temperature butter. Karkanian knew that as soon as he turned on the motor, the noise would act as a homing beacon for Archangel. He didn't have time for anything fancy with the saw. He had to make one quick cut, lift the severed head by the hair and, when the tall man came bursting through the door, have his machine pistol ready in the other hand. He was counting on the shock value of the decapitation to freeze Archangel for a second or two, long enough to nail him in the face with a full-auto burst.

He swept the woman's hair up over the top of her

head so it wouldn't tangle in the blade as it passed through, then he pushed the front of her throat against the saw teeth. Figuring that a running start might get the job done even faster, he pulled her throat back about a foot.

That done, he double-checked his machine pistol, which sat on the counter on the other side of the saw: safety off, selector switch to *F*, pistol grip facing him.

Satisfied that everything was ready, Karkanian reached for the power switch.

BOLAN MOVED QUIETLY to the corner of the kitchen where the room made a sharp dogleg to the left. In front of him was the open storage area for dry food-stuffs. Along the near wall was a thick, metal-clad door. The heavy jackets hanging on coat hooks beside it told him it was a meat locker. The caged light over the door was lit, which meant someone was inside with the light on.

There was no way out.

No window.

No other door.

Maybe that's what Karkanian wanted.

As Bolan jerked open the door, the band saw started up. Karkanian looked over his shoulder, stunned by the premature intrusion. He was poised to push the woman's neck through the blade, but his hands were no longer touching her. Surprise had made him pull back just a little.

A little too much.

In that same second, whether she felt the sting of the saw teeth or the grating noise of the motor startled her awake, the woman moved. Before the killer could push her forward, she twisted up from the counter. His lunge forward actually helped her get her head around the saw blade.

As Karkanian pushed against empty air, he drove his hand through the whirring blade. Flesh and bone from the webbing of his thumb to the middle of his forearm seared away in an instant. His blood sprayed the ceiling, walls and the back of the woman's head.

Mouth agape, the serial killer watched half his arm fall to the floor, then he reached for the machine pistol.

The Executioner took the easy head shot, sending a 9 mm through his right eye and into his brain. Karkanian fell away from the howling saw onto his face on the butcher-shop floor.

As he turned off the saw, Bolan saw the woman was shivering. He cut her bonds and helped her off the counter.

"Come on, let's get out of here," he said.

Back in the kitchen, where the light was better, he could see she had an inch-long, superficial cut across the middle of her throat. Her pallor told him that she was going into shock. He took down one of the butcher's insulated jackets and slipped it over her shoulders.

"You need to sit very quietly until help arrives," he told her. He helped her over to the rice bags. "It shouldn't be long now. I've got a few more of these guys to take care of."

"I'll be okay," she told him. "I'll be fine."

Bolan checked his machine pistol's magazine. Before he hit the mill, he needed to visit Legion's ammo wagon.

"Stay here and keep warm," he told her, then he hurried from the kitchen. In the parking lot outside the cafeteria, Karkanian's Winnebago was a smoldering ruin. He gave it a wide berth. As he neared the side door of the other RV, all the mill's lights went out.

CHAPTER TWENTY-TWO

After the second shot cut a keyhole-shaped slash through the sheet-metal wall above his right hand, Gummy Nordland got his butt in gear. He was already four stories up the ladder, much closer to the catwalks above than to the plant floor below, so going down was out of the question. Movement was in order, a moving target being more difficult to hit. He couldn't move very fast, though. Because of his shot-up calf, he had to rely on his arms to pull himself from rung to rung.

Two stories farther up, the top of the ladder ended in a narrow steel catwalk, which was his original goal. Nordland figured he'd make an indistinct, if not completely invisible target if he went belly down on the grating and stayed very still.

Trying to rally the mill workers with the public-address system had proved worse than useless. It had been a waste of precious time. All the employees wore ear protectors and couldn't hear the loudspeaker. And even if he'd managed to rally them, then what? The automatic weapons were all outside, out of reach. Would he have asked them to take on the killers with broom handles and shovels? Fat chance.

Another bullet zinged at him, this one clanging into

the rung six inches above his head. The impact rang in his ears and rattled through his hands. The bullet was embedded in the ribbed steel. He could see the tail end of it sticking out of the hole it made. The shots were falling closer as the guys in black found the range. The sons of bitches were making a game of it, taking single shots to stretch out the torture instead of blasting him off the ladder in one quick barrage. If they hit him any place, even an arm or a leg, he knew he'd have a hell of a time hanging on. He knew he'd probably fall, and it was a long way down.

What Nordland wanted to do, and couldn't, was to twist around on his perch and shoot back. It would just be a waste of bullets. He couldn't aim while hanging on with one hand and standing on one leg.

Then the inevitable happened.

The top of his right shoulder exploded in pain, as if he'd been slammed with a ball-peen hammer. The bullet cut through his shirt and put a half-inch-deep crease in his skin and muscle as it tracked on through to the wall. Nordland's right hand failed him, and he started to slip.

The chief was determined not to take the big fall, not to die in a heap of splintered bones like poor Lyla Bamfield. He caught himself with his good left hand and as his full weight came down on that shoulder, he found the next rung with the toe of his shoe. He pulled himself as close to the ladder as he could get.

A shuffling sound made him look down. He saw an orange dot bobbing across the mill floor under him. It was the top of a worker's hard hat. The guy was running past the foot of the ladder, in a big hurry to get someplace. Somebody on the far side of the plant shouted an oath, then a burst of machine-gun bullets whanged into the base of the steel wall. They missed the worker, though, and he kept right on going. The guy ducked through a doorway, and two seconds later all the lights in the plant went off and the whine of its machinery died away.

Dizzy from his wounds and disoriented by the sudden total darkness, Nordland clung to the ladder for dear life.

"I THINK YOU GRAZED HIM," Butcher Boy said to the player who had just taken a shot. "Now I'll finish the job."

As he started to draw a bead on the target, Butcher Boy saw the guy in the orange hat running across the back of the plant. He had a funny, loose-jointed gait. "Damn! There goes a live one!" he cried, dropping his aim point and thumbing the fire selector switch to burst mode. He knew that the far end of the plant was supposed to be Wavy Hair's responsibility, so technically he was poaching on another player's turf, but he figured what the hell.

He ripped off a 3-round burst that never quite caught up to the target. It nipped at the guy's backside as he disappeared into a doorless doorway.

When the power went out, there was a kind of ominous clunk, almost an inanimate gasp as hundreds of thousands of circuits switched off. While his eyes tried to adjust to the change in conditions—there wasn't even faint starlight filtering down, so it was blacker than black inside the plant—the dynamos in the massive machinery wound down, then stopped. It took a few seconds for him to realize that his vision wasn't going to get any better; under the circumstances, he was seeing as well as was possible. Which wasn't at all. He might as well have been struck blind.

"No big deal," Butcher Boy said to the others. "Give me a second. I'll unchain the hangar door and one of you guys can duck out and pick up five NODs from the van."

Extending his arms in front of him and waving his hands, he slide stepped until he finally made contact with the plant's interior wall. He felt along the corrugated steel until he came to sliding doors and the chain. As he fumbled for the padlock, behind him, in the dark, he could hear running footsteps. Tiny quick steps, like so many mice.

It didn't matter to him. There was nowhere to go. Then he unlocked the padlock and pulled the chain through the door handles.

Over his shoulder, he said, "One of you go. I don't care who does it. Just hurry."

"Me, I'll go," a player piped up from the darkness.

As they pushed the hangar door open, he squeezed through the gap. "Back in a flash," he said.

BOLAN STEPPED out of the RV with his night optical device pulled down over his eyes and extra, full magazines for the H&K tucked in his pants pockets. Right away he locked on to the car and the van parked next to the plant's side entrance. The hoods of both vehicles glowed yellow hot in the infrared sensors. They hadn't been sitting there for long.

As he approached the car, he saw the blown-out

tires, the missing window glass on all sides and the pockmarks of dozens of bullet holes. When he looked inside, he saw guns and ammo, which meant only one thing: that the sedan was one of Legion's rolling armories. If the driver's door, which stood wide open, was anything to go by, this one had been abandoned in a hurry.

The Executioner rounded the rear of the car, making sure no one was hiding behind it. He noticed the length of chain stretched across the outside of the plant's huge double doors. It seemed an unnecessary precaution, not to mention a violation of fire code, unless you were trying to keep somebody inside from getting outside.

Legion didn't want the ducks fleeing the shooting gallery.

At the sound of approaching footsteps, Bolan moved quickly back to the cover of the car's front fender.

A single player, sans NOD, rounded the corner of the plant and headed for the van. The guy opened the rear doors, which faced Bolan's position, and started rooting around inside. The Executioner let the guy continue his search undisturbed, while he drew a solid bead on the back of his head using the sedan's front fender as a gun rest.

When the player finally straightened and turned, he had his hands full of gear.

Bolan's SMG coughed once. The killer's head snapped back as a parabellum round caught him square in the middle of the forehead. He fell back against the van's open doors, and as he did, his arms opened wide, dropping the stuff he'd gathered. Rubber legged, he slid over the bumper and fell to the ground.

The Executioner crossed over to the fallen player and saw all the NODs on the ground. The guy had come out of the dark plant to get them, which meant that the Legion killers inside were blind.

It was turnabout time.

He gathered up the NODs and picked up three more the player had left in the van. After he had thrown them as far into the darkness as he could, he headed for the corner of the building that the player had come around.

When he stepped past the corner and out into the parking lot, he could see the edge of another pair of hangar doors between him and the water end of the mill. Figuring that the four boys waiting for their infrared goggles would be standing right by the door, perhaps with ready weapons, he decided to try another way in.

Bolan retraced his steps to the shot-up sedan and the chained entry. The chain was hardened steel and looked tough. The lock was massive, but it wasn't bulletproof. He fired at it point-blank, and it sprang open. Then he carefully eased the chain loop from over the doorknob and opened the man-size, inset door a crack.

He looked onto a curious and confusing landscape. There were enormous yellow shapes: oblongs that loomed many stories overhead, great, hulking lemon-colored boxcars with open maws. Because of the heat they gave off, they were painfully bright. The cooler objects, the ramps, the floor, the structural bracings, were a deep green. Against the glow of the background heat, it was difficult to make out human shapes.

Yellow on yellow.

Soft as a breeze, Bolan slipped through the doorway.

"KEEP YOUR SEPARATION," Wavy Hair warned his two pack-mates. "Make sure you stay an arm's width apart."

He and the others were searching for the guy in the orange hard hat and for the switch that would turn the power back on. Wavy Hair knew the doorway the guy went through was somewhere just ahead because he was running for it as the lights went out.

Darkness had forced them to form a three-man skirmish line. It was the only way to keep their quarry from slipping past them. It had also forced them to sling their machine pistols for fear of accidentally shooting one another.

Wavy Hair suddenly stopped. "Hold it," he growled. "I thought I heard a step."

"Which way?"

"Behind us."

The three of them listened intently. They heard the rumbles and sighs of massive boilers cooling down, the popping of metal pipes as they contracted. But no footsteps.

Wavy Hair shook off the unsettling feeling that they were being followed. He was letting the darkness spook him. "Come on," he said, "it can't be much farther."

It wasn't.

His left hand found the doorless doorjamb. He reached out with his right and gripped the shoulder of the player next to him. "Here it is," he said.

He waited until the others found the opening in the wall, then he tapped one of the men on the arm. "You stay at the door," he said. "Make sure the bacterium doesn't slip around us and get away."

Wavy Hair heard the rasping sound of honed steel sliding from a ballistic nylon scabbard.

"He won't get by me," the player said.

Wavy Hair reached out and found the other player's back. "Take the right side of the room," he told the man. "I'll take the left."

"Check," came the reply.

As Wavy Hair moved into the room, he pulled out his Recon Government SOG knife from its inverted shoulder sheath. The weight of the razor-sharp commando knife felt good in his hand. He stepped forward into the blackness, unsure exactly which room he was entering. In the confusion of the chase, he hadn't seen which doorway the guy had ducked into. He knew the mill floor plan, though, and that told him what the possibilities were, which, in turn, helped him interpret what the fingers of his hand touched.

Steel boxes were set in the walls.

Boxes as high as he was tall.

And the fronts of the boxes were missing, and his fingertips brushed over hundreds of tiny trip levers.

They were the switches on the fuses that controlled the flow of power through the pulp mill. Because the power was off at the main, he didn't have to worry about accidentally completing an electrical circuit with his searching fingertips.

"Do you know where we are?" he asked the other killer.

"Power-supply room."

"If you think you've found the master switch," Wavy Hair told him, "give me a shout before you pull it. I don't want to get fried."

"Ditto."

Wavy Hair advanced along the wall, letting his fingers brush over the power panels. He figured the worker who had run in here probably had a hiding place all picked out before he killed the lights, under a desk or workbench. Behind a tool cabinet. Maybe there was even a closet at the back end. What there wasn't was an exit.

Then he heard a strange noise behind him, a rasp, then a soft rustling. A breath of breeze touched the back of Wavy Hair's neck, sending a chill down his spine. Something had moved back there, in the blackness by the doorway.

Wavy Hair forced himself to calm down. It was just the guy he'd left back there shifting around. If it was anything important, the sentry would have let out a shout for sure, no doubt a whoop of triumph while he got busy stabbing with that combat dagger of his.

Wavy Hair's toe stubbed into something solid, and the impact jolted up his leg. "I'm at the back wall," he said, directing his voice across the room to where he thought his counterpart was. His fingers traced the outline of a wall cabinet or locker. He kicked at its base, making sure there was no hiding place, before he moved on. He continued another few feet, then paused. Holding his breath, he listened for the sound of the mill worker's breathing and for the footsteps of his companion along the opposite wall.

He heard nothing.

His fingers grazed the edge of a low counter- or desktop. He reached lower and felt a drawer handle, then two more. He slid his hand along the face of the bottom drawer to an opening, the kneehole of a desk, which was blocked by the legs of an office chair.

Wavy Hair rolled the chair back, knelt and speared his blade into the opening. It met no resistance. He got down on his hands and knees and thrust deeper. The tip of his knife scraped against the wall.

Damn, he thought. As he pulled back, his hand brushed over something on the floor. His fingers returned to it.

"I found his hard hat," Wavy Hair announced. "Stay on your toes. He's in here somewhere."

As the killer straightened, something flashed behind him. For the briefest of instants, he glimpsed the desk in front of him and the back of the office chair. Then the blackness closed in again.

The flash was accompanied by a coughing sound and the metallic plink of a shell casing as it hit the floor.

AGAINST THE FOREST GREEN of the plant's far wall, Mack Bolan saw moving figures. Yellow. With arms outstretched.

A skirmish line of three blind men.

With machine pistols.

The Executioner crossed the mill floor, closing in on them. When the players stopped suddenly, so did he. When he was thirty feet behind them, Bolan recognized Wavy Hair by the sweep of his forelock. The man had turned and looked right at him without seeing.

Bolan raised his weapon to fire, but had to hold up as Wavy Hair and one of the others moved through the open doorway ahead. The third guy stood as a sentry in front of the entrance. In his right hand was a sliver of green.

Cold steel.

The Legion killer wasn't expecting someone to try to take the knife away from him in the dark. Accordingly his grip on the handle wasn't firm.

The Executioner moved cat-quick, catching the flat of the blade between his fingertips and jerking it away before the player could react.

The guy didn't know what to think or do. Suddenly the knife was gone, his hand empty. He knew he hadn't dropped it because it would've made a sound when it hit the concrete. It was more like it had been vacuumed away. But by what?

He opened his mouth to call out to the others.

Bolan struck with the double-edged dagger. Aiming the point like a bullfighter, he placed the steel in exactly the right place, sliding it with a soft rasp into the man's throat to the hilt. The killer didn't cry out; he couldn't. It was hard to scream with a blade through your voice box.

The Executioner twisted the man out of the doorway and as he did, he finished the kill stroke. Then he held the guy against the base of the wall and let him bleed out. It was over in a few seconds. The only noise had been a swish of fabric against fabric.

After lowering the body to the floor, Bolan stepped into the doorway. He could see three bright yellow blobs in the low-ceilinged room. The two that belonged to Wavy Hair and his partner moved along opposite walls, searching stealthily. The third blob was on the floor in the middle of the back wall, curled into a ball.

The Executioner walked soundlessly down the center of the room, straight to the desk under which the mill worker had taken cover. Before he rolled back the office chair he knelt and whispered, "They're coming. Take my hand."

The worst thing that could've happened was that the guy would've made a ruckus, bumping something under the desk, letting out a yelp, thereby alerting the players to his presence. But he didn't. Maybe he was too scared to move. If he was, he got over it quickly. When Bolan put out his hand, the worker took it. He led the guy back to the entrance and parked him against the wall.

When he reentered the power-supply room, Wavy Hair was straightening from the desk. His fellow player was a little slower, not quite yet to the corner. Bolan cut in front of the guy, careful of the unsheathed knife in his left hand. He raised the silenced machine pistol in one hand and fired once, the muzzle-blast flashbulb bright in the black room.

IF WAVY HAIR HAD BEEN looking in the right direction, in the light of the flash he might have seen the tall man dispatch his partner: a vague outline of broad shoulders, outstretched gun hand and the insectlike headpiece of the NOD.

But he was looking the wrong way. And when he turned toward the light, it was black again.

"Hey!" he said. "I told you no guns in here!"

He expected an explanation, maybe even an apology. He got nothing.

The chill rippled down his back again.

"Hey, answer me! Where are you?"

When Bolan nudged him behind the ear with the hot gun muzzle, Wavy Hair nearly jumped out of his skin. He slashed out with the SOG knife, while with his other hand he made a grab for the machine gun slung over his shoulder.

The Executioner had anticipated that. He deftly flicked out with the dead player's blade and slit the strap. Before the killer could catch it, the H&K clattered to the floor.

"Who the fuck are you?" Wavy Hair yelled.

"A creature of the deep."

Bolan heard a sudden intake of breath. Wavy Hair had figured it out. He knew whom he faced, he knew that there would be no mercy for him, as there had been none for his brother. The yellow hands moved in a sweeping circle, trying to make contact, to bring feet and forearms into play, as well as the edge of cold steel. Bolan stepped out of reach.

He watched as the killer grew more and more agitated, swinging and slashing in wilder and wilder arcs. Wavy Hair knew that Death was coming for him. It was the same terrible foreknowledge that sooner or later had come to each of his many victims.

Mack Bolan didn't prolong the man's agony. It wasn't in his nature to torture his fellow creatures.

With a careful one-handed shot, he blew the man's brains into a far corner of the room.

"WHAT IS KEEPING that guy?" Butcher Boy asked.

The other players had no answer. The man who'd gone for the NODs had been out there a long time.

"I'll go get the damned things myself," the German growled. He flipped his machine pistol's selector switch to autofire and stepped through the gap between the sliding doors.

Keeping close to the side of the building, he walked to the corner and peered around it. In the starlight he saw the vague outlines of the van and the sedan. They weren't what caught his attention. Beyond them, across the parking lot, the torched Winnebago lay on its side, still spitting occasional flurries of sparks into the sky.

A short distance away sat an undamaged RV.

In the feeble glow of the Winnebago's embers, he moved to the cover of the Legion van. As he rounded its back bumper, he saw the figure crumpled there. A quick check told him the player was stone dead and worse, the NODs he'd been sent to collect were missing.

Then he noticed something glistening along the ground beside the hangar doors, a silvery snake, twenty feet long. It was the chain he'd fastened. The lock was nowhere in sight.

After checking the sedan, Butcher Boy carefully advanced on the apparently operational Winnebago. When he saw the number on the license plate, he knew from a very short process of elimination that the destroyed RV was the one Karkanian had been driving.

The German climbed into the RV through the side door, ready to open fire, but the vehicle was deserted. He fumbled his way forward. Finding the switch on the dashboard, he turned on the Winnebago's interior lights.

The store of ammo and extra weapons were slung

all over the rear of the RV. He could see none of Legion's night optical devices among the confusion of bullets, magazines and machine pistols. As he rummaged around in the debris to make sure, he found something that made his mouth go dry—a man's wet clothes.

Butcher Boy raised the shirt to his face, sniffed at it, then touched the sleeve with the tip of his tongue.

It wasn't just wet.

It was wet and salty.

Through the RV's bullet-cracked front windshield he could see the burned-out hulk of the other Winnebago, and he had no doubt who was responsible for the disaster.

Archangel.

And Archangel was inside the mill.

As BOLAN STEPPED OUT of the power-supply room, he picked up the dead sentry's SMG and slipped its ballistic nylon sling over his shoulder. Then he scanned the mill floor. He was glad he'd taken the time to toss away all the other NODs. Now that he was accustomed to an infrared interpretation of his surroundings, it was easy to pick out mill workers in hiding. It would have been easy for Legion, too. The only safe place for the workers was up against the boilers whose lingering heat would mask their presence. The workers weren't thinking about that, of course. It didn't even occur to them that the men who hunted them might be able to see in the dark, might be able to pick them out against the tiers of chemical drums, behind the protective bars and grilles of the silent machines, like daffodils in a green meadow.

Looking up at the crisscrossing catwalks high overhead, Bolan saw more daffodils. Those guys were hoping that height and darkness would protect them. There was even a guy way up on a ladder, but he wasn't moving. He was frozen there fifty feet above the floor.

With a NOD, they were all potential targets.

But they weren't the targets Bolan was interested in.

He walked down the wide aisle between the outside wall and the sides of the huge processing machines. As he approached the end of the building, the hangar doors came into view. In front of them stood three men holding subguns. If they were waiting for the player he had shot, he wouldn't be coming back. Instead, they would be joining him.

Because they were standing so close to the door, and because the door was open, the Executioner didn't want to risk a long-distance attack. It could give one or more of them the chance to slip out. If they did that, they could lead him on a merry chase through the nearby woodlots, merry and time-consuming.

So he moved in closer, angling toward the tiers of stacked chemical drums, close enough to hear them talk.

''I think we got the sorry-ass, raw end of this deal,'' the one on the right said. ''While the other players are racking up big scores in the town, we get stuck with a few sailboats and this stinking mill.''

The one in the middle agreed. ''Who decided who went where? That's what I want to know. Is somebody playing favorites, or what?''

"I've heard of stranger things happening," the first guy replied.

"I don't know about you guys," the one on the left said, "but I don't feel so bad. When Butcher Boy had his back turned, I managed to pick myself up a nice memento over in the storage shed."

"Yeah," the player on the right said, "the walls have ears and so does your pants pocket."

"Did you get a rightie or a leftie?" the middle one asked.

"I took the pair. Makes a better-looking wall mount. You know, more balanced."

"Well, I got diddly," the guy on the right said. "If the NODs would ever get here, I might find something I like, too."

"What's keeping Butcher Boy?" the middle guy asked.

"Maybe he fell down the same hole as what's-his-name," the player on the left suggested.

"It couldn't be that dark out there. Maybe something happened. Maybe we should go out and have a look," the guy on the right said.

"What are you going to be able to see?" the ear collector asked. "For Christ's sake, keep your shirts on. Butcher Boy will be back in a minute."

With a resounding clunk, the power came back on. For a few seconds, everyone in the mill was as blind in the light as they had been in the dark.

Inside Bolan's NOD, it was even brighter.

He stood in the open, not fifty feet from the trio of armed murderers, dead in the water. When he moved, it was like he'd planned it all along, calculated the degree of turn, the numbers of steps, the required burst of speed. But it wasn't planning, it was instinct. He knew where the nearest cover was and he made for it. Blinded but not disoriented, he flipped off the NOD as he lunged for the tier of barrels.

The players' eyes recovered faster than his but they weren't expecting to find him there when the flashbulbs stopped going off in their heads. Startled by his nearness, they jerked back in reflex, defensively raising their weapons to their chests instead of lowering them to bring the business ends to bear.

In the end, it all balanced out, with him diving blind and them unable to take advantage of a sitting duck.

As the Executioner dived behind the chemical drums, three subguns stuttered, thunking into the steel. The barrels at his heels instantly sprung a dozen leaks. He whirled and stuck his machine pistol around the corner, touching off a short unaimed burst to keep them off him while his sight fully returned.

As the black blur of the barrels came into focus, he turned and ran for the mill's wall. The barrels were stacked fifteen drums high, and there were four times that many on each side of the block. No way could the players shoot over them and hit him. They could, of course, round the perimeter and sandwich him between their guns, which was exactly what they were doing, if they had any sense.

As Bolan ran, he unslung the second machine pistol. When he reached the corner of the stack, he was ready for Legion. He wasn't ready for the six mill workers who were hiding in the narrow gap between the barrels and the wall. They blinked at him from the middle of the row and slowly raised their hands in surrender.

"Get down!" he shouted.

As he raised the machine pistol in his left hand, the workers scrambled to hit the deck, fearing the worst.

On the other side of the block of barrels, somebody yelled, "Now!"

The Legion players thought they had worked it all out. At the signal, they would charge him in unison, coming at him from both sides of the tier. They figured he would either panic and retreat in one direction or the other, and either way he'd end up in somebody's sights. Or that he would stand and fight one opponent while the other got the drop on him.

They figured wrong.

The Executioner stood facing the corner of the tier of barrels, a subgun in each hand. By tipping his head a little left or right, he could pick up a running target. He picked up one right away. A man in black darted out along the side of the tier, firing as he charged. Because he was running, he couldn't shoot straight.

Bolan, who was standing with knees bent, didn't have that problem. As slugs sailed wild into the mill wall, wild and high into the sides of the barrels, he aimed low and pinned the trigger, letting the muzzle creep lift the line of slugs from the floor through his target. Bullets stitched the man from crotch to hairline, and he crashed in a rag-doll heap.

More bullets ripped past Bolan's back.

The other two guys came at him down the narrow gap. He couldn't walk his fire into them because of the workers on the ground, so he stepped away from the corner of the tier and, holding the weapon steady, saturated fifteen feet of path with slugs. The players ran into the hellstorm and absorbed multiple hits as he emptied the H&K's magazine. The last killer dropped a few feet from where the mill workers lay.

Bolan stepped over the workers and checked the bodies. When he was sure they were dead, he told the workers to get up off the floor. They looked shaken and pale. "Come on," the Executioner said, "let's get you guys outside. You'll be safer there."

BUTCHER BOY CAME OUT of the power-supply room on the run. Even so, he wasn't quick enough to get a shot off at the man in the NOD on the other side of the plant. He watched as Archangel darted along the stack of drums, watched as his pack-mate tried to run him down, and saw the player get killed for it.

At that point, he moved closer to the cover of the mill wall. He couldn't see the back corner of the block of drums because of stacked boxes in the way. He could hear, though.

More autofire clattered along the wall, then stopped abruptly.

Maybe his players had gotten the bastard, he thought, disappointed that the prize might not be his.

Butcher Boy sneaked around the pallets and, seeing no sign of Archangel, slipped quickly over to the towering wall of drums. As he moved to the corner, he heard Archangel's voice.

He flattened his back against the barrels, holding his machine pistol at head height. When the first mill hand appeared, he turned and saw the gun muzzle, but he was too startled to say anything. Then the next guy bumped into his back, pushing him forward. Six of them filed past the submachine gun's barrel and didn't make a peep.

When the flow of workers stopped, Butcher Boy made his move.

He stepped around the corner with the weapon poised. The man who called himself Archangel had a subgun in either hand, but his hands were at his sides, the muzzles pointing downward.

"That will do," Butcher Boy said, taking aim at Bolan's chin.

The tall man stopped and tensed.

"No way you're fast enough," Butcher Boy told him. "Drop the guns or I'll shoot your arms off."

Bolan let the machine pistols fall to the concrete.

"Come to think of it," the German said, "maybe I'll shoot your arms off anyway. It sounds like fun."

"Lower your weapon."

The voice came from the corner of the block of drums.

Butcher Boy looked over his shoulder and saw a .45 automatic pointed at his head. The guy who held it two-handed was all shot up and dirty.

"I'm a police officer," Gummy Nordland said. "I'm ordering you to drop your weapon or I'll fire."

Butcher Boy considered his options. The hated enemy stood in front of him. The threat of death stood behind. And he made his choice.

First things first.

Nordland's Government Model Colt .45 boomed as the blond man started to pivot toward him. The

230-grain full-metal-jacket round caught him high in the cheek, and passing through, blew away the far side of his head.

"Son of a bitch," Nordland said, lowering his pistol. "I didn't want to do that. Bastard left me no choice."

Bolan picked up the guns he'd dropped. "You did the right thing, Chief. I owe you one."

"You owe me nothing, bud. You saved my hash a dozen times over tonight. Without you, these people might have killed the whole damned town."

"You look kind of wobbly," Bolan stated.

"I lost some blood. I'll be okay."

"Why don't you sit down over there and take a load off? Meanwhile, I'll get one of these mill workers to give a shout on the PA system and tell his friends it's safe to come out."

"Sounds like a plan to me, bud."

EPILOGUE

As the Justice Sikorsky helicopter circled in for a touchdown in the mill parking lot, the white circle of its spotlight swept over the burned-out Winnebago. Hal Brognola could see a charred human body on the ground behind it. Nobody from the Bureau had been here with the crime-scene tape yet. Or maybe they had run out of the stuff. As Brognola had just seen first-hand, Port Flattery was covered with it.

The helicopter landed a short distance from the smoking hulk. As the big Fed stepped out, a man in a blue FBI windbreaker and billcap greeted him. "Got somebody over here you should meet, sir."

Brognola followed him to a minivan the tactical squad had commandeered. Inside, in the middle seat, was a blond woman with a badly bruised face. She was shivering under a heavy oversize coat. Beside her sat a big man with bloodstained pants and shirt. He had his arm around her shoulders, hugging her.

"Sir, this is the police chief who took down most of the bad guys," the agent told him. "Chief Nordland, this is Harold Brognola."

"Call me Gummy," the chief said. He tried to raise

his hand in greeting but got it only partway up before the shoulder wound stopped him. "Shit."

Brognola leaned in to grip his hand. It was rough-skinned, like a beat-up old hunting boot. "I'm Hal. Glad to meet you, Gummy. Sorry it couldn't be under better circumstances. Looks like you had a time of it here."

"It was living hell, and that's the truth. But what that agent just said is wrong. I didn't handle all those terrorists by myself. I can't take credit for that."

"I know. I've just come back from town. The people of Port Flattery did a remarkable job. You should all be proud."

Nordland started to say something more on the subject, then changed his mind. After a pause, he said, "Have they located my missing officers yet?"

"I'm afraid so, Chief," Brognola replied. "Both of them were found dead in Flattery Park along with one of their squad cars. The other cruiser was left abandoned at a park-and-ride lot near the main highway."

"So at least one of them got away?"

"Looks like it, but we can't tell for sure yet. Chief, I don't want to keep you or the lady here any longer. We're going to get you both some medical attention. I'll be talking with you again soon."

Nordland nodded and, as the van's door slid closed, he cradled the woman tighter.

Brognola watched the minivan leave, then returned to the helicopter. Inside, he reconnected to the scrambled line to the White House. At the President's request, he had been giving him updates on the half hour.

"What have you got, Hal?" said a familiar though drained voice. "How many people did we lose?"

"I'm afraid it's still hard to say, sir. We won't know for sure until well after the sun comes up. We lost too many, for sure, but not as many as we could have, all things considered."

"And you say the folks out there stood up to the bastards?"

"Yes, sir. Made them turn tail."

"Well, that's a bright spot. A town full of heroes. They won't be able to scrape the press out of their hair for months."

"Yes, sir."

"What about this character on death row? Pickett, is it?"

"He's got an appeal filed for a new trial, but it won't go anywhere. Not when we have proof that he arranged for the murders of witnesses. He'll be checking out, on schedule."

"Good enough," the President said. "I want you to thank your people for me. I know things got fluid on us, but they rose to the challenge and did their usual excellent work. And, Hal, I want you to give my special regards to your man. My special regards and thanks."

"I'll do that, sir. You can count on it."

Take
2 explosive books plus a mystery bonus
FREE

James Axler

OUTLANDERS™

DOOMSTAR RELIC

Kane and his companions find themselves pitted
against an ambitious rebel named Barch, who finds a
way to activate a long-silent computer security
network and use it to assassinate the local baron.
Barch plans to use the security system to take over
the ville, but he doesn't realize he is starting a
Doomsday program that could destroy the world.

Kane and friends must stop Barch, the virtual assassin
and the Doomsday program to preserve the future....

One man's quest for power unleashes a cataclysm
in America's wastelands.

After the ashes of the great Reckoning, the
warrior survivalists live by one primal instinct

JAMES AXLER

DEATH LANDS ®

Way of the Wolf

Unexpectedly dropped into a bleak Arctic landscape by a
mat-trans jump, Ryan Cawdor and his companions find
themselves the new bounty in a struggle for dominance
between a group of Neanderthals and descendants of
a military garrison stranded generations ago.

Desperate times call for desperate measures. Don't miss out on the action in these titles!